Now &
THEN

Now & Then

A PARKER CITY MYSTERY

by

Justin M. Kiska

Cover Photo (original) by Hamidreza Torabi via Unsplash

First edition

ISBN: 978-1-947915-96-1

Cover art by Level Best Designs

This book was professionally typeset on Reedsy.
Find out more at reedsy.com

To Jessica – "Spain thanks you for your service."

Prologue

Spring 1981

One by one, he watched from the shadows across the street as the self-important members of the Parker Historical Society's board of directors left the old converted townhouse in the middle of the city's historic district. A waste of a building, he thought to himself with more than a little contempt. If he'd had his way, it would have been torn down years ago. But nothing ever changed in Parker. The powers-that-be wouldn't allow it. If the status quo shifted even slightly, there was a chance they could lose their influence and ability to control everything that went on in the town.

First to leave, clearly in a rush to get on his way, was Howard Worthington. A tall, distinguished man with whom he'd had the opportunity to speak on many occasions. If he was forced to admit it, Worthington was a decent guy overall. But he was still one of *them*. As the patriarch of one of the city's founding families and president of South Mountain Bank & Trust, he was nothing more than a stuffed shirt getting rich off the backs of everyone around him. Although, he did have excellent taste when it came to cars. Worthington's shiny new Mercedes 280SL was parked in the small lot next to the building. A mechanical thing of beauty, the Cherry Red roadster glistened in the light of the street lamps. What he would have given to get behind the wheel and take it for a spin. For a moment, enticed by the luxury toy, he almost forgot the reason he was there. He needed to focus and not let himself be distracted.

As the little convertible sped off down the street, a few more of Parker's self-proclaimed social elite emerged chit-chatting about God-only-knows-what. No doubt the conversations were benign and of no real importance in the grand scheme of things. Heaven forbid these *important* people spend any of their valuable time discussing the city's real problems, instead opting to debate the theme of that year's fundraiser or how it was beyond necessary to refinish the Wooton Cabinet Secretary Desk that the society purchased the year before for a reported $10,000!

The darkened alley provided the perfect vantage point to watch every move these people made. Smirking, laughing, *thinking* they were better than they were. He knew each and every one of them. They all had their dirty little secrets they didn't want anyone to know. But in Parker City, everyone knew everyone else's business. It didn't matter how hard one tried to hide it.

There was one thing he knew for certain. People were creatures of habit. Whether an individual following their daily routine or as a group, each person doing what they always did—like a cog in a machine—patterns always emerged. You just had to pay close attention and look for them. That's exactly what he'd been doing…watching. By doing so, he'd learned a great deal about his *subjects*.

As expected, fifteen minutes after the meeting was scheduled to conclude, everyone had left but *her*. Staying behind after the meeting was part of the routine *she* always followed. She would be the only person left in the building after the mousey receptionist who greeted everyone with that stupid toothy smile left. With the front door now locked, the lights still burned bright on the third floor where the group had its small office. That's where he would find her.

"It's time. Go now."

The voice constantly in his head was more forceful than ever. It was always there, whispering in his ear and telling him what to do. Over the last few days, the voice had been getting louder and louder. It was becoming unbearable. He had to do this tonight to make it stop.

"Go now!"

Checking to see that no one was on the street, he stepped from the shadows, leaving the safety of the alley and its evening camouflage. Even if someone did see him crossing the street, what would it matter? He certainly didn't look suspicious and quite frankly, anyone he ran into would probably know him and not think twice about seeing him out and about. Everyone in Parker City knew everyone else. Which is exactly why it was so difficult to keep secrets.

Hiding in plain sight, he quickly made his way across the street.

Taking a deep breath once he reached the sidewalk, he disappeared once again into the shadows that filled the empty parking lot beside the old house. Having sat through a boring history lesson about Parker City once, he remembered the wrinkled old historian standing at the front of the room telling everyone how there used to be another building where the lot was now. It started out as a stable for the household's horse and carriage before it was turned into a garage for the family's fancy new Buick touring car. Eventually, it ended up being used for storage until one hot summer night a group of students from Hammermill College, just north of the city, burned it down while protesting the Vietnam War. It was one of several buildings that had been damaged that night. Luckily no one had been hurt, but two dozen college kids were arrested and brought up on charges after the incident.

The back yard, at one time the location of countless garden parties, was now full of weeds and overgrown bushes that needed serious pruning. The only thing that looked remotely tended to was a small footpath from the parking area to a back door. Now an emergency fire exit, it was once the servants' entrance into the kitchen. Filled with file cabinets and dusty boxes, the kitchen had long ago been converted into a storeroom. The latch on the door was old, almost as old as the place itself, and easy to pop with a good hard shove. No bars on the windows, no burglar alarms to worry about going off—this was too easy, he thought to himself with a smile. He quietly eased the door closed behind him. The doorknob dangled in its place, having almost come off in his hand. The entire place smelled old. That was the only way he could describe it. There was something about the smell that forced him to think back on all the times he'd been forced to visit his grandmother.

So full of random boxes and bins, he found it difficult to squeeze his way through the storage room. Already anxious, he began to be overtaken by a feeling of claustrophobia. After a few deep breaths, he pressed on and out of the room. Following the empty hallway, he passed room after room filled with antique sofas and chairs, Chippendale sideboards, and paintings by local artists no one would ever hear about outside of Parker. Moonlight provided the only light with which to navigate the first floor. Slowly creeping down the main hall, strange shadows danced across the walls and ceiling around him. They could have been ghosts guiding his path, their eerie shapes pointing the way.

He couldn't help but feel as though this were the opening scene of a horror movie or some murder mystery. It was certainly the perfect setting.

When it was first built, just a few years before the turn of the century, the house on Braddock Street was one of the most magnificent, and certainly most modern, in the city. Three stories of polished mahogany hardwood floors, marble fireplaces, electricity in every room, a kitchen (with a refrigerator), and a bathroom on each floor made it the envy of almost everyone in town.

Almost one hundred years later, visitors to the historical society were greeted in the foyer by a portrait of the original owners, Theodore and Miriam Garrett. A successful attorney, Theo Garrett had been appointed to the Circuit Court for the district covering Parker County by Governor Elihu Jackson. He was a fierce jurist whose time on the bench earned him the reputation of being a "hangin' judge." By the time he retired, he'd sentenced more men to maximum sentences and years of hard labor than the other two judges with whom he served combined.

The house had remained in the Garrett family until the judge's great-grandson donated the property to the Parker Historical Society for its permanent home several years earlier. It was now a museum dedicated to the history of the small western Maryland city.

Vivid black and white photographs depicting life in Parker City during its earlier days hung on the walls throughout the house. The opening of the first Woolworth 5 & 10 Cent Store; the groundbreaking of the Harlequin Theatre; a parade for troops returning from Europe after World War I; a visit from President Franklin Roosevelt were all forever frozen in time.

Having been through the building on a number of occasions, he was familiar with most of the displays. But tonight was not an educational visit during which he'd be wasting time paying homage to the past.

"Don't touch anything."

The voice was just as anxious as he was.

Starting up the grand staircase to the second floor, he moved slowly to keep the old wooden step from making too much noise. The worn carpet runner masked his footfalls as he climbed the treads, the smell of dust and stale air following his every step. A slight moan from one of the warped boards stopped him dead in his tracks. Frozen, not breathing, he waited to make sure she hadn't heard him. After several tense moments, he allowed himself to relax. The unnerving groan that had stopped his heart hadn't carried upstairs. Or, more likely, as with anyone that spent a significant amount of time in the old house, she was probably used to hearing creaks and squeaks and didn't think twice about them. He still had the element of surprise on his side.

"Be careful. Be quiet!"

Taking a tentative step, then another and another, he began to climb once again. Counting the steps as he went, he tried to remain focused. Reaching the landing on the second floor, he paused to listen. It was eerily quiet. That only added to the mood. A momentary surge of excitement filled his body.

The rooms on the second floor were where the historical society's various displays and exhibits were open to visitors. The residents of Parker City and the surrounding county were proud of their home and its heritage. The area had first been settled as a small trading post on the Tasker River in the early 1700s. It hadn't officially become a city until 1785, a mere two years before thirty-nine prominent men signed their names to the country's new Constitution some hundred and twenty miles away in Philadelphia. With its roots firmly embedded in the early days of America's republic, combined with its proximity to the nation's capital and the part it had played during the Civil War, history was indelibly and proudly woven into the fabric of Parker.

Up and down the hall, dim lights glowed in each room. One of which was the library, where all the official documents and papers had been collected, including tax journals and census records dating back to 1790. Looking through the leather-bound folios, one could trace property ownership, business contracts, and families back to some of the city's earliest days. The pages were yellowed and brittle with age, but the handwriting was still remarkably clear.

Having started as a rural community, with farming still a very important part of the local economy, a rift had begun to grow as more commercial and manufacturing businesses began to open. It was a battle that had been fought time and time again—old versus new, the past versus the future. The small town community values that gave Parker its character were being engulfed by the encroachment of the Washington suburbs as they spread out in all directions. Parker City, in particular, was turning into a very big small city.

Even as Parker City and County glacially clawed their way into the future, there was an old guard dating back to the days of the original trading post that still held most of the power. Five families were credited with the founding of the city: The Bakers, the Mosses, the Worthingtons, the Tildons, and, of course, the Parkers. If one were to go through all of the documents the society had amassed over the decades, the names of those five families would appear on deeds and transactions generation after generation after generation.

Across from the hall, in what was once the bedroom of Theo and Miriam's only daughter, was a place visitors could see original clothing from different periods in Parker's history. A waistcoat that belonged to Thaddeus Parker, the city's first mayor, hung on a dress maker's form in a glass display cabinet in the center of the room. The rust colored vest had been immaculately preserved, as had Thaddeus' pipe, which was displayed in a box on the fireplace mantel next to a little gold plaque. Beside the fireplace hung bullet-riddled jackets from a pair of Civil War uniforms, one from the north and one from the south. The tattered and bloodstained pieces belonged to brothers Joseph and Jeremiah Woodley. One fought and died for the Union, the other for the Confederacy. They were stark reminders that the history the region was built upon was not always pretty and peaceful, but bloody and tragic.

A favorite room through which visitors could stroll was the Map Room. From the first hand-drawn map of the trading post along the Tasker River to the current layout of the city, the growth of Parker could be tracked over the last one hundred ninety-one years. Every major addition of land was recorded and exhibited on large maps along the walls.

There was even a rumor that one of the maps from the days of the Civil War, of which the society housed three, contained hidden clues to the legendary lost Confederate Treasure. No one had ever actually uncovered any secret messages or treasure maps, so most people just chalked it up to being an old wives' tale. Though there were some old timers around that swore by the myth.

Throughout the house, there were so many remarkable pieces from the past, all of which deserved attention and any of which could be viewed as a doorway to history. None of it was of any interest to him. It was on the third floor where his interest lay. He was there for a reason. There was no more time to waste.

The closer he got to the top of the wooden stairs, with all the lights still burning bright on the third floor, the more difficult it became to disappear into the shadows and hide in dark corners.

"It's time."

The narrow stairs opened onto an equally narrow hallway. Covered with many more black and white photos, it was almost impossible to see the sage green wallpaper which had been recreated to match the design of a cloth covering that once hung on the plaster walls. Pieces of furniture, each with its own story, cluttered the already cramped passage. Staying as close to the wall as possible, it was an obstacle course trying to avoid tripping over any of the antique pieces.

At the end of the hall, Theo and Miriam's bedroom had been converted into a conference room where the board would hold its monthly meetings. The most striking features, certainly Mrs. Garrett's favorites, were the oversized windows looking out on the front of the courthouse across Braddock Street. A small decorative park with rose bushes and a water fountain marked the path for those on their way to court. In the spring, as the flowers bloomed, it made for a beautiful picture.

Along with an old wooden conference table and matching chairs, some of the more priceless pieces in the society's collection were kept in the conference room where they could only be enjoyed by a select few. It was all such bullshit, he thought, passing by the open door, glancing in just to make certain he hadn't miscounted and no one had stayed behind.

The sound of shuffling paper was coming from the room next door. That's where she would be, in the office. He could hear her humming something horribly off-tune. A combination of anxiety and excitement brought on by the thought of her just around the corner caused his chest to tighten. He needed to get his breathing under control.

"Calm down. You can do this."

Standing in the doorway, he was finally able to see her. The surprise was going to be better than he imagined.

Beverly Baker was standing with her back to the door, next to a small desk in the center of the room. A former beauty queen, Beverly spent hours every morning doing her hair and make-up, selecting the perfect outfit, and picking just the right accessories. Image was everything, and the process was her daily ritual. Other than being a platinum blonde, in no way natural, she bore a striking resemblance to Linda Gray, who had recently risen to fame playing Sue Ellen Ewing on *Dallas*. Big hair, shoulder pads, and all. It was a comparison Beverly relished.

Physically attractive, her personality left quite a bit to be desired. The current matriarch of another of the city's founding families, she'd once been referred to as a viper disguised as a southern belle. Those words were uttered on more than one occasion by none other than her late father, state Senator Wilson Lee Baker. Like father, like daughter, they both had the ability to be charming and affable, but both commanded and demanded respect and obedience. Senator Baker had been a shrewd negotiator in the halls of the state capital, but when talking failed, he didn't see a problem using a little blackmail now and again to get what he wanted. It was the Baker family motto—do whatever it takes to achieve your goal. If that meant screwing over someone to get ahead, so be it. It was a lesson he had instilled in his four children from a very early age.

Following the senator's sudden death after suffering a massive heart attack, as the eldest child, Beverly had taken over the family's considerable holdings, the vast majority of which were in real estate. According to records in the clerk's office at the courthouse, the Baker family was one of the largest private landowners in the county.

As he slid into the room, she had a copy of the day's newspaper open in front of her, reading something she deemed worthy of her precious time. When she finished reading, she closed the paper and tossed it on the desk. With her paper shield gone and nothing distracting her senses any longer, Beverly's body stiffened ever so slightly. Did she know she was being watched? Could she sense him? He wondered what horrible thoughts might be running through her mind at that very moment.

He hadn't moved, hadn't made a sound. He was barely breathing. But she knew he was there. If he were able to see his own reflection in a mirror, he would have seen the horrifying grin on his face. It was a combination of pleasure and complete evil. He was reveling in the moment.

"Hello, Beverly."

Chapter One

Then...

The flood several years before had a devastating impact on the city. Rural in its beginning, it had slowly and painfully begun to suburbanize, becoming a bedroom community of the nation's capital. Not even thirty thousand people had called Parker City home before the Great Flood. After, the population was even less.

The waters had been like an invading army, pushing through the streets, displacing families and literally washing away businesses indiscriminately, leaving much of the oldest parts of the city in ruins. At the heart of the downtown sat the Center Square of Parker. From the four corners created by the intersection of Commerce and High Streets, rose four classic Pre-Civil War buildings. When first constructed in the 1800s, shortly before the war, they had been the tallest and most magnificent Parkertons had ever seen. Several architectural historians had even featured the Center Square and its antebellum structures in their works chronicling the region's design history.

For all their original splendor, after the five days of heavy rain and thunderstorms finally subsided, the once grand structures found themselves under nearly four feet of sludge-like water. Three years later, a shadow could still be seen on the stone and granite facades from where the water level had remained for days. It didn't matter how many times the buildings had been cleaned, hints of water damage lingered as a haunting reminder of the devastation Mother Nature had the ability to inflict. Like apparitions never willing to move on to the next world, buildings that once glimmered in the sun sat cold and dark.

It was the same story for most of the buildings along the main streets near the Tasker River. Boarded-up windows, crumbling exteriors, and a general sense of despair hung in the air along the once bustling commercial corridor.

The floodwaters had barely receded before Parker City's mayor, Charlie Oland, publicly committed to a complete restoration and revitalization of the area hit hardest by the storm. He devoted much of his time to the plans, meeting with elected officials at all levels—city, county, and state—to try and convince them to appropriate more tax dollars for recovery programs. Members of Congress even received personal visits in the hope of finding federal funds to help rebuild. There were those that said if sheer will alone was enough to restore what had been lost, then the mayor's would undoubtedly turn things around.

Even with his efforts to breathe life back into the devastated streets, the historic downtown area remained a virtual ghost town. There was very little to bring people to the blocks surrounding the Tasker River any longer. The prosperity Ronald Reagan had promised the year before when he was elected to the White House still had major hurdles to clear if things were going to improve. At least that was the case in Parker City.

With the abandoned buildings, dark alleyways, and empty thoroughfares came the crime one would expect in any depressed urban setting. Each evening, as the sun retreated below the horizon, prostitutes took their places on various corners, gangs of young hoodlums roamed freely, and drug deals were made openly on the streets. Not that many people were around to bear witness. No matter what the mayor and chief of police did, crime continued to be the only viable business downtown. Unable to put an end to the illegal activities, the Parker City Police Department was at least able to contain the illicit goings-on to the crippled blocks bordering the river. It was a small victory. A very small victory in a much bigger war city officials were losing.

Though the center of Parker remained an albatross around the necks of city officials, other areas on the outskirts of the city's limits were showing signs of life and beginning to grow. Housing developments were springing up on the north and west sides of the city, manufacturing facilities had opened along the southern corridor, producing everything from furniture to machine parts, and a brand new 800,000 square foot shopping mall was under construction on the east end.

Visionaries, like Mayor Oland, truly believed Parker City could have a prosperous future. Skeptics said that future hinged entirely on the restoration of the downtown. What had become the dismal symbol of the city needed to change before anyone would ever be able to believe in better days to come.

Chapter Two

The scene was the same for Ben Winters every morning as he drove his beat-up police cruiser to the Parker City Police Department. What were once busy streets lined with stores and restaurants, which he remembered from only a few years earlier, were now empty storefronts with plywood covering the windows and graffiti scrolled on the walls. Most days he used to have breakfast at a little diner, the Silver Griddle, just off the Center Square. The place wasn't much to look at, but the home-cooked food was incredible. There was usually a wait just to get a table or for an empty seat at the counter. But it was always worth it. After Ben had his fill of eggs and bacon, he'd grab a cup of coffee to go and walk to the station only a few blocks away.

That was before the flood. Nowadays, Ben would drive down the same street hoping to see any sign that business was returning. But there never was. Day after day, the dire situation never seemed to improve. Everything still looked the way it did the day before—miserable.

On that particular morning, the sun rose on a much cooler than expected spring day. With a crisp breeze blowing in from the mountains to the west, a chill was in the air. On the ground, frost had formed on the grass overnight, turning Jefferson Park into a field of glistening white crystals. It was a beautiful scene, but completely unwanted. The park's signature feature, a broken down battlement in the middle of an open stretch of land, sat covered with a thin layer of icy dew. The left-behind remnant of the Civil War looked as though it had fallen under the spell of a wicked ice queen. It had been a particularly cold winter, so when the temperature began to rise and everyone turned their clocks forward, no one wanted to look back. Spring had finally arrived. That's what made the cold-snap that morning so frustrating.

Jefferson Park, the thirty-acre expanse in the middle of the city, divided old downtown Parker from the newer sections of the city. It was all very confusing if you hadn't lived in Parker your entire life. Just like residents of Manhattan gave direction using uptown and downtown as opposed to north or south, natives understood the distinction and those who weren't natives, well, no one really cared what they thought—in Manhattan or Parker City.

As the clock on the dashboard rolled over from five-fifty-nine to six o'clock, Ben rattled by a deserted Jefferson Park. His patrol car, one of the oldest in the fleet, had taken what felt like an eternity to start that morning. Luckily, his use of that particular vehicle was only temporary because the department was in the process of transitioning over from the old Plymouths of the '60s to Ford's new Crown Victoria line. As head of the PCPD's new undercover detective squad, consisting of only himself and his partner, he had been promised a brand new unmarked '81 Crown Vic. He'd even gotten to pick the color—a golden-tan.

Joining the police force right out of college, Benjamin Adam Winters first served as one of the department's twenty-five uniformed patrolman. Not being a hotbed of criminal activity, the department didn't have individual specialized divisions like in other, larger cities. Uniformed officers handled all the cases and calls regardless of the severity.

One of Ben's very first calls after putting on the badge was to the scene of a robbery at the local High's convenience store. The following day he was called to help an elderly woman get back into her house after she locked herself out when she went to collect her mail. The day after that, he was put on a traffic assignment. Uniformed officers with the Parker City Police did it all.

However, shortly after returning from a conference of Mid-Atlantic city mayors, Charlie Oland decided to make some changes. The mayor's grand vision for Parker and its future was beginning to spill over into every aspect of the city's operations and functions. He instructed his police chief to create a detective squad whose purpose would be to act as the department's criminal investigative unit. He wanted Parker City to be on par with its neighbors and didn't want any department to fall behind, whether police, fire, Planning, or Parks and Rec. Mayor Oland was forward thinking. That was a fact with which no one could argue.

Chief of Police Edgar Stanley, on the other hand, was not forward thinking. He also didn't like politicians interfering in the way in which he ran his department. On more than one occasion, and to the face of more than one mayor, he would say he'd been there long before them and would be there long after. Even though he served at the pleasure of the mayor and city council, no one had ever actually tried to challenge the entrenched chief.

The best way to describe Edgar Stanley was as a surly, miserable sonofabitch out of place in his own time. The form of policing he subscribed to was much more in line with that of the New York City police at the turn of the century, when rules could be bent—if not outright broken—to achieve a goal. It was that type of policing which a young Teddy Roosevelt set out to bring to an end when he became police commissioner. Much in the same way Charlie Oland wanted to modernize the PCPD. It wasn't corruption he was fighting so much as breaking the belief that the old ways were the only ways.

Stanley liked doing things the old way. His way. If it had worked for the last twenty-five years, he saw no reason it wouldn't work for the next twenty-five. But the mayor was dead set on the city having its own detective squad. So if appointing a couple of detectives would get the young, idealistic mayor out of his hair, then so be it. He'd put up with worse ideas.

After reporting to work one morning six months ago, Ben and his partner, Tom Mason, had been summoned to the chief's office and the new detective squad was created. Even though it was made very clear that Stanley was completely against the idea. Neither Ben nor Tommy took it personally, but at twenty-six, they were both the youngest members of the department and too inexperienced to see they were being set up for failure. It was their age that made them the best fit for the mayor's vision of a modern police force, though. At the same time, their youth was the reason they'd had difficulty working alongside some of the more senior members of the PCPD. Just like the city as a whole, it was old versus new, the past versus the future—a constant, ongoing struggle.

If the experiment with a detective squad ended up being a success, the chief would have no problem taking credit. If it failed miserably, then Detectives Winters and Mason were too young and it was the mayor's fault for trying to fix something that wasn't broken in the first place.

The scrutiny Ben and his partner had been under since that fateful meeting with the chief had been intense. Luckily, the most difficult cases they had faced were nothing more than a few break-ins and the theft of a car. So far, they had a perfect track record, but there was no way to keep up that winning streak forever. Ben understood; he was a realist. Eventually they would come across a case they couldn't close. He just hoped it didn't happen any time soon.

On the bright side, now the chief only grumbled when he saw Ben and Tommy in the hallway, as opposed to mumbling something derogatory under his breath. The detectives were willing to take what they could get.

The Parker City Police Department was headquartered in a two story brick building just around the corner from City Hall. The station wasn't fancy or very spacious, but it served its purpose. Even after a recent renovation, the building was still woefully lacking. The chief had been lobbying for close to a decade to get the mayor and city council to approve the money to build a new headquarters. The current station had been built in 1895. Some joked that's when Stanley had taken over as chief of police. Year after year though, the council would come back and say the department could either have the money to build a new station or have the money to cash paychecks, but they couldn't have the money for both. That's not to say Mayor Oland didn't try to find money for other programs and equipment, the city just couldn't afford to build a state-of-the-art law enforcement complex.

As Ben turned the cruiser into the parking lot the department shared with City Hall, he thought to himself that the building looked exactly like a police station should. It was solid and secure, a good old-fashioned red brick building on a stone foundation. If it weren't for the bars on the basement windows where the holding cells were located, someone who didn't know might have thought it was a small school. Designed by the same architect that designed City Hall, the two buildings shared some of the same features, but the PCPD was nowhere near as opulent. It was more of a bastard stepbrother. City Hall had white marble columns and hand-carved engravings along its stone parapet, while the station was lucky to have a roof that didn't leak. City Hall was fronted by a beautiful park with rose bushes and a fountain, while the station had a cracked sidewalk with a tree root growing out between two of the cement slabs. And at night, City Hall was illuminated by floodlights, while in the darkness the station went from looking like a little schoolhouse to looking like a creepy mental asylum.

Be it ever so humble, Ben thought to himself as he parked the car.

Chapter Three

At that time of day, with the sun just barely above the eastern horizon, the station would still be blissfully quiet. Except for those needed to keep things running overnight, a skeleton crew at best, the place was practically deserted. That's how Ben liked it. He liked to start his day early, using the calm of the morning as time to focus and plan his day, as much as he could. As a police officer, there was no way to know for certain what your day would be like. Anyone who wore a badge would say they liked the quiet, uneventful days. Their families also liked those types of days. When a shift was uneventful, it meant everyone got home safe.

Letting himself in through the parking lot entrance in the back of the building, Ben said good morning to the booking officer on duty, the first person anyone arrested overnight would face. Unfortunately, Sergeant Ronald Rodgers didn't have that pleasant of a face.

"Quiet night?" Ben asked, glancing at the bulletin board next to the door to see if anything of interest had been posted since he last checked.

"Not a peep," answered the sergeant without looking up from his crossword puzzle.

"Is the chief in yet?"

That got him to put his pencil down and raise his eyes over his horn-rimmed glasses. "What do you think, Winters?"

Ron Rodgers had been on the job longer than Ben had been alive. A round man with a big bushy mustache the color of ash and not a single strand of hair on his head, he was usually sarcastic and dismissive when he spoke to Ben. Unlike with others at the department, it wasn't personal.

Sergeant Rodgers was naturally sarcastic and dismissive with everyone. At his age, with retirement right around the corner, he just didn't care that much anymore. Even so, he was a fixture in the PCPD and pretty much ran the place during the night shift. Why he'd never been promoted to a rank higher than sergeant was still a mystery to Ben. Though he had heard rumors about a long-standing feud between Rodgers and the chief. Something to do with a squad car running out of gas while the two were in pursuit of a suspect. Or something to do with a broken coffee mug. It all depended on who you asked.

Ben couldn't remember the last time Chief Stanley had gotten to the office ahead of him, let alone before ten o'clock. It was a luxury the chief enjoyed being the top law enforcement officer in a small city with very little crime.

The early morning quiet of the police station was relaxing to Ben. It helped him think. Some people couldn't handle silence. They always needed some sort of noise in the background. Ben could never understand that. Too much noise made it difficult to concentrate. He liked to think.

Walking down the hall, a familiar smell lingered in the air. The same one he smelled every morning. It was hard to describe exactly, but it always made him think of a musty library or old elementary school. There was something institutional about it in his mind. After all the time he'd spent in the building, he thought he'd be used to it by now. Yet, every morning it still took him by surprise.

The detective squad had an office on the second floor in the center of the building. The space was slightly larger than a storage closet. It had just enough room for two desks next to each other, a couple of file cabinets, and one trash can. Because of its location, it had no windows or natural light of any kind. It also boasted a door that squeaked no matter how much WD-40 was put on the hinges and a hideous green vinyl linoleum floor. Thankfully, the air conditioning worked in the summer and the heat in the winter, even if the air vent rattled nonstop.

The rest of the building was much the same—functioning but falling apart. Even with some recent work that had been done on the station, it still had issues. Cramped quarters could either help to improve comradery or exacerbate minor grievances and turn them into bigger problems than necessary. For the most part, the PCPD handled the lack of space well. Ben and his partner were just lucky to have the small amount of privacy they did.

Hanging his coat on the hook behind the door, Ben tossed his briefcase on his chair and headed for the break room down the hall. After a particularly restless night, he was in desperate need of a strong cup of coffee. For whatever reason, he hadn't been able to sleep. He spent most of the nighttime hours staring at the ceiling of his bedroom. Something had been bothering him, but he didn't know what. A very uneasy feeling had settled in the pit of his stomach and had kept him on edge all night, watching the hours painfully tick by. The hope was a shot of good old-fashioned caffeine would clear his head and settle his nerves.

On the hunt for coffee, he passed a row of empty offices. One by one they'd begin to fill as the department's command staff rolled in. But for now, he was on his own. At least that's what he thought.

As he got closer to the break room, he could smell the unmistakable scent of fresh coffee. Somebody on the second floor was already at work. Pushing through the break room door, it was no surprise to Ben to find Captain Nick Brent, the department's operations commander, standing in front of the old coffee maker with an empty mug waiting for the machine to finish brewing. In Ben's mind, he was easily the hardest working man on the force.

At six-foot-four and barrel-chested, the former Navy man was an imposing figure. Even though it had been almost two decades since he was in the service, he kept his hair trimmed short and close to the scalp, making up for it with a thick ginger mustache. Brent was number two in the department and the chief's right-hand man. Chief Stanley set the direction for the officers and made the big decisions, but the captain was the one that ran things day-to-day. No one understood how he did it, but he kept up with all of the department's crime statistics, worked as the liaison to the Parker County Sheriff's Department and Maryland State Police, taught a class at the police academy, personally reviewed the daily incident reports, and found time to go out on patrol when a shift was short a man. Ben didn't think he ever slept.

He could be a gruff old bear, certainly as old school as Chief Stanley, but everyone in the department liked him. More importantly, they respected him. When the idea of creating a detective squad was initially proposed, Brent had been the first to warm to the idea. The more he thought about it, the more he liked it. He had been very supportive of Ben and Tommy, giving them whatever resources he could spare when needed.

"Good morning, sir," Ben said, watching the captain fill his cup with the steaming hot brew. "The coffee smells good this morning."

"I was visiting my sister in Seattle a couple weeks ago," he started, skipping over the pleasantries of a greeting and pouring an obscene amount of sugar into his cup, "and she took me to this little coffee shop. It was pretty good, a hell of a lot better than this stuff. But the picture on the cup was some sort of weird mermaid creature-thing. And it rained every day. Very depressing." He paused just long enough to drink half the cup in one gulp, then added, "It was all too hippy-dippy out there if you ask me."

Captain Brent had an interesting way with words Ben, thought to himself as he filled his own mug, taking in the glorious smell of the fresh coffee. Its rich aroma alone filled his entire body with a welcome sense of calm.

The two spent the next few minutes talking about the opening of baseball season and whether the Orioles' recent trade of Kiko Garcia for Chris Bourjos would make any difference to their chances of winning the pennant. Neither was holding out much hope. Ben had barely touched his coffee by the time the captain had finished off his first cup and poured another, followed by a third to take with him back to his office.

Left alone in the break room, Ben took a few minutes to flip through the morning edition of the *Herald-Dispatch*, giving the caffeine a chance to kick in. By the time he got to the sports section, he was feeling much better and was ready to take on the day.

Chapter Four

Ben closed the file folder and tossed it on top of the stack with the others. Chief Stanley wanted updates on everything on which the squad was working. It still struck him as amusing when someone referred to the detective *squad*. There were only two of them—Detective Sergeant Ben Winters and Detective Tom Mason. "Squad" just sounded better, he guessed.

Like in any bureaucracy, all the reports would have to work their way up the chain of command. First, they would land on the desk of the Field Services commander, Lieutenant James Dennis, Ben's supervisor, then move on to Captain Brent, Dennis's supervisor. Finally, they would reach the chief, who may or may not actually read the reports. There were also weekly in-person briefings he would deliver to the command staff, which was basically just him repeating what he'd already written in his reports. Ben knew for a fact Stanley never paid attention to what he was saying in those meetings. Half the time, he'd sit thumbing through the paper, completely ignoring Ben or whoever happened to be speaking.

By eight o'clock, the station had come to life. Voices filled the hallway outside Ben's door, phones rang more frequently, and the mimeograph machine across the hall was running at full speed. The peace of the early morning had disappeared for another twenty-four hours.

As Ben opened the next file, Tommy Mason strutted into the office as only he could. With a bold swagger, Ben's partner exuded a cock-sure attitude. The look of a horny schoolboy plastered on his face.

"Guess who got lucky with who last night," Tommy teased through a grin that would put the Cheshire Cat's to shame.

"Whom," Ben said, not looking up from the form he was filling out. "Guess who got lucky with *whom*. And my guess is you with Shirley from down in Dispatch."

"How the hell, man? How did you know that?" Tommy asked, marveling at Ben's Sherlockian skills.

"You're wearing the same thing you had on yesterday and you smell like Chanel, which Shirley wears so much of, you'd think she bathed in it every morning."

"That's why you're the *chief* detective in this department, my friend," Tommy said, dropping into his chair and kicking his feet up on the desk. A few more inches to the left and he'd have knocked over the pile of papers Ben laid there for him to read.

Ben Winters and Tommy Mason had gone to school together, graduated from the police academy together, and joined the force together. Both were attractive young men, but each in his own way. Ben was average height, fit, and had a full head of thick auburn hair. Tommy was six-foot-two of pure muscle and his dark brown, almost black hair was already starting to gray, along with his Tom Selleck-inspired mustache.

Clean-cut and straight-laced, Ben looked like the boy next door. The kind of guy every girl wanted to take home to meet her parents. Tommy, on the other hand, was the athletic type—the star of the football team—and the guy every girl wanted to make out with under the bleachers.

When they were still on patrol, Ben's uniform was always crisp. Tommy's could usually use another minute or two under the iron. It was the same story now that they wore suits every day. Ben always tried to look as sharp as possible, wanting to project a serious image to combat the disadvantage of his age and youthful appearance.

Tommy didn't think what he was wearing mattered, which is why he didn't care if he showed up to a scene with his pants a little wrinkled or a stain on his tie. He didn't understand why they couldn't dress more casually like some of the guys on *Hill Street Blues*. Ben kept explaining that wasn't how real detectives dressed, just the ones on television. Tommy still thought it would be more comfortable. He absolutely hated wearing a tie and knew how good he looked in a leather jacket.

Regardless of what they were wearing, both understood the only way to earn respect was with results. They knew the odds were stacked against them from the start, and most of the people in the building were expecting them to fail. On the one hand, the patrolmen who were passed over when the squad was created were jealous; on the other, the brass didn't like the mayor sticking his nose where it didn't belong and telling them how to run the department.

No one ever accused Ben of being a stick in the mud or not being able to let loose when not on duty. On occasion, some of the guys called him "Opie," referring to the young character Ron Howard played on *The Andy Griffith Show*, but he was no redheaded little tot and could drink any of them under the table and keep going. In addition to his professional achievements, he'd also won the title of Beer Pong Champion back at the police academy. But it was Tommy who was always the life of the party, and the guy with whom all the girls wanted to spend the night. Ben knew when to be serious; Tommy didn't care. They were the perfect team, the perfect balance for one another.

As the morning went on, Ben continued digging through the stacks of papers, hoping to eventually unearth the hideous beige laminate top of his desk. He couldn't believe the amount of paperwork that came with his job and didn't want to imagine what it would be like if Parker City had any serious crime. The next thing he was going to ask for was a secretary—which he already knew there was no chance of getting.

Beside him, Tommy was clicking away on their new computer. He despised the machine and was in no way comfortable typing. Using both of his index fingers and only his index fingers, he slowly and painfully entered the information into the appropriate flashing boxes on the screen, cursing under his breath with each keystroke. He didn't pretend to understand how the thing worked or where the numbers and letters he was typing went, but Ben promised the computer was going to make their jobs a lot easier. Tommy had no idea how, but he trusted his partner, so he kept hitting the keys, one at a time, swearing with every stroke.

"This thing is nothing like my Atari," Tommy groaned, standing and stretching his arms. "With something as *sophisticated* as you keep telling me this thing is, I should at least be able to play *Space Invaders* on it when I need a break."

Leaning back in his chair, tossing his pen on the desk, Ben made a very good point. "If you were able to play video games on the computer, you wouldn't get any actual work done."

"I'm not disagreeing with you," Tommy responded without hesitation. "But right now, I'm going to stretch my legs and grab a coffee. You want one?"

"I could use a refill," Ben said, handing him his blue and white Baltimore Colts mug.

"Still a Colts fan? That's just sad. The Redskins are going all the way this year, dude," he shouted from halfway down the hall.

According to the clock above the door, it was almost ten. The morning was flying by. Ben's plan was to have everything finished by lunchtime because he had been requested at a budget meeting that afternoon. There were a number of city council members who wanted to be walked through the PCPD's budget request for the coming year, and one of the subjects to be discussed was the needs of the new detectives. There was no telling how long that was going to take, so he wanted a clear schedule for the afternoon.

When Tommy returned, he had a fresh cup of coffee in each hand with a glazed donut balanced carefully on the rim of each mug. Handing Ben his mid-morning snack, he said, "Something's going on over at the old Garrett House. Shirley came up to tell the LT about a call that just came in. Patrol says it could be a possible break in."

"And she came up to tell Dennis about it in person?"

"She came up for the donuts and ran into Dennis. You know how he doesn't like first-floorers up here, so she needed a cover story."

"Oh, the intrigue of the Parker City Police Department." Ben rolled his eyes and took a bite of his donut. It might have been a cliché, but the PCPD did have good donuts.

He hadn't even had a chance to swallow when Lieutenant Dennis marched into the makeshift office, red-faced and visibly agitated. To be fair, that was the way he usually looked. A tall, stick-figure, with a pointy nose, and slicked back hair, he was a man in a perpetually bad mood.

"Winters, Mason, get over to the historical society," he barked. "It's time to earn your stripes. Somebody killed Beverly Baker. Don't fuck this up."

Chapter Five

At first, Ben wasn't sure he'd heard the lieutenant correctly. Beverly Baker was as well known in the city as the mayor. And in some circles, she was considered more important. He'd never met the woman personally, but knew her by reputation. She sat on the board of trustees of Tasker Valley Memorial Hospital and Hammermill College, chaired nearly every major social function in the city, and was the president of her family's company. Beverly Baker was a pillar of the community. The thought of someone having killed her was hard to believe at first blush.

Competing thoughts raced through Ben's mind as he opened the bottom desk drawer and retrieved his service revolver, a Smith & Wesson .357 Magnum. Holstering the weapon, he grabbed his jacket and headed out the door. Tommy was already a few steps ahead of him. Their pace quickened with every step. They were practically jogging by the time they reached the parking lot.

Climbing into the driver's seat, Ben said a silent prayer that the engine would turn over by at least the third try. They needed to get to the Garrett House as quickly as possible. Now was not a time for the old car to have a temper tantrum and not start. As if it understood the importance of the situation, the engine sputtered for a brief second, then roared to life with the first turn of the key. It was a small miracle. Ben thanked whichever divine power had intervened and answered his prayer.

The PCPD was by no means a large metropolitan police department. The incidents it handled were minor compared to those of nearby cities like Baltimore and Washington, DC. So Ben wasn't entirely surprised to find at least half the force already on the scene when they pulled up in front of the historical society. The sudden death—or murder, as it was being reported—of such a prominent figure was bound to bring everyone running. Ben counted six patrol cars parked haphazardly along the street and could hear more sirens approaching in the distance. Officers had already begun cordoning off the immediate area with yellow crime scene tape. A number of passersby had gathered, drawn to the morning's police activity. The onlookers were being corralled on the sidewalk across the street so as not to interfere with arriving personnel.

Getting out of the car, Ben scanned the scene. He was taking it all in, making mental notes about everything he saw. The activity was frenzied and could quickly turn into a circus if someone didn't take control of the situation.

Walking toward the fury of activity, Ben clipped his badge to the lapel of his jacket, making it easily visible. Even though he knew it was all in his mind, the weight of his service piece seemed to become heavier and heavier with every step he took closer to the scene. Was his heart beating faster, as well? Or was that in his imagination too?

From behind his sunglasses, Tommy was surveying the scene in his own way. Besides the small army of city police, two county sheriff's deputies had arrived, and a Maryland State Police trooper was pulling up with his dome light swirling. Not seeing any of the department's brass there, it was going to be him and Ben—specifically Ben—who would need to take command and get things organized.

Easily recognized by the two patrolmen keeping the growing crowd of sightseers at bay, the detectives ducked under the police tape and stepped into the ensuing chaos. It was going to be a baptism by fire for the fledgling detectives.

The weight of the situation grew heavier with each step they took. All eyes were on Ben and Tommy now, literally and figuratively. Much like Chief Stanley, not many of the boys in uniform understood why the department needed a detective squad. Everything had been perfectly fine the way it was, and to call two guys in a storage room a "squad" was just laughable.

The other side of the argument was that if the mayor was going to force such a unit on the department, then why were two of the greenest officers given the job? The rank and file of the Park City Police had not taken the announcement well. A few had been congratulatory, whether sincere or not. Most, however, were openly hostile. The more senior members of the department took offense that kids, as they referred to them, were going to be running around pretending to be Dick Tracy. The younger officers, on the other hand, were jealous as hell they hadn't been the ones tapped for the new job.

The first few months had been miserable, especially for Tommy. He used to love going out and grabbing a beer with the guys after their shift, standing around the water cooler telling dirty jokes, or hanging out in the locker room talking about that weekend's football game. A huge Washington Redskins fan, this was a very important part of his fall and winter. Once he exchanged his blue and gray uniform for a few suits from the Sears catalogue, he felt like he was on the outside looking in. The upside was that all the women around the station—the secretaries and dispatchers—didn't have a problem with his new position. He was their very own Thomas Magnum, but with a badge.

Ben had adjusted to the resentment and hostility a lot quicker. He'd always wanted to be a police officer. Even as a little boy he could remember dreaming of growing up and being just like the guys in the pages of his comic books. Every time a new crime thriller opened in the movie theaters, he begged his father to take him to see it. As a kid, he had romanticized wearing the badge and being a police officer. Looking back, he understood that now.

Now, after a few months in their new positions, things were cooling off. Most everyone saw that neither Ben nor Tommy weren't stepping on anyone's toes or trying to look like a pair of heroes. They stuck to their assignments and turned in results. However, even though the majority of the department had started to come around and accept their new roles, some of the old-timers—the fossils of the PCPD—weren't going to cut them any slack whatsoever. Some even went out of their way to hassle the pair.

Sitting on the front steps of the townhouse, the detectives found a visibly shaken patrolman. Ben guessed, judging by the shaking hands and complete lack of color in his face, he was the one who found the victim. His pasty complexion also led Ben to believe he'd never seen a dead body until today.

"Hey, Pete," Ben started, "you alright?" He put his hand on the officer's shoulder.

Peter Vernon had joined the force the same year as Ben and Tommy. The difference was he'd already been in uniform for a number of years, serving as a sheriff's deputy one county over. In comparison, Harrison County made Parker look like an international metropolis. The biggest crime spree in Harrison had dealt with in recent months was a sudden rash of cow tipping. When they first heard about the incidents, Tommy thought it was a joke. But it turned out there was a gang of teens harassing farmers and causing general upheaval on their lands.

"Ben." Vernon stopped, catching himself. "I mean, Sergeant, or um, Detective Sergeant…" He wasn't sure if he was going to pass out or throw up.

"Ben's fine, Pete. I'm still just Ben." Giving the officer a chance to compose himself, Ben pulled a small notebook from his jacket pocket. "You want to start at the beginning? Tell us what happened."

Taking a deep breath, Officer Vernon began by saying, "Everything was just like always this morning. I was doing my usual circuit through the city. I start coming down Braddock, and all of a sudden I see a woman run out in the middle of the street. She was screaming like mad."

The officer paused and took a deep breath.

"Did you see where see came from?" Ben asked, not wanting to press too hard but still needed to collect as much information as possible.

"Yeah," Vernon said, shaking his head. "It was Lucy Jenkins. She came running out of the historical society there. We go to the same church. I know her."

Ben nodded and gave him a reassuring smile. "What happened then?"

"Like I said, she was screaming and ran right out into the middle of the street. She was almost run over by a delivery truck. The truck slammed on its brakes and I had to swerve so I didn't rear-end him. It was lucky no one was behind me.

"So, I jump out of the car and pull Lucy onto the sidewalk. She's sobbing and all I can make out is her saying, 'upstairs, upstairs.'"

Looking around, Tommy assumed Lucy Jenkins was the woman sitting in the backseat of the one patrol car with a blanket wrapped around her shoulders. "You say you know this Lucy Jenkins? Does she work at the historical society?"

"Yeah. She's the secretary," the officer said, nodding. "I didn't want to leave her by herself, so I radioed for assistance. Dunkin rolled up a few minutes later, so I left her with him and went to check out the building."

Tommy was beginning to feel that if they needed to coach every detail out of Vernon, it was going to be quite some time before they got into the townhouse to see for themselves what had everyone in suck a state.

Silently motioning to Ben, Tommy let his partner know he was going to head inside to have a look around. There wasn't any reason both of them needed to hear Vernon's every move, and Ben was better at taking statements, anyway. If it came to it, he'd take Lucy's statement. He was always much better with the female witnesses.

Tommy nodded to another uniform officer standing at the front door as he stepped into the old house. He just wanted to take a cursory first look around. Cautiously making his way through the first floor, he found the back door wide open. Its lock was smashed and dangled from the doorframe. Clearly the entry point for whoever broke in. On the second and third floors, nothing looked as though it had been disturbed. At least as far as he could tell.

The place was dark and musty. The dust hanging in the air was making his eyes water. Morning light shining through the thick lead-glass windows filled the house with odd shadows. That alone was enough to set anyone on edge. Reaching the third floor, the Tommy thought his mind was playing tricks on him because he would have sworn he felt a cold chill run down his spine. At the end of the hallway, he found the empty meeting room. Again, nothing looked out of place. Then, in the small office next door, he found

Beverly Baker.

Chapter Six

Now...

Nearly four decades after that terrible spring in 1981, not only had the events that transpired been largely relegated to legend, Parker City was unrecognizable. Nearly tripled in size, the city was booming. Residents who had moved north from the Washington suburbs, bringing with them their families and their money, far outnumbered native Parkertons. Though there was still something of a divide and mistrust between those who had been born and raised there and the more recent transplants, the city and surrounding county had become a thriving mini-metropolis in Western Maryland.

The residential explosion in turn had ignited an economic boom.

The plans that Mayor Charlie Oland put into place during his administration had also paid off, helping to pave the way for a downtown that was thriving like never before. It had taken longer than he would have liked—thirty-plus years and three more mayors, to be precise. But shops of every kind, galleries, and fashionable eateries filled the once empty, dilapidated buildings ravished by the Great Flood of '78.

On any given day, the streets bustled with life and activity. It didn't matter if it was a weekday or weekend. Downtown Parker City had returned from ruin. From restaurants bearing the names of nationally renowned chefs to expensive antique stores, the once bleak and desolate void of nothingness was in the middle of a modern renaissance. In the end, against all the odds and naysayers, Charlie Oland had had the last laugh as his dream of a prosperous downtown had come true.

The resurgence underway in downtown Parker, however, paled in comparison to what was happening throughout the rest of the city—now the second largest in the state. Not only had a number of national corporations opened regional offices there, but two Fortune 500 companies were headquartered in the city's south side commercial district, an area home to high rise office parks with highly sought after addresses by up-and-coming businesses.

Most striking of all was what had happened along the Tasker River itself. Office and condo buildings lined its banks. The stunning modern architecture cut into the sky, creating a skyline no one would have imagined so many years earlier when the entire area was under water. Even the new City Hall, a gleaming glass and steel structure, had been built along the river bank. The shadow it cast over the Tasker River was symbolic of how the city had rebuilt and would never be at the mercy of the river and its waters again.

No one was happier about Parker City's new Golden Age than the current mayor, Gregory Oland, son of the former mayor. Following exactly in his father's footsteps, Greg had attended the University of Maryland and Georgetown Law, then briefly practiced law privately before running for Parker County State's Attorney. After a couple of terms as the county's top prosecutor, he set his sights on the mayor's office. Whether his path was of his own choosing or his father's design was never quite clear.

As Parker City's chief executive, though, the second Mayor Oland proved himself to be his own man. He guided the city through the national economic downturn, being as tough with his budgets as he had been with the criminals he sent to prison. His aggressive austerity measures during the worst of the financial crisis kept the city afloat and poised for a boom when the markets began to turn around, which is exactly what happened.

People began to say the Olands had a sixth sense when it came to seeing Parker's future. No matter how outlandish or unpopular the idea, they always knew what was best for the city, even if the city didn't know itself.

Their plans proved it time and time again. Some wondered if Greg Oland's son would also have "the gift" and be a third-generation mayor one day.

It went without saying Charlie Oland was exceedingly proud of his son. To see an Oland back in the mayor's office filled his heart with joy. He would always think of Parker as his city. He's the one who'd rebuilt it, after all. Even now, in his late seventies, he would still walk down the street, shaking hands and talking to everyone with whom he crossed paths. He was still as well-known as ever. And just as influential.

The Olands had become Parker's modern political royalty. They were the future. Gone were the days when the city was run by just a few powerful families. The old guard had finally fallen…to be replaced with a new guard.

Chapter Seven

Like everything else in and around Parker, the police department had grown and become a model police force, just as Charlie Oland had envisioned during his term in office. Well-funded, well-staffed—just over two hundred strong—led by a progressive chief, the PCPD had been built into a prime example of a modern urban police agency.

As had always been the case throughout history, with Parker's growth came the inevitable pain of increased criminal activity. It was the nature of any developing community. More people, plus more commerce, equaled more crime. It was a very simple equation. From only two detectives when the squad was first created to thirty in the current Criminal Investigations Division, PCPD detectives handled cases dealing with everything from property damage to homicide. Compared to other cities of similar size, however, Parker's crime stats were much better. A fact the chief didn't mind pointing out from time-to-time.

The days of only a handful of patrol officers on the street were a thing of the past. Four rotating platoons now covered Parker City's forty square miles twenty-four hours a day, seven days a week. Whether in patrol cars, on foot, riding bikes, or zipping around on Segues, at any given time, a police presence on the streets was evident. The chief wanted his men to be out in the community as much as possible. He wanted there to be a good relationship between the department and the residents and merchants of the city. The more the officers were on the street talking to people, getting to know them and their neighborhoods, the safer everyone felt.

The policies put in place by the chief even extended to how the department dealt with the ever growing minority and immigrant population. Such strides had been made in connecting with these communities that the U.S. Department of Justice used Parker City and the PCPD as an example for how police and multi-cultural communities could work together.

When Parker built the new City Hall, the PCPD got the new station for which it had been lobbying for so long. "New" being something of a relative term. After the city's government offices moved to the Charles F. Oland Building along the river, referred to by some as the Ivory Tower, the old City Hall had been renovated and become the home of the PCPD. It was a stately headquarters, retaining all the building's original, and expensive, decorative features including hardwood floors, crown molding, granite fireplaces, and marble columns. The grand old building now just happened to be retrofitted with the most technologically advanced law enforcement and communication equipment available.

A beautiful example of post-Civil War architecture, the building provided a picturesque backdrop for outdoor events held on its front lawn. Until City Hall had moved, the park served as the location for the swearing in ceremony of the mayor and members of the city council every four years with all its pomp and circumstance. A number of honors had been bestowed on citizens over the years there, as well as proclamations that served very little purpose other than making for good press.

Since becoming police headquarters, security had tightened and all major events were either held at the Oland Building or the Harlequin Theatre. An exception having been made, that afternoon's gathering in front of the police station was entirely appropriate. Blue and white bunting decorated the park, with rows of white folding chairs filled by local dignitaries and VIPs, and a podium set up on the front steps for the speakers to honor the retiring Parker County Sheriff, Thomas Mason.

"As state's attorney for eight years," Mayor Greg Oland was saying, reminiscing, and making it a point to draw attention to his own service to the community, "I was privileged to work with Sheriff Mason on a regular basis. It was an honor to work with a man of such distinction and devotion to protecting and serving the residents of this county. From his earliest days as one of the first detectives with the Parker City Police Department to his tenure as the most popular sheriff in our county's history, he has given so much of himself to this community."

Oland knew how to lay it on pretty thick when needed. For the last seven and a half minutes, the mayor had been recounting story after story about the outgoing sheriff, praising him up and down, leaving no positive adjective unsaid in his remarks. At one point he actually used the word "gecorennes!" Whoever had written his remarks had no doubt had a thesaurus, or an old English dictionary, open next to them.

Sitting in the front row next to Tommy, Ben Winters thought that if he didn't know the guy, he would have thought he was the second coming of Christ by the way Oland was gushing about him. The sheriff's popularity in the county was very high, and he was leaving the job on his own terms before the county executive decided it was time to appoint someone younger.

As his partner for so many years, it was only natural that Ben would be on hand to say a few words. Who better to talk about Tommy Mason than his best friend?

Following the case in '81, the two had worked to build up the detective squad, proving the importance of a well trained and equipped investigative unit. As the city and the police department grew, both Ben and Tommy rose through the ranks. There was one advantage Tommy always had over Ben, though. He knew how to work the system. He was the more personable of the two and far more politically savvy. As their careers took off, he made sure to always remain friendly with the powers-that-be, whomever that happened to be at the time. It helped to provide cover and grease the wheels for Ben and himself when they needed help with an investigation.

Detectives Ben Winters and Tommy Mason made quite the names for themselves through a number of high-profile cases and a stint on a federal task force, both becoming highly sought after for their expertise, experience, and ability to close difficult cases.

Following a particularly nasty campaign several cycles back, the newly elected county executive cleaned house, removing the heads of all major departments, including that of the sheriff's office. Because of his connections, ambition, and sterling reputation, Tommy was appointed and sworn in as Parker County Sheriff.

Fifteen years later, after four decades in law enforcement, he was ready to sail off into the sunset, figuratively speaking, and enjoy a well-deserved retirement. To honor his years of service, a number of activities had been organized, culminating with the public event in front of the Parker City Police Department, the place where his career began.

Mayor Oland was coming to the end of his remarks, preparing to introduce Ben, who would in turn introduce Tommy for his farewell.

"It's now my honor to introduce a man who knows Tom better than anyone else. A brother in blue, his former partner, and a man who himself will be following the sheriff into retirement in just a few months, Ben Winters."

The mayor stepped away from the microphone as Parker City Police Chief Benjamin Winters walked to the podium.

Chapter Eight

Ben didn't like speaking to large crowds, or in public in general, for that matter. He was much more comfortable in an interrogation room, face-to-face with a suspect. The person in the hot seat could very well have been a psychotic serial killer, but in that room, he was in full control. It was the same when he had to take the stand and testify in court. That was part of the job. But standing in front of a group of people, even with a prepared speech in front of him, set his nerves on edge for some reason he never understood.

In his position as Chief of the Parker City Police Department, he knew there was no way to actually avoid speaking in public—no matter how hard he tried. So when he did, he did so very begrudgingly. On the occasions he was able, Ben was more than happy to have the deputy chief stand in for him.

When he'd been approached about speaking at Tommy's retirement, though, he was all too happy to accept the invitation. The situation was completely different. Not only was Tommy a good friend—more of a brother, really—he had done an outstanding job running the sheriff's department. From cleaning up internal matters within the agency, the reason he'd been appointed sheriff in the first place, to more recently dealing with the heroin epidemic spreading along the east coast. He deserved recognition for his efforts, and that's why Ben *wanted* to say a few words.

Tommy had become a very popular figure, not just in Parker County, but throughout the national law enforcement community. Not only was he a past president of the National Sheriffs Association, he had also served on a blue ribbon presidential commission charged with making recommendations to address the growing opioid crisis that was plaguing large swaths of the country.

Even though his job had become very political, the law always came first. It didn't matter who broke it, how much money they had, or what fancy title might be in front of their name. If they committed the crime, Sheriff Thomas Mason was going to make certain they did the time. A philosophy Ben shared whole heartedly. A criminal was a criminal was a criminal. Not that the two were heartless and didn't take extenuating circumstances into consideration. But it was the people who thought they were above the law that raised their ire most.

With both of their retirements coming so close together, a number of news stories had begun popping up chronicling the men's careers. The *Washington Post* had just run a feature article on the two outlining the major cases on which they'd worked and the impact they'd each had on the departments they now commanded.

As with any press he ever received, Ben hated it. He much preferred to stay out of the spotlight and focus on doing his job. Tommy was much more open to being the center of attention. Using the press had helped to get him into the sheriff's office, so he was always willing to provide a quote or give an interview. He'd even become something of a regular on the cable news channels as an expert on topics related to crime and policing.

Regardless of his desire to remain in the background whenever possible, Ben had a sterling reputation. Administratively, he had proven himself to be extremely skilled when it came to organization and management. Not only was he able to identify the best and brightest, he was able to convince them to join the PCPD. The command staff alone was made up of a number of decorated police veterans. It was the high regard in which Ben Winters was held that drew so many talented individuals, who could easily work in bigger and certainly more well-known agencies, to the city's police force.

From the top brass all the way down to the patrol officers on the streets, as chief, Ben had instituted policies of rigorous training and continuing education. The captain of the Professional Standards Division, who oversaw all of the departments' professional development and training, was one of Ben's closest advisors. The PCPD's training program had become an example for other departments across the country. Ben was extraordinarily proud of the strides the department had made during his tenure. The PCPD of today was nothing like the one he and Tommy joined in their youth. It was forward-thinking and modern. Long gone were the days of being afraid to try something new just because that's not how it was always done in the past. Innovation now drove the department.

Ben was never one to take the credit, however. He knew how to delegate and rely on the expertise and abilities of his top people. Micromanaging the PCPD was not his style. He provided guidance and made the tough decisions when needed, but on a day-to-day basis, he put his trust in the men and women around him.

As a former investigator, Ben couldn't help but still involve himself in major cases from time-to-time. Most detectives working a case resented having a superior officer looking over their shoulders, let alone the police chief himself. That certainly wasn't the feeling of the detectives of the PCPD. They welcomed their boss's assistance. He never tried to run the investigations, never wanting to interfere, but would be there to provide counsel after reviewing the evidence. For the younger detectives, it was like a master class in criminology. No professor could teach what Ben knew from his decades as an investigator on the street. The advice and guidance he was able to provide to his men was priceless.

Mentally, Ben had never been as sharp. Physically, the story was slightly different. Even though he was still fit, for the most part, his stomach had rounded out a bit more than he would like and the wrinkles around his eyes were more pronounced. Most telling perhaps was the dull gray that had completely replaced the shiny auburn of his hair. The stress of his chosen profession had caused the change to occur much quicker, but that had nothing to do with the aching knees whenever it rained. Ben was not enjoying getting older, especially when it appeared as though his friend was frozen in time.

As if they'd been reading his thoughts, Ben heard a Kathleen Turner-esque voice from behind him say, "Do you ever wonder how he still looks so young? Did he discover the Fountain of Youth and not tell anyone?"

Laughing, Ben turned to see the Chief Judge of the Parker County District Court standing there, a glass of champagne in one hand and a plate of hors d'oeuvres in the other. Lydia Strauss might just be the only person in the room with the ability to make a comment like that since she'd been on the bench for close to thirty years and known Ben and Tommy for almost as long. Not to mention, she herself was now in her seventies but looked a good twenty years younger.

"He looks just like he did forty years ago when we first joined the force," Ben said, shaking his head in mock disbelief. "He just doesn't age."

"Take it from someone who knows, Ben," she said with a wicked smile, "I wouldn't be surprised if a face-lift and tummy-tuck may have taken place at some point."

Chapter Nine

Following the official ceremony with all its pomp and circumstance and all the glowing speeches of praise, the VIPs were invited to a private reception on the third floor of the PCPD. The stately suite of offices once occupied by the mayor when the building was still City Hall, now belonged to the chief of police, explaining why he had an antique crystal chandelier hanging in the center of his office, along with an Italian marble fireplace and a hand-painted mural on the ceiling. Even more grandiose and out of place in a police station was the adjoining executive conference room. A pair of oversized pocket doors usually separated the spaces, but when opened, the two rooms created a magnificent reception venue. An elite party of fifty or so could easily mingle and float between the two spacious rooms. A working office, though. Ben never hosted receptions. But again, this was a special occasion.

During his years as sheriff, Tommy made a lot of powerful friends. Not only was the lieutenant governor on hand to pay tribute to his service, the Executive Director of the National Sheriffs' Association, the Maryland State Police Superintendent, and the Director of the FBI were also guests. Tommy was nothing if not well connected.

Ben was in the middle of a conversation with the president of the Chamber of Commerce and one of the two congressmen at the reception when the man of the hour tapped him on the shoulder and asked if he could interrupt.

"Have you had a chance to catch up with Alan yet?" he asked, as the man at his side shook the chief's hand.

"Director Rigley, welcome to our little part of the world," Ben said with a smile.

"Director Rigley? Really, Ben?" The goatee-sporting, linebacker-looking gentleman in a well-tailored Brooks Brothers suit shook his head in mock exasperation.

"I have to show some respect for the head of the FBI…even if it's you," Ben said as the brawny black man engulfed him in a bear hug. "How're you doing, Alan?"

"Two years on the job and I'm finally starting to feel like I'm getting the hang of DC."

"Not like sitting in your cushy office in Alexandria, is it?" Tommy pointed out with a good-natured jab at his old friend.

"Those were the days, boys. Those were the days. I actually had time to eat breakfast, lunch, *and* dinner back then."

Alan Rigley had been a federal prosecutor when he first met the two working on a task force targeting corruptions in the Capital Region. Bringing down several government officials, a handful of DC lobbyists, and even some Wall Street executives who had been working together put Alan on the fast track to becoming U.S. Attorney for the Eastern District of Virginia. From there it was a tossup as to whether he would end up as Director of the Federal Bureau of Investigation or Attorney General of the United States. Many insiders believed he could have his pick, and in the end, he went with the Bureau. Rigley openly admitted that he liked putting bad guys away and thought he could do more good heading up the FBI. Plus, he couldn't tolerate the idea of sitting through White House Cabinet meetings.

His first couple of years in the J. Edgar Hoover Building, leading the nation's federal law enforcement agency, had been an active one. By all accounts, Rigley was making just enough friends and just enough enemies in Washington to show he was doing a good job. Being the first African-American to lead the Bureau, he was also making history.

The three men had become friends and stayed in touch, managing to get together for a beer whenever they could find the time in their schedules. But those get-togethers had become fewer and farther between. The growing demands of their jobs had turned an e-mail every now and again into their best means of staying connected.

After catching up as much as they could in fifteen minutes, Alan apologized for having to leave. Only half-jokingly, he said his staff only allowed him out for a couple of hours at a time and he had a tight schedule for the rest of the day. In fact, his next stop was a meeting with the president at the White House in a little over an hour, so he was already cutting it close. Even a convoy of big black SUVs carrying the Director of the FBI could only move so fast in all the traffic around Washington. Regardless of the use of flashing lights and sirens.

"Impressive turn out," Ben said as he scanned the crowd.

He and his former partner had tucked themselves away in a corner of the room so they could watch the guests mix and mingle. Ben was still nursing his first glass of champagne. Tommy was working on a scotch and soda.

"Everybody loves me." Tommy smiled, then finished off what was left in his glass. Ben couldn't help noticing that his friend seemed slightly distracted. It would have been hard for anyone else to notice with the way Tommy had been working the room, but Ben could tell when he had something on his mind.

"The mayor had some nice things to say about you. Did you write his speech for him?"

It was subtle, barely perceptible, but Ben noticed Tommy's reaction at the mention of Gregory Oland. There had definitely been a slight pursing of the lips. The chief didn't know of any bad blood between the two, but obviously there was a story.

"He's a twit," Tommy said after clearing deciding not to say what he had originally intended.

"He's a politician," Ben answered very matter-of-factly.

"He's running for congress and wants everyone to think he's tough on crime. Did you count how many times he mentioned he was the former state's attorney? Five. In ten minutes."

"Like I said, he's a politician," Ben repeated with a shrug, taking a small sip from his glass.

"I guess I'm just getting crotchety in my old age. But he's nothing like his old man. Charlie was the real deal."

"He was a politician too," Ben casually pointed out.

"Yeah. But there was something different about him. He at least seemed honest." Abruptly changing the subject, Tommy asked, "Are we still on for golf Saturday?"

Ben didn't want to push the subject, so he went with the flow, saying, "Nat's going shopping with her sister, so I have the entire day to help you kick off your retirement. I thought we could grab a late lunch at The Landing afterward."

"Good. I love their crab cakes."

As quickly as he'd changed topics the first time, he did again. This time his mood became much more serious.

The mischievous twinkle perpetually in Tommy's eyes had suddenly dimmed, as if a dark cloud was passing in front of the sun.

"I've been thinking about Beverly Baker," Tommy said. His voice was just loud enough to be heard over the buzz filling the room.

A jolt ran down Ben's spine at the mention of the name. He couldn't even remember the last time he'd thought about that case. Even though it was decades old, just hearing the name made his stomach twist into knots. Beverly's murder had been the beginning of everything.

"While I was packing up my office, I came across some old papers that got me thinking…"

Before he could finish, the pair found themselves being joined by the mayor and his ever-present campaign manager. "Tom, if you could spare a minute, the lieutenant governor's getting ready to leave and was hoping to get a picture with us." Ben was sure the photo would end up on an Oland for Congress campaign flier in the near future.

Even in a room full of people, Greg Oland's voice, calm and cool, cut through the noise with ease. "Five minutes, tops. Then you two can get back to your serious conversation. What are you talking about, anyway? Ben looks like he's seen a ghost."

"Just talking about old times, Mr. Mayor," Tommy said through a forced smile. "Let's go take that picture. We shouldn't keep the lieutenant governor waiting."

Tommy handed Ben his empty glass and allowed the mayor to guide him through the crowd. The lieutenant governor was waiting out in the hall for their photo-op. Left alone in the corner, Ben felt like he'd been kicked in the gut. Beverly Baker was the first victim during that dark spring in 1981. In an instant, all the memories came flooding back along with the emotions it originally stirred in him. The case had been officially closed, but questions still lingered. There were a few details that never did sit right at the time with the two young and inexperienced detectives. What could Tommy possibly have found that brought all of this up again now?

Chapter Ten

Then...

Walking into the historical society's small office and joining his partner, Ben immediately saw Beverly Baker's lifeless body lying on the floor with two very unhappy looking officers kneeling over it. The mood in the room went from somber to outright cold as all eyes turned to the pair of detectives. They might as well have been under a microscope. Everyone was watching them, judging every single move they made. Lesser men would have buckled under the immense scrutiny and pressure, but Ben and Tommy didn't have time to think about that. They had a job to do.

"Look who it is, the department's golden boys," Buck LuCoco, one of the sour faced patrolmen, sneered. "I figured it was only a matter of time before you two showed up."

Over three hundred pounds, LuCoco used the edge of the desk to heave himself to his feet. Winded just from standing, he wheezed his way over, getting as close to Ben as his stomach would allow. A senior member of the PCPD's good-ol'-boy network, he had been one of the most vocal of those opposed to Ben and Tommy's promotions to detective and had never let up on his criticism.

"I think you boys might be a little out of your league here. Why don't you let us experienced coppers take care of this one? You can go back to filing your reports on missing pets."

Before Tommy could even open his mouth in defense, a powerful voice took them all by surprise, echoing off the walls, making the whole room feel as if it was shaking. "I'd like to point out that Detective *Sergeant* Winters outranks you, *Officer* LuCoco. And even if he isn't willing to remind you to respect his stripes, *I am*. Are we clear?"

The chastised officer's fat face turned as red as the shag carpet on the floor when he saw Captain Nick Brent's imposing figure filling the doorway. The anger in his voice was only matched by the fire in his eyes, visible even through his sunglasses. If there was one thing the captain was not interested in, it was a pissing match between his men. LuCoco's juvenile antics had been going on long enough, and he didn't have any more patience for them. He was beginning to think it might be time for the patrolman to put in his papers and retire.

LuCoco's massive size was dwarfed by Brent's commanding presence. Ben thought he could actually see LuCoco shrink in front of their eyes as the captain stared him down.

"Sir, Captain, I was just saying, um…" The officer stumbled, looking for his words, trying to figure out how to cover his ass, while the other patrolmen in the room quickly busied themselves.

Brent wasn't interested in hearing what the man had to say. Clearly in no mood to deal with anyone's childish jealousy issues, he ordered LuCoco and anyone else who felt the way he did to clear out. Beverly Baker, one of the most important people in Parker City, was dead. That meant there was going to be no time for petty dick measuring on this case.

With LuCoco gone, Captain Brent turned the scene over to Detective Sergeant Winters, who began assigning duties, including sending one officer to call for the coroner. Ben's mind was racing, making mental lists of everything they needed to do and everyone they needed to interview.

"Captain," Ben said, turning to a new page in his notebook, "would you please contact the State Police and have them send over their Crime Scene Unit? We're going to need them to process the entire office."

"And the storage room downstairs," Tommy added. "The back door was bashed in. We could get lucky and there may be some fingerprints."

Not having its own crime lab team to collect and analyze fingerprints or blood types or the facilities to examine and store a body, the Parker City Police relied on state agencies for these services. It wasn't very often the PCPD required them, but when it did, Brent acted as the liaison between the departments.

"I'm surprised they aren't here yet," Brent said. "I would have thought the trooper downstairs would have already called this in. I'm sure they'd love to come in and take over the case."

"This is our jurisdiction," Tommy answered. "Let 'em try to strong-arm their way in."

"I'm sure it won't come to that," Ben said, his tone firm and matter of fact. "But if they could send CSU over as soon as possible…"

Before continuing, Ben took a deep breath to help slow his heart rate. It had been racing since the moment he'd arrived on the scene. Closing his eyes, he blocked out all the sounds in the room. He wanted to look at the crime scene with as little distraction as possible.

At first glance, the room itself looked undisturbed. They were going to need to speak with members of the historical society's staff to see if anything was missing. Until then, they couldn't rule out a robbery gone wrong. There were certainly enough valuable antiques in the building to make it a target.

"Has anyone gone through the building yet to see if anything has been disturbed? Any displays broken into? Exhibits messed with?" Ben asked the men gathered in the room.

Tommy was the only one to speak. "I did a quick walkthrough before I got up here. Nothing looked out of place to me, but then again, I don't know how everything should look."

"Dunkin, would you and Bateman do another sweep, floor-to-floor, please? Anything that looks like it isn't right, let me know. It doesn't matter how trivial you think something might be. If you can tell something's been moved, for any reason—like there's no dust on it, make a note of it and we'll check it out."

After the officers left to start their walkthrough, Tommy asked, "You do realize, you basically just sent two men to examine the dust in an old museum?"

"That's not exactly what they're doing, but until we can speak with someone who knows the building and its exhibits, we have to start somewhere. When we're finished here, we'll go talk to the secretary. Hopefully she'll have calmed down a bit by then and be able to talk."

Jotting some quick notes in his notebook, Ben wanted to get all of his initial thoughts and observations on paper. He needed to make sure he didn't miss anything. No detail was too insignificant at this point. A case could turn on the smallest piece of evidence. One of the reasons for his promotion was because the mayor wanted a specialized investigative team that did things properly and could focus on the details of a case. If Buck LuCoco was in charge, it would all have been handled in a lazy, slipshod manner.

Slowly and methodically, he began examining Beverly's body and the surrounding area.

Lying face up on the plush, yet worn, carpet, she looked almost angelic. It was a little hard for Ben to believe, having heard so many terrible stories about the woman. Right then, in that moment though, she looked so peaceful and serene. There was no denying she had been an attractive woman, and if he hadn't known, she could have simply been taking a nap. Or, more apt for Beverly Baker, lying in wait like a predator, luring her prey in before pouncing. But there was no life left in her slender body now sprawled on the floor.

To her left, next to her outstretched arm, was the telephone receiver. The cradle still sat on the corner of the desk, the cord that connected the two pulled from the base of the phone. To her right was an antique pistol with what looked like blood and a few strands of blonde hair on the handle. Her head ever so slightly turned to the side, Ben could see a spot behind her ear and down her neck where blood had dried, matting her hair and turning it crimson.

"What do you make of this?" Ben asked, pointing at the gun.

"That's a Burlwood Stock Colonial Flintlock Officer's Pistol," Tommy answered without skipping a beat.

For the briefest of moments, Ben didn't know what to say. He hadn't been expecting such a detailed response. "How the hell do you know that?"

Jerking his thumb over his shoulder, Tommy casually said, "I read it on the plaque there on the bookshelf. I'm guessing that little display thing's where the gun usually sits. Judging by the blood and hair there on the handle," he held it up with a handkerchief and examined the piece more closely, "it looks like someone used it as a club. They'd have had to hit her pretty hard to cause that kind of wound—to draw blood like that."

"Yeah, but I don't think that's what killed her," Ben said. "Look here."

Using his pen to push away some of her hair, he exposed dark red marks ringing her neck. The coroner would be the one to determine the official cause of death following the autopsy, but in Ben's opinion, she'd been strangled. He was certainly no medical expert, but the telltale signs were right there in front of him.

Ben examined the body from a number of angles to be certain nothing had been overlooked. Then, stepping back and looking at the scene from a wider perspective, he surveyed the entire room from all directions. From the corner of his eye, Ben could see the other officers in the room shaking their heads as he walked around them, standing and kneeling in different spots to get alternative vantage points. He knew he must have looked ridiculous, but after doing so, he finally thought he could see the full picture coming into focus and had a theory of how things happened. It wasn't hard to imagine. He just let his mind arrange the various puzzle pieces, coming up with the most likely version of events. More often than not, it was the simplest answer. There wasn't always a complicated and convoluted solution.

"Here's what I'm thinking," Ben began as he slowly started walking through the room, enacting his theory. "Beverly was working here in the office alone. Her killer comes in and startles her. A natural reaction, she goes for the phone to try and call for help. The killer grabs the flintlock pistol from the shelf—a weapon of opportunity—and uses it to hit her on the back of the head, knocking her to the ground. Then he—assuming it was a *he*—pulls the cord from the phone, turns her over, and strangles her with it."

Tommy's eyes narrowed as he looked down at Beverly's body. He'd been in agreement with Ben up until the very end. Crouching down, he carefully examined the phone cord. "There's one problem with that theory. The marks on her neck don't match the spirals of this cord. I don't think it's the murder weapon."

"Okay. So then what *did* the killer use?" Ben asked, looking around the office for something that could match the shape of the ligature marks.

Kneeling once again to examine Beverly's neck, from the angle Ben was at, the marks took on an all too familiar shape. Without actually touching the body, he placed his hand above the dark abrasions and saw that his fingers lined up exactly the way he thought they would. The bruises around Beverly's neck were caused by fingers, impressions left by the killer's own hands. It was a chilling revelation.

Had the blow to the head not knocked her unconscious, she would have been staring directly into the eyes of her killer, gasping for air, no doubt struggling to pull his hands away from her throat.

If she'd been conscious during the assault and fought back, judging by her well-manicured nails, she could easily have scratched her attacker, leaving her own marks on his hands or face. Even if she did try fighting the killer off, without enough air she would have been unconscious in a relatively short period of time. Only a matter of seconds, actually. The more she struggled, using up the oxygen in her body, the quicker she would have passed out. After that, it wouldn't take long to finish her off. Most people didn't realize how quickly someone could be strangled to death. Longer than in the movies, but not by much.

"That was easy," Tommy said with a wry smile. "We figured out *how* he did it. Now we just need to figure out who did it and why. Was she a target? Or just in the wrong place at the wrong time?"

"Well," Ben said, thinking about what this particular method of murder could mean. "When it comes to strangulation, it's personal. Especially when you do it with your bare hands. In this case, I think someone wanted to *feel* the life leave Beverly Baker's body. I don't think it can get much more personal."

Chapter Eleven

The State Police's Crime Scene Unit arrived shortly after Captain Brent had contacted his counterpart at the Parker County Barracks, where the team assigned to cases in Western Maryland was headquartered. It took much longer for the state coroner's van to arrive at the scene. Coming from Baltimore, the assistant coroner explained there had been an accident on Route 70, bringing traffic to a standstill. The delayed arrival gave the CSU team time to do an extremely thorough examination of the crime scene before the body was removed.

Officers Dunkin and Bateman agreed with Tommy and reported back that nothing appeared to have been disturbed anywhere else in the building. The only sign of any damage was in the storage room on the first floor where the outside door had been forced open. Wanting to take a look for himself, Ben took a few moments to poke around in the room full of old cardboard boxes and file cabinets. The only thing without a thick layer of dust on it appeared to be the door handle. The knob hanging precariously from its place, along with the small shards of wood from the doorframe, made it seem reasonable to guess this is how the intruder entered the building. Ben wanted to make sure the handle was dusted for prints. It could be the best chance they had at finding a decent, useable fingerprint.

Finding his partner standing in the entry hall, Ben asked, "What are you thinking?"

Chewing on his lower lip for a moment, Tommy finally said, "I think it is safe to say the killer did not have any allergies."

Ben raised an eyebrow.

"Because no one allergic to dust would be able to breathe in this place," Tommy finished. "It's like they haven't dusted since some of this stuff was new. And the whole place smells like my grandmother's house. Someone needs to open some windows and air this place out."

"What you're saying is you haven't found anything else useful? Like another way the killer could have gotten in and out?"

"I checked every window and every door. The only one that shows any sign of being touched is the one back in the storeroom That's how our guy got in. Other than that, the only other thing that seems out of place is the dead body upstairs."

Ben rolled his eyes.

Heading back up to the third floor, the CSU supervisor, Lieutenant Clover, was waiting for them. He was a gangly looking state trooper with aviator glasses much too large for his face, a ridiculous comb-over, and a handlebar mustache.

"My guys have found more than fifty prints in the office," he said, not looking up from his clipboard and certainly not sounding too pleased. "Most of which are only partials at best. I don't think they're going to be much help. There's just too many. And we won't have anything to compare most of them to."

Ben suddenly felt deflated. He'd been certain the forensic team would find something of value after processing the room. But it turned out that finding too many fingerprints was as bad as finding none at all.

"What about the pistol?" Tommy inquired. "Were there any prints on the pistol?"

Scanning down his paperwork, Clover answered dryly, "No."

"Dammit," Ben said under his breath. "That means either the killer wiped the gun down or was wearing gloves."

"Did you find any blood other than the victims?" Tommy asked. Again, trying to sound hopeful.

"Nah. And there wasn't much of that. We bagged the pistol. It clearly has blood and hair on it. You saw that. But until we test it, we can just assume it belongs to the vic. Nothing other than that though."

"So, we've got a pretty clean crime scene?" Ben asked.

"More or less," he said with a slight shrug, then headed down the stairs.

"Make sure someone dusts the back door for prints," Ben called after him.

"Is it me, or does it seem like that guy doesn't like his job very much?" Tommy asked when the lieutenant was out of earshot.

"Yeah. I got the same feeling," Ben agreed. "Hopefully his report will have a little more detail. Maybe *something* useful."

"At this point, I'd be happy with a rough estimate of the size of the killer's hands," Tommy said as they rounded the stairs on their way down to speak with Lucy Jenkins. "It would at least be something to work with. And, as you are technically my supervisor—being the lead detective and all—I would like to request that our next crime scene have an elevator. I'm tired of walking up and down all these stairs."

Ben couldn't help but laugh. If it wasn't for Tommy's attempts to lighten the mood, the gravity of the situation would be crushing. Ben was thankful that his partner always knew how to help relieve some of the tension when it was building up.

That was certainly turning out to be the case now. It didn't look like the physical evidence, what little there was, was going to help the investigation very much. It wasn't like in the movies where a bloody hand print pointed them directly to the murderer.

Chapter Twelve

Lucy Jenkins was a petite woman made smaller by the fact she was currently wrapped in a large blanket. All the detectives could see of her as they approached the squad car in which she was sitting were her red curls puffed up over the folds of the thick gray material. Ben felt bad for having kept the woman waiting for so long, but in a murder investigation, things could not be rushed.

"Miss Jenkins," Tommy said with his most gentle smile, "my name is Tommy Mason. This is my partner, Ben Winters. We're detectives with the PCPD. Would it be alright if we ask you a few questions?"

It appeared as though the woman had regained her composure, though the earlier trauma had clearly taken its toll. The young woman looked worn and like she was ready to curl up in bed and pull the covers over her head. Clearly, she'd been crying because long rivers of blue mascara streaked down her cheeks.

"Can we get you something?" Ben asked. "Some water? A cup of coffee?"

"No. Thank you. I'm okay." Her voice quivered ever so slightly as she wiped her eyes with the palms of her hands.

"I understand you're the secretary for the historical society. How long have you had that job?" Ben wanted to ease into the questioning. He didn't want to start out by asking about the gruesome scene she'd walked into that morning.

"Um, about two years now."

"And what are your main duties?"

As she listed the usual administrative tasks a secretary performs, Ben jotted down anything he thought he might need to reference later.

"Now, as for Ms. Baker, did she often spend time in the building alone?"

"As the society's chairwoman, she would come and go as she pleased. She usually stayed for a little while after board meetings. Like last night. I left and locked up after the other board members, but Ms. Baker was still working in the office."

"So, there was a board meeting last evening?" Ben said. "Did anything interesting or out of the ordinary occur?"

"Not really, but…well," Lucy answered, then stopped. It was clear to Ben and Tommy she was weighing very carefully what she could and should say.

"Lucy, my I call you Lucy?" Tommy asked in a tone as smooth as silk and gentle as cashmere. "We would appreciate anything you can tell us. Whether you think it is significant or not, the smallest detail could help."

The secretary's expression eased, a smile almost appearing on her lip. Once again, Ben thought, another woman has fallen to the charms of his partner.

"Nothing happened last night," she began, "but there'd been some problems recently. Ms. Baker had a falling out with Mr. Worthington, another member of the board."

"Mr. Worthington?" Ben asked. "Would that be Howard Worthington, the bank president?"

Lucy nodded. "A few weeks ago, they had some sort of fight. It didn't have anything to do with the historical society. But people talk. It was about some business deal or something. Mr. Worthington was the chairman of the society. But Ms. Baker was furious, so to get back at him and embarrass him, she called for the board of directors to strip him of his chairmanship and give it to her."

"I can imagine that caused some tension," Tommy offered.

"How did Mr. Worthington respond?"

With a small shrug, Lucy said, "He didn't seem to care that much. Or didn't show it. He's always been very nice to me."

"Did anyone else on the board have a problem with Ms. Baker?" Ben asked.

There was that look again. Lucy wasn't sure what she should say.

After a moment, she said, "Ms. Baker was very demanding. No one ever said anything to me, but I've overheard some of the board members saying some things about her."

Not wanting to push too much harder at the moment but knowing he may need to speak with the secretary again in the future, Ben said, "Thank you, Lucy. This has been very helpful. Do you think you would be able to give one of the other officers the names of all those at the meeting last night?"

Without any better place to start, Ben thought the board members were as good a place as any.

Walking back toward the townhouse, Tommy frowned. "We're supposed to think that a banker killed a socialite over an argument about who was going to be the chairman of a small town historical society?"

Ben shrugged as he flipped his notebook closed. "The Bakers and Worthingtons are seriously rich people. Who knows what would make one of them snap? Money makes people do weird things…so I've been told."

As the detectives were discussing what affected the mental state of the wealthier classes, Chief Stanley arrived in full bluster. He was in a fury and started barking orders the minute he stepped out of his car and his feet hit the pavement. For a police chief who prided himself on presiding over a city with very little serious crime—not that he'd really been personally responsible for that fact—the murder of a powerful member of the community was not the kind of black mark he wanted on his record. Stanley wanted details about everything that had been discovered so far. More importantly, he wanted answers.

All eyes once again turned to Ben. This was the first time he ever had to brief the chief face-to-face. With Tommy at his side to help fill in any blanks, Ben tried to be as clear and concise as possible. Stanley was not known for being very detail oriented, so Ben didn't want to lose his attention. By the time he'd completed explaining the working theory, Ben thought the old man was going to have a stroke right there in front of him. Standing in the little foyer of the historical society, the chief exploded when he was told the detectives were going to interview the president of South Mountain Bank

& Trust.

"You think Howard Worthington killed Beverly Baker? Are you kidding me? Do you have your head up your ass, Winters? Howard-fucking-Worthington! The man owns a bank. His family is one of the oldest in the county. Howard-fucking-Worthington!"

"Chief," Ben tried to explain but couldn't get more than a word in.

"You're going to go in accusing a man like him of murder? You think that's going to end well for you? First, he'll bury you. Then he'll come after me. He's a personal friend of the mayor's! They golf together every weekend!"

"Chief, we aren't saying…"

"Dammit! How could this happen? Beverly Baker…killed…dead. Beverly-fucking-Baker. I've already been on the phone with her sister, who was inconsolable, by the way. When she couldn't talk anymore—because she was sobbing hysterically—her brother got on the phone and reamed my ass out. This kind of thing shouldn't happen to people like them. The mayor is going to shit himself when he finds out what's happened. Then he's going to shit on me for letting it happen. And how am I supposed to tell him that you think Howard Worthington did this? I'm not going to have those two families on my ass. "

Captain Brent, the voice of reason, finally spoke. "No one is saying Howard is a suspect, Ed. Detectives Winters and Mason are going to have to talk to everyone who was at the meeting last night. They're just starting with him because he'd recently had a problem with the victim. That's all. It's the same thing I'd do. I don't think any of us here think that pencil-pushing desk jockey is even capable of something like this. But they have to start somewhere."

Stanley finally took a breath and thought for a moment before saying, "Of course, he's not. He's too afraid of getting his shoes dirty to kill anyone."

Ben prayed no one saw him roll his eyes.

The chief's logic was astounding. Not to mention, it seemed like he was more concerned with angering the Bakers and Worthingtons than actually catching the killer. The longer they stood there, the more flush the chief's face became. Ben could swear he was so irate he actually saw smoke coming out of the man's ears.

"Sir, Tommy and I are just going to ask him if he saw anything out of the ordinary last night when he left. I promise you, we're not going to accuse anyone of anything until we have some sort of evidence."

"And naturally," Tommy chimed in for the first time, "you'll be the very first person we tell when we do have evidence."

Stanley bit down hard on what was left of his cigar. He always had the stump of one in his mouth, yet no one could remember ever seeing him light a new one.

"Don't fuck this up, you two," the chief growled as he turned and stormed up the stairs, wanting to see the scene of the crime for himself. Brent followed close behind to keep him from verbally, or physically, assaulting anyone else. "Beverly-fucking-Baker!" They could hear the gruff voice trailing off as it traveled up the steps.

Ben turned to see a puzzled look on Tommy's face. "What's wrong?"

"That's the second time today someone told us not to *fuck this up*,'" Tommy pointed out. "I don't understand. Do they think we *want* to fuck this up?"

Chapter Thirteen

Once Beverly Baker's body was secured in the van and ready to be taken away, the assistant coroner found Ben to give him his initial thoughts after conducting the on-site examination. He agreed with the detective's speculation that it appeared as though the victim had been strangled to death.

"Of course," he continued, "the official autopsy will confirm the actual cause of death. There's always a chance we've missed something, but this one looks pretty cut-and-dried to me. I'd be surprised if the autopsy concludes anything other than strangulation."

"The sooner we can get your report, the better. Not that I want to put any pressure on you, but any information that could be useful…" Ben's voice trailed off as he took in the other man's expression. Clearly, this was a request with which he was used to hearing. No doubt, everyone felt their case was the most important.

Ben and Tommy watched the coroner's van pull away and begin its journey back to Baltimore as they themselves were leaving the historical society's townhouse.

"It looks like a storm might be coming," Tommy said, using his chin to gesture toward the sky where a thick black cloud was now creating a giant shadow over Parker City.

"Isn't that apropos?" Ben said under his breath.

No sooner had he uttered those words, a chilling wind caused the old shutters on the historical society's building to rattle. Followed by a flash of lightning and a prolonged rumble of thunder off in the distance.

Walking toward their cruiser, Tommy pulled a pack of Newport cigarettes out of his jacket pocket. Taking one for himself, he offered the pack to Ben.

"No thank you," Ben said, appreciating the friendly gesture. "But you know my answer."

"Old habits," Tommy answered. "I promise you, one day you're going to need one."

This was a common ritual between the two. Tommy always offered, even though Ben never accepted. In fact, he'd never smoked a single cigarette in his life. As for Tommy, he couldn't remember a time when he didn't smoke.

The pair's first stop was going to be the station so they could collect their thoughts and come up with a game plan. Ben tossed Tommy the keys. Maybe he'd have better luck getting the engine to turn over on the first try.

When they reached the car, the two were met by a jean jacket clad "pretty boy," as Tommy would later refer to him. Leaning against the driver's door, the Tom Cruise wannabe was flipping through a little spiral-ringed notepad, clearly waiting for them. Right off the bat, Ben knew he didn't like this guy, whoever he was. There was something about the smirk on his face. He was cocky, arrogant, and definitely full of himself. Three words that all meant the same, but this guy deserved all of them. Ben was good at reading people, especially when they so blatantly projected their persona to the world.

"Can we help you with something?" Tommy asked, exhaling a puff of smoke as he stared the man down.

"Detectives, Roger Benedict, with the *Herald-Dispatch*. Any comment on the horrible murder of Beverly Baker? Inquiring minds want to know."

He was a reporter, and not only did he already know there had been a murder, he already knew who the victim was. That didn't sit well with Ben.

"How do you know about that?" Tommy snapped.

"No comment," Ben answered at the same time.

"It's a small town, Detectives. *Everybody* has heard that someone killed the Wicked Witch of Western Maryland. It's about damn time something interesting happened in this pathetic little burg. I finally have something to write about other than whose pig won the blue ribbon at the county fair."

Instinctively, Ben reached out, grabbing his partner's arm to stop him from pulling his gun. He didn't think Tommy would actually shoot the little shit, but he couldn't take the chance of having a second homicide on his hands right now.

"Like I said, we have no comment," Ben answered as calmly as possible. He wasn't prepared to give anything up at this very early stage. "This is now an open investigation. When we have something to report to the press, we'll let you know."

"Now get your ass off our car," Tommy ordered, flicking his cigarette butt at the reporter's feet.

"Look guys, I'm just trying to do my job. We could help each other out. Share information."

"You think you have information we need?" Tommy was getting angry. The tone in his voice was all too clear.

"I found out Beverly Baker was dead before anyone else, didn't I?"

The reporter was certainly a condescending little prick.

"And how exactly did you do that?" Ben asked, genuinely curious.

The reporter's response was a smile that would make the Devil himself shudder. Trying to remember his high school lit class, Ben thought about Milton's description of Satan in *Paradise Lost* as the most beautiful of the angels before his fall.

"Let's just say someone whispered it in my ear."

"Can I shoot him now?" Tommy asked.

For the briefest moment, Ben found himself actually contemplating the ramifications of letting Tommy shoot the man…in the foot.

Chapter Fourteen

Now...

The case had been over thirty years earlier, so the mention of Beverly Baker after all that time had knocked Ben on his heels. The three murders that occurred in the spring of 1981 made it one of the darkest times in Parker City's recent history. One that few people wanted to remember. Even though the case was officially closed, Ben still kept a copy of the file in one of his desk drawers. Why? He could never really say. And while few of the new suburban transplants knew of the events which had unfolded almost four decades earlier, lifelong Parkertons would never be able to erase the black mark of the past.

Usually laser focused, it took a lot to sidetrack Ben Winters. But his assistant, Corporal Drew Collins, had noticed the chief had become distracted. At one point, while talking to the president of the Parker County Chamber of Commerce, he lost his train of thought not once but twice. Each time stopping mid-sentence while he tried to remember what he'd been saying. For the life of him, Drew couldn't figure out what had caused the chief to become so preoccupied. If anything serious had come up, he certainly would have known. The chief was usually so in tune with what was going on around him. The young officer had never seen him this way in the three years he'd been Ben's executive assistant.

It was an enormous responsibility, being the chief's assistant. Sitting outside the boss's office, he got to see and hear everything. He kept Ben's schedule, read all the reports Ben read, and usually accompanied him when he left the station to visit crime scenes. Drew was only the chief's third assistant since he'd taken over the department. The previous two had been civilians, but when Ruth Edelstein finally retired, Ben decided to find his new executive assistant from within the ranks of his department.

Looking like he could still be a student at Hammermill College, Ben was concerned Drew might face the same issues he and Tommy had back when they were first made detectives. His worries were short-lived. As a corporal, he was already a senior patrol officer, so had put in his time. And Drew was a natural when dealing with the other members of the department. Straight out of the gate, the young man had proven to be efficient, responsible, and capable of handling excessively stressful situations. Many times he knew what the chief wanted before Ben knew himself. The young officer was taking the opportunity to learn everything he could from the living legend that was Ben Winters.

"Sir, is everything alright?" Drew asked when he was able to pull Ben aside at one point, making it appear like he was delivering an urgent message. "You just called Councilman Crum by the wrong name."

"I did?"

Drew nodded.

"That would probably explain the strange look on his face," Ben said, clearly trying to laugh off the situation and move on.

After another glass of champagne, Ben did his best to put Beverly Baker out of his mind as the reception started running well into the late afternoon. This was a rare occurrence when one considered most of the guests were people who could usually only spare fifteen minutes at any one event. It showed the respect Tommy had earned during his years of service. Although the sheriff would have said it was because his friend had spared no expense and put out a great spread. Good food and free alcohol always kept people around.

A number of VIPs had come and gone, but once the caterers stopped replenishing the buffet table, the party began to wind down. Conversations continued into the hall as everyone left the third-floor suite of offices and headed for the elevators.

Ben kept an eye on his former partner, whose mood had also changed. However, he was much better at masking how he was feeling. Tommy had always been good at compartmentalizing. But having known him for so long, Ben could tell the ghosts of the past were haunting him. No one else may have noticed, but he could see it in his friend's eyes.

"I can't thank you enough for this, Ben," Tommy said as the last of the guests were leaving. "I never thought this day would come."

"You thought you were going to drop dead at your desk?"

"Something like that."

"Do you want me to have one of my guys take you home? I think you finished off two bottles of champagne by yourself."

Tommy laughed. "People can't get drunk off champagne. Google it. It's a scientific fact."

"It really isn't."

"I know. But *I* can't get drunk off champagne. I'm fine. Really. I ate more than enough of those little chocolate cake bites to soak up the booze. And whatever that pretzel wrap thing was, fantastic with that spicy mustard. I stuffed a few in my pocket to take home with me."

Both men stood looking out the oversized windows at Parker City's skyline. This was far from goodbye. They were still going to see each other all the time; more now that they actually had free time. The momentary nostalgia was because this was the end of an era. It was time to start a new chapter. Tommy joked that he might write a book about some of their cases. Ben pointed out—in the way only a friend could—that he'd actually have to read a book first before he could write one of his own.

Breaking the silence, Ben turned to Tommy, looking him squarely in the eyes and asked, "What's wrong? What could you possibly have come across after all this time?"

"We got it wrong, Ben."

"What does that mean?"

"Neither of us was ever really happy with the way the case ended. You know that," Tommy paused, then cleared this throat and started to say, "I had a conversation with…" but was interrupted by Ben's assistant.

"Sorry to bother you," Corporal Collins said, clearly anxious. "There's a situation at the hospital. A patient is holding some nurses hostage in his room."

"Tasker Valley Memorial?" Tommy asked.

"Yes, sir. Someone from the psych ward. ESU is on the way."

"That's square in your jurisdiction, Ben," Tommy said, patting his friend on the shoulder. "You should go take care of this. We'll talk later. My things already over thirty years old. Another day isn't going to make much of a difference right now. Besides, it's just a theory. It could just be the delusions of an old copper on his way out the door."

Ben didn't like having to end a nice day this way, dealing with a hostage situation at the hospital, let alone walking out on his friend when there was obviously something he thought they needed to discuss. The PCPD's Emergency Response Team was trained for situations like these and would take point, but he wanted to be there. Something like this needed his attention, and Tommy understood. He'd had more than his fair share of crises pop up out of the blue over the years. Whether a sheriff or a police chief, you were always on call. It was nothing like a typical nine-to-five office job.

"Do you want to come along for the ride?" Ben asked as he grabbed his jacket from behind the door on his way out of the office.

Shaking his head, Tommy said, "For once, I think I'm just going to go home and enjoy my evening. I don't know if you've heard, but I'm retired."

"Not until tomorrow, you're not!" Ben shouted from halfway down the hall.

Chapter Fifteen

Knowing his friend wouldn't mind, Tommy decided to make use of the now empty office. The caterers were still in the conference room cleaning up what remained of the scrumptious buffet, but all he needed was to borrow Ben's computer. Logging on to the Sheriff's Department's server, he quickly checked his Emails.

Nothing.

He'd literally received no new emails during the reception. It wasn't too long ago that he was getting a hundred a day.

"I'm not even officially out the door and I've already been forgotten," he said to the empty room.

Picking up the phone on Ben's desk, he paused. It was completely digital. There weren't any buttons to push. Everything was done on a giant LED touch screen. Staring at the glowing list of icons, he had to search for what looked like a keypad. Hoping for the best and that what he was about to push didn't set off alarms and lock down the entire building, he pressed the screen. The image of a traditional keypad appeared.

"This thing is just ridiculous," he said, dialing his office number. He just wanted to check in to make sure nothing had come up during the retirement festivities.

Looking at his watch, it was only a little after four-thirty. He couldn't think of the last time he'd called it a day that early. Then again, he only had one more official day on the job. His office was already empty. His deputy, who was taking over for him, was already starting to run things, so he could take the rest of the day off. Part of him wanted to stop by the hospital to see if there was anything he could do, but he didn't want to get in the way. It was Ben's department that handled these incidents within the city limits. If the PCPD needed anything, they'd call.

Tommy had spent a lot of time reminiscing over the last several days. His had been a long and active career. Not all of the memories were good. He'd seen more than his fair share of the worst parts of humanity. Drugs and gangs were always on his mind, especially in recent years as the opioid epidemic exploded and the international criminal gang MS-13 was beginning to gain a foothold around Washington. Either could destroy a family; both could destroy society.

Tommy shook away the thoughts of Doomsday, replacing them with the memories of how he'd seen communities come together after a crisis. He'd seen enough good to balance out the bad, he reminded himself as he eased into traffic on the highway.

Several years ago, following his third divorce, Tommy Mason moved into a quaint three-bedroom rancher in Middleboro, a town just west of Parker City. It had only been recently that Middleboro's population saw a significant increase. Like all the other little hamlets in the county, it started out as a small farm town with a Main Street that had the town hall, a couple of churches, a diner, and a fire station. As Parker City grew, the development spilled over its borders. First one small shopping center opened, then another, then a golf and tennis club. After that came the flood of new homeowners, turning Middleboro into the place for young, up-and-coming professionals to build their mini-mansions.

No one argued about the beauty of the houses, with their columned porticos and ornate stone facades, but they were all crammed so closely together a person could look out their side window and practically touch their neighbor's house. Tommy never understood how "kids," as he referred to them, could afford such grand homes. When he was in his twenties and just starting out, he could barely afford the little trailer he rented.

The sheriff's house was in one of the older neighborhoods, so there were no five and six thousand square foot homes to be found anywhere on his street. He liked his house. He'd tried the downtown townhouse with his first wife; a historical 1913 house with his second; and a farm with his third. The ranch was by far his favorite. He never thought he'd enjoy spending time outside mowing the lawn or planting trees, but he'd really taken to it on his days off. Coming home in the evening, with the stars shining brilliantly in the sky and a cool breeze blowing down from the nearby mountains, he'd sit outside on his back patio with a cup of coffee and let the beauty of his couple of acres carry away the stress.

Pulling his Tahoe into the garage, he grabbed his briefcase and dress jacket from the backseat. It was rare to find him wearing a uniform anymore, opting for a suit and tie—he never thought he'd see that day. For special events, like his retirement reception, he'd dust off his brown and tan dress uniform with all the medals and ribbons.

In the kitchen, he found his mail on the counter and a note from his housekeeper saying she was going grocery shopping on Monday, so if there was anything specific he wanted, he should make a list.

Tommy was the kind of guy that didn't care if piles of clothes built up on the floor or dirty dishes sat in the sink for a couple of days. It was one of his most annoying traits according to all three of his former wives. Having a housekeeper to take care of things like the laundry, cleaning, and shopping was nice. Less for him to worry about and as an added bonus his house always smelled like citrus.

Marriage never agreed with Tommy, but that didn't stop him from trying it a few times. It became apparent very early on that he and his first wife weren't going to last. They were young and in lust. Not love, lust. For the first week after they were married, while on their honeymoon in the Bahamas, they couldn't keep their hands off one another. It was the second week when they actually had to return to real life and try living together that the problems began. Both had serious independent streaks, and neither was willing to give up their particular way of doing things. Marriage number one ended a year after it began.

His second wife thought she could handle him being a police officer, and she did pretty well for the first few years. It's when Ben and Tommy began working on higher-profile cases and started to find themselves more and more in the spotlight that the marriage began to come apart.

As for wife number three, there wasn't much he could say other than he thought the third time would be the charm. For a while, he thought he found *the one*, even if he hated living out on that damn farm. She was a freelance travel writer, so would be gone for extended periods of time, giving him the best of both worlds. He was happily married but still had all the freedom he wanted while she was away. In the end, she realized she liked being away more than living on the farm.

It was at that point Tommy decided there would be no more wedding bells. Period. He would find his own perfect home and go back to playing the field like he did when he was younger. Not that his job as the county's top cop allowed him a large amount of personal time. That didn't stop him from always showing up with an attractive woman on his arm at official functions, though.

Changing into a polo shirt and jeans and grabbing a beer out of the refrigerator, he threw together a sandwich for a quick dinner. He was still pretty full from the food at the reception, but the thought of a pastrami sandwich made his mouth water. More often than not, he would eat dinner at his desk in the study, one of the bedrooms he converted into a home office. The FOX News Channel, his preferred media outlet, was running yet another special report on the upcoming presidential election.

His housekeeper kept the small house spotless and free of all clutter, but the study was off limits. To the casual observer, his home workspace was chaos. County maps hung on the walls with different colored pushpins marking the locations of various crimes and other incidents. His desk and the bookshelves along one side of the room were piled high with teetering stacks of papers and books. But Tommy knew what everything was and in which pile it could be found.

Leaning back in his chair and putting his feet up on his desk, he started thinking how tomorrow would be his final day as Parker County Sheriff. It was such an odd thought. Not having to worry about receiving a phone call in the middle of the night telling him something terrible happened somewhere in the county.

Thinking about that, he grabbed his cell phone and sent off a quick text message to Ben: *How's it going?*

He hadn't heard anything from his office about what was happening at the hospital, which was good. It meant the city police didn't require any assistance. He just wanted to check in.

After forty years on the job, he wasn't sure how he was going to feel about retirement. He'd already had some offers from a couple of companies looking for a security consultant, whatever that meant. It would definitely bring in a nice retirement income, but he was thinking it might be time to take a break—a real break. He'd already made plans to go down to Florida to visit his sister for a few weeks, then after that he would just see what happened.

His cell phone buzzed. Looking at the screen, he read Ben's response: *50-50 chance might need to breach. Don't WANT to use force on a mental patient! May have no choice.*

If he was feeling anxious about retirement, he couldn't imagine what Ben was going through. Out of the two, Ben was unquestionably the workaholic. Tommy was willing to bet a small fortune that not having to get up in the morning and go to the office was going to drive his former partner crazy. This in turn would drive Natalie crazy. He did not envy her.

Chapter Sixteen

The sun had dropped behind the mountain range hours earlier, leaving Middleboro wrapped in a cool spring evening. Eerily quiet, a strong breeze rustling the trees was the only interruption to the almost deafening silence. Enjoying a cup of coffee next to the flickering flames dancing around the small fire pit, the sheriff reclined in an oversized lounge chair on his patio. The air was crisp and filled with the scent of the fresh kindling on the fire. Tommy felt completely relaxed and knew there were going to be a lot more nights like this.

Watching the brilliant sunset cast its golden rays across the valley, Tommy found himself thinking about some of the people he'd put away over the years and the people he'd been able to help. Like anyone else, he'd had his ups and down, but wouldn't go back and change a thing. It was odd how nostalgic he was feeling. He was never one to look back, but in recent weeks, it felt like that's all he was doing. He just figured after forty years of waking up and putting the badge on every morning, it was bound to happen. What would it say about him if he didn't take some time to reflect on all those years?

Finishing off his coffee, he put the fire out and headed inside for the night. The smoke from the ashes trickled upward, disappearing into the black sky as dew was beginning to form on the freshly cut grass.

From across the street, a figure hidden in a patch of trees watched as the old sheriff doused the fire. He'd been there since just after sunset, using the shadows and inevitable darkness to conceal himself amongst the cluster of maple trees.

Watching the sheriff sipping his coffee all evening brought back a rush he hadn't felt in decades. A rush he never thought he'd feel again. He was the hunter stalking his prey…again. This time, there was no voice whispering in his ear, though. He knew what to do.

He was surprised by how well the sheriff had aged. Other than his hair being a little grayer, he looked just like he did all those years ago. The first time they met. Since then, Detectives Winters and Mason had gone on to have very distinguished careers. Careers that had been very public and very easy to follow. He'd been keeping tabs on them for a long time. It was something of a hobby. Some people liked to bird watch. Others liked to collect stamps. He followed the adventures of Benjamin Winters and Thomas Mason.

The neighborhood was still. The night was clear and cool. Except for a few houses along the street where the flickering glow of a television hinted that someone was still awake, the rest were dark, everyone already asleep. He needed to be careful. Someone could be out walking their dog, and he couldn't be seen in Middleboro outside the sheriff's house. It wasn't like before when he could walk down the street and still be invisible. Hiding in plain sight was no longer an option.

Pulling the hood of his windbreaker over his head, trying to obscure as much of his face as possible, he quickly crossed the street looking both ways to make sure no one was out and about at that time of night.

Keeping to the shadows, he ducked around the side of the house, past the smoldering embers in the fire pit. Staying close to the house, he moved quickly, his heart beating faster with every step. Waves of familiar feelings washed over him. It was all coming back to him.

The French doors from the back yard to the kitchen were unlocked. How stupid could the sheriff be? What's the first thing the police always told people? Lock your doors!

He smiled as he slipped into the empty kitchen. Steven Colbert's opening monologue was coming from the other room. The minute he entered the house, he smelled something odd and out of place. The scent was sweet and spicy. It was cinnamon. Looking around, he saw a cinnamon scented candle burning on the counter. That was a surprise. He would never have thought big, manly Thomas Mason liked scented candles. You learn something new every day, he thought.

Peering around the corner into the living room, he saw the television was on, but the room was empty. Listening, he tried to tune out the late night comedian talking about the upcoming election. Where was Mason?

Just as he was about to step into the living room, there was a sudden movement in the darkened kitchen behind him. Without warning, Tommy lunged from the shadows. The sheriff was strong, and for an old guy, still in great shape. His muscular arm wrapped around the intruder's throat as the two fell forward, landing on the sofa.

"What are you doing in my house?" he snarled, yanking the hood from the intruder's head and turning him over in one mighty move. Tommy's eyes narrowed. "You sonofabitch! It was you! Of course, it was!"

Tommy was about to bring his fist down on the man's face with all the force he could manage when a sharp jolt of lightning shot from his stomach into his chest. Reflexively, he reached for the pain and pulled back a hand covered in blood. A crimson stain was quickly spreading across the lower half of his shirt. Tommy's eyes fixed on the bloody knife in the intruder's hand.

Before he could react, a second thrust forced the blade through fatty tissue, then muscle. The shock forced him backward, almost tumbling over the armrest of the sofa. This gave his attacker just enough wiggle room to free himself from under Tommy's weight. Leaving his weapon where it was, lodged in the sheriff's gut, he found his footing and raced for the kitchen.

Whether it was all the years of police training or the adrenaline now surging through his body, Tommy pulled himself together. With the knife in his stomach and the pain radiating throughout his body, his fight-or-flight response had kicked in. He was ready to fight. He just wished his Beretta wasn't locked in the gun safe in his study.

Tommy needed to make a split-second decision. Go for his gun or go for the intruder? There was no way he was going to let this guy get away again.

Following the killer into the kitchen, Tommy was barely through the door when the cinnamon scented candle in its heavy decorative glass jar crashed against his temple, knocking him first into the wall, then to the ground. He lay there crumpled in a heap on the cold floor. The blood running freely down the side of his face from a deep gash over his eye pooled on the tan tile underneath him, mixing with the blood seeping from the wounds in his stomach.

"You had a good run, Tommy boy." The voice coming from above him faded in and out as he tried to remain conscious. "Too bad you aren't going to make it to your last day on the job. Kinda like getting tackled on the one yard line, isn't it?"

For the briefest of moments, Tommy thought he was getting a second wind, and the pain was beginning to subside. The horror came a second later with the realization that he was just numb and starting to feel very cold.

"Ben's going to get you, you prick." Tommy's voice was barely audible.

"What's that? Ben? He's next."

Tommy watched the dark figure walk to the sink and pull the blinds over the window open. Still holding the thin nylon cord in his gloved hand, with a single yank he pulled it from the plastic track. Stretching the cord out and wrapping the ends around both hands, he slowly made his way back to the sheriff.

"No reason not to keep with tradition, wouldn't you agree?"

Once, twice, three times he wrapped the cord around Tommy's throat and began to pull. He'd missed this feeling. The others had tried to put up a fight, though. The sheriff was already half dead because of the amount of blood he'd lost. But it was still satisfying.

For the first time, Tommy knew he wasn't going to be able to talk his way out of the situation. He never thought it would end like this, but it hadn't been an empty threat that Ben was going to take this guy down. It was a promise. He knew his friend, the man that was closer to him than a brother, wouldn't rest until he got this guy.

And even though he had all the confidence in the world in Ben, he was still going to help him out one last time. Feeling the darkness taking hold,

Tommy used every last ounce of strength in his body to pull the knife from its resting place in his stomach. With one final motion, he took a slice at his killer. It wasn't much, but he knew he'd got him. The knife struck with enough force to make the dark figure let out a sharp howl.

Knowing he'd made his mark both in life and on his killer, and that Ben was going to bring this guy down, Tommy Mason closed his eyes. Exhaling his final breath, he slipped away with a cocky smirk lingering on his lips.

Chapter Seventeen

Then...

Howard Worthington, his "new-ish" wife, and baby daughter lived in a ten thousand square foot mansion on a sprawling estate. As one of Parker's original founding families, the Worthingtons, like the Bakers, were part of the fabric of the city, woven into every aspect of life. The Worthingtons, Bakers, Parkers, Mosses, and Tildons built Parker and in many ways still controlled everything that happened in one fashion or another.

The sheer size of the new Worthington House on the city's north side was scandalous during its construction. No one needed something so ostentatious was the popular refrain. Loudest of all being the voice of Beverly Baker. Not one to hold a grudge against those who had urged the city's planning and permitting department to reject the design of the massive house, Howard made it a point to invite even the most vicious of critics to a five-star housewarming gala. And on the day of the party, everyone showed up wanting to get a look at the inside of the modern marvel. It gave him great pleasure to see them all green with envy.

It was no secret that Howard Worthington loved having things that were shiny and new. From his house to his cars, he liked having the latest and greatest of everything. Even though he had more than enough money to buy anything he wanted—and usually did—he never acted that way. He was friendly, charming, and always ready with a smile, a kind word, and a large check for charity. By all accounts, he was a decent man and an honest banker.

His family built South Mountain Bank & Trust on the foundation of a true desire to help the community and those who lived there. The philosophy paid off. As SMB&T grew, becoming one of the region's largest financial institutions, so did the Worthingtons' net worth, which was on full display as Ben and Tommy drove their sputtering squad car up the drive to the enormous art deco home sprawling out before them.

"I think I should've been a banker," Tommy said, clearly in awe of the architectural masterpiece. "This place looks like a spaceship."

"A little out of place for Parker City," Ben pointed out. "This is the kind of house a Hollywood movie star should be living in."

"Just because it's a little different, doesn't mean there's anything wrong with it."

"I didn't say there was. It's just that this house doesn't fit around here. I'm surprised he was able to get it built at all, knowing how the city doesn't like anything *new*."

The two detectives continued their bickering about the house's right to exist within the city limits of the historic Western Maryland town as they climbed the steps to the front door. Ben noticed a number of cars parked around the circular drive. The one that caught his eye was the cherry red Mercedes Roadster. Knowing he'd never be able to afford something like that on his salary, he could only imagine what it would be like zipping around on the country roads with the roof down on a sunny day.

Tommy was also eyeing the car, thinking about what it would be like behind the wheel. It would definitely be a chick magnet. Not that he needed any help in that department, but he knew what it would do to Shirley and the other girls in Dispatch to see him drive up in that beauty.

Ben rang the bell. From inside they could hear the muffled sound of chimes. Ben would have sworn it was the melody of one of Beethoven's symphonies. Through the glass door, they saw an older man appear. He was wearing a plain white shirt and black tie under a gray vest, with the gold chain of a pocket watch dangling from one pocket to the other. His stiff movements gave him away immediately.

"The butler did it," Tommy said under his breath as the door opened.

"Can I help you?" the manservant asked, giving the two the once over with a critical eye.

"I'm Detective Winters. This is Detective Mason," Ben said from behind his badge. "We're with the Parker City Police. We need to speak with Mr. Worthington."

"Is he expecting you?"

"We called his office, and they said he was working from home today," Tommy offered.

"This is regarding…?"

"A criminal investigation," Tommy said, not doing a good job of hiding his growing frustration.

Before Tommy was able to say anything else, Ben explained, "This is an official police matter. There's been an incident involving one of Mr. Worthington's acquaintances, and we need to ask him a few questions."

"Right this way, Detectives. If you wait here, I'll see if Mr. Worthington is available."

The butler disappeared back down the hallway from which he had come, off to announce the arrival of the authorities. As he walked away, Ben took a second look at the odd figure. He wasn't the stereotypical English butler one would have expected. Sure, he dressed the part, but his build was of a former wrestler, big and burly. And the scar running down the side of his face made Ben wondered if there was some underground butler fighting ring he didn't know about. But what did he know? Maybe he'd received the scar defending the honor of a former employer.

Standing in the center of the sleek white foyer, the two police detectives found themselves admiring all the paintings hung on the walls. Not that either of them could identify any of the pieces, but they knew they had to be originals. Worthington didn't do anything half-way, so buying a cheap piece of art to put on display in his home didn't seem like his M.O.

"How much do you think one of these pictures goes for?" Tommy asked, realizing how jealous he'd be to know the answer.

"I don't even want to think about it. But I do like that one."

"It's just a bunch of colored squares. I don't get it."

Before the two were able to get into a critical discussion of the Picasso, the butler returned accompanied by the master of the house himself.

Howard Worthington looked exactly like what Ben thought a bank president should look like. Clean cut, hair that didn't move, tanned skin, all wrapped in an air of confidence. Even working from home, he was wearing a shirt and tie, albeit underneath a pink cardigan.

"Howard Worthington," he said, introducing himself. "Captain Brent said you would be stopping by today. Please, come into the library."

Had the captain's call been a warning, or was he trying to clear the way for the young investigators so as to not create any backlash from questioning such a prominent figure? Ben was willing to give Brent the benefit of the doubt for the time being.

The two-story library just off the main foyer was easily three times the size of Ben's entire apartment. One full wall was floor to ceiling windows looking out over the front drive, the other three were covered with bookcases filled by every kind of text imaginable. For the highest shelves, there was even a rolling ladder like in the movies. A matching pair of white leather sofas sat facing each other in the center of the room. Worthington sat with his back to the windows and gestured for the detectives to have a seat opposite.

From where they were sitting, the light filtering in from the windows cast a glow around Worthington, making him look almost heavenly sitting there, legs crossed, arms stretched out to either side on the back of the sofa. He was a man at ease and completely in command of his surroundings. Ben got the impression this was a man comfortable wherever he was. There was something else. He gave off a warm and fatherly air.

"Can I offer either of you something to drink? Water? Coffee? Fredrick can make a mean martini."

"No, thank you, Mr. Worthington," Ben answered.

"Sir," Tommy began, being as professional as possible, "I'm Detective Tom Mason with the PCPD. This is my partner, Detective Sergeant Ben Winters. We're here to talk to you about Beverly Baker."

"Tragic," Worthington said. "Beverly was not a nice person. In fact, she was a horrible human being. But no one deserves what happened to her."

"You know what happened to Ms. Baker?" Ben asked, taking out his notebook.

"Nick…I'm sorry, Captain Brent, told me when he phoned."

Ben was starting to wonder if there was anyone in the county that didn't know what had happened to Beverly Baker.

"We understand you and the victim recently had a falling out, and she replaced you as chairman of the Parker County Historical Society."

"Serving on the historical society's board is just something I do because there has been a member of my family on it since it was founded. Believe me, if I could convince my sister to take my place, I would. As far as being its chairman, it was just my turn at bat. No one else wanted it at the time. So, if you're suggesting that I might have killed her because she had the board remove me as chair, I'd have to tell you I had better motives."

Both Ben and Tommy were surprised at the matter-of-fact nature of his statement. When being questioned by the police, most people became defensive and tried not to say anything that might incriminate themselves. Worthington openly admitted he had reason to kill the victim. There's no way this case was going to be that easy, was it?

Not entirely sure what the correct follow up question should be, Tommy simply asked, "Could you please elaborate on that?"

Starting from the beginning, the banker, as cool and casual as could be, explained, "South Mountain B&T has been working with the Baker family and their companies for generations. In fact, SMB&T has provided funding for all the city's notable families to grow their own business—helping them become some of the largest in the region. Over the last year, though, Beverly went on something of a buying spree. She purchased huge tracts of land all over the county. I felt she was overextending herself. So, when she came to me this last time to help finance yet another acquisition, simply to stick it to one of her rival developers, I denied the loan."

"I'm guessing Ms. Baker didn't take that well," Ben said.

Worthington laughed. "Beverly took the loan rejection as a personal insult and a slap in the face to her entire family. Since then, she's been badmouthing me around town to anyone who will listen."

"And that's why she used her influence to take over the leadership position at the historical society?" Tommy asked, realizing how ridiculous it sounded.

"In her twisted thinking," the banker said with a crooked smile, "it was retaliation."

He went on to explain how the two hadn't even spoken since that fateful meeting at the bank that ended with her storming out of his office, slamming the door so hard it knocked his original Rothko, a prized piece of his art collection, off the wall.

To Ben, it sounded like Beverly Baker actually had more of a motive to kill Howard Worthington than the other way around. He couldn't imagine someone committing such a terrible crime over the chairmanship of a small historical society. But in the world of the rich and powerful, where status mattered more than anything else, all bets were off.

After listening to the story, neither Ben nor Tommy got the feeling Worthington had anything to do with Baker's death. Whether it was the fact he seemed so charming and open about everything or their guts telling them this just wasn't the guy, they both had the feeling Howard Worthington was a dead end. That would no doubt make the chief happy.

To cover all their bases, though, they still asked the obligatory questions. Where had he been the previous evening? Could anyone corroborate his whereabouts? Did he see anything suspicious when he left the meeting? Having gotten their answers, all of which they would need to verify, they thanked him for his time and made their exit.

Forty minutes after arriving, the detectives felt certain they had all the information they needed and could report back to the chief that Howard Worthington was not Beverly Baker's killer.

Chapter Eighteen

Several hours at the crime scene, followed by the time spent speaking with Howard Worthington, put it well past lunch by the time Ben and Tommy returned to the station. Running on only a few cups of coffee and a couple donuts, it was the adrenaline that was keeping them going. With that starting to wear off, they were both starting to crash and feel the weight of events on their collective shoulders. Unfortunately, food wasn't going to be an option any time soon.

The moment they walked through the door, they were informed by the desk sergeant on duty that the chief wanted to see them in his office.

"It goes without saying, Stanley sounded pretty…agitated," Sergeant Shepard said. "He was swearing more than usual."

"Is that even possible?" Tommy asked, only half joking.

"No doubt he wants a full report on our conversation with Worthington." Ben sighed. "At least he should be happy when we tell him we don't consider him a suspect."

The closer the detectives got to the chief's office, the louder they could hear Stanley's voice. Even with his door closed, there was no muffling his deep growl. He'd obviously not had a chance to cool down since they'd seen him at the crime scene.

Positioned outside Chief Stanley's office was his secretary, a wiry little woman named Mildred Greene. As far as anyone within the Parker City Police knew, she'd been with the department since it was founded sometime in the early 1800s. An institution, she was a woman no one dared cross. Her temper could be just as fiery, if not worse, than Stanley's. And like her boss and his ever-present cigar, she was never without a lit cigarette dangling lazily from her lips.

Seated at her desk behind several stacks of papers and an old Adler typewriter, Mildred glared up at Ben and Tommy over the rims of her out-of-style eyeglasses. Without a word, she jerked her head toward the chief's door, letting them know they could go in. Her fingers never once stopped, continuing to tap away at the keys in perfect rhythm.

"I don't think she likes us," Tommy whispered as they passed into the preverbal lion's den.

Chief Stanley was finishing a telephone call as they entered. It didn't take a detective to figure that out. He slammed the receiver down onto the cradle so hard the desk shuddered. Ben seriously thought the desk might collapse.

"Sit," the chief barked. "Alright. What did he have to say?" No reason to point out who *he* was. Ben knew exactly who the chief was talking about.

Ben started at the beginning and recapped the interview with Howard Worthington as Tommy sat quietly. Going line by line through his notes, Ben wanted to make sure not to leave anything out. He'd be putting all of this in a report later, but for now, the chief wanted to hear it all firsthand.

"He admitted quite freely that he disliked Beverly Baker. They'd had a big falling out over a business deal that he refused to finance. Then, to get back at him," Ben paused, "she forced the board of the historical society to strip him of his title and position as chairman."

"And that's why you thought he killed her?" Stanley snapped.

"We're going to need to speak with everyone who was at the meeting last night. We just started with Howard Worthington because we learned he and the victim had a recent dust up," Ben tried to explain one more time.

"So now you're satisfied that he didn't kill her?"

"After speaking with him, we don't believe he is our killer."

"If you had just listened to me in the first place, you wouldn't have wasted your time...or his," the chief growled.

After Stanley heard everything he wanted to hear, he dismissed the young detectives. But before the door closed behind them, he made it clear they needed to solve the case as quickly as possible. And though he didn't say it, they knew if they didn't, they'd be handing in their badges.

"Where to next?" Tommy asked as he and his partner left the chief's office.

"Do you have the list of people at the meeting last night?"

Tommy flipped through his notebook to the page with the names of all the historical society's board members. Aside from Beverly Baker and Howard Worthington, there were five other members—Dr. Edmund Kane, president of Tasker Valley Memorial Hospital; Professor Daniel Epstein, chair of the History Department at Hammermill College; Dorothy Elizabeth Parker, philanthropist and matriarch of the Parker family; William Laney, executive director of Tasker Valley Civil War Museum; and Bruce Maitland, managing partner with Tildon, Harlow & Maitland Attorneys at Law.

Tommy ticked off the names one at a time, noting that Lucy Jenkins, the society's secretary, had also been at the meeting taking notes, along with the organization's accountant. All of whom would need to be questioned.

Ben rubbed his eyes with the palms of his hands. It was going to be a long day, but if he and Tommy divided the list between them, they could cover more ground in a shorter amount of time. The odds of any of these people being the killer didn't seem very likely, but it was possible one of them had seen or heard something.

Each taking half the names, they split up heading out to see if they could come up with any leads that might point them toward Beverly Baker's killer or, if nothing else, a possible motive other than she just wasn't a nice woman.

Chapter Nineteen

Now...

To the surprise of many, Ben Winters wasn't all business all the time. Even though he'd spent countless hours at the office or investigating in the field, he'd managed to find himself a woman he didn't think he could live without. Natalie was his safe harbor. After everything he had seen on the job, no matter how bad or disturbing, he'd be able to come home to her and she was always able to make him feel better. He had no idea what life would have been like without her.

Ben couldn't even count the number of times he'd described her as a saint for putting up with him. Not that Natalie ever corrected him, she was just happy to be there for the man who felt he single-handedly needed to save the world.

The two met briefly during the terrible spring of '81. Natalie Kirkpatrick was a young teacher at Tasker River High School at the time. After their initial encounter, they kept running into each other while out shopping, at the library, on dates. It was as if the universe was subtly trying to nudge the two together whenever possible. During one of their chance encounters, Natalie asked Ben to come and speak to some of her classes about what it was like being the chief detective with the Parker City Police Department. He was all too happy to oblige.

From there, some would say, the rest was history. As Ben's career in law enforcement took off, Natalie climbed the ladder in academia, becoming a vice principal, then principal, finally retiring from the Parker County Public School System as an assistant superintendent of schools. She'd even found time to teach some classes at Hammermill College while Ben was off fighting crime.

Even though both had been career oriented, they'd made time to start a family, agreeing it was one of the best decisions they'd ever made. Their oldest, Andrew, was a first year cardiologist at Rush University Medical Center in Chicago, while their baby girl, Emma, was general counsel for a technology start-up in San Francisco. Ben always joked that if anything ever happened to his or Nat's pensions, the kids would be able to take care of them. After Ben finally hung up his holster for good in a few months, he and Natalie were planning a trip out west to spend some time with both the kids.

The couple still lived in the same house they first bought after they were married. Only a couple blocks east of Jefferson Park, it was a Post-Civil War Second Empire style house they purchased for next to nothing because of the state it was in. It was a fixer upper before fixer uppers were in fashion. The investment had come back to them exponentially, as the houses along East Branch Avenue were now some of the most sought after in the downtown area for their historic value and detailed architecture. Even the current Mayor Oland lived just down the street from Ben, albeit in a house three times the size.

Working regularly on the weekends, Ben allowed himself Friday mornings off to spend with Nat. She'd fix them a big breakfast, usually more food than two people should eat by themselves. When the weather was nice, they'd finish eating and go for a walk to Jefferson Park. When it wasn't so nice, they'd sit and have coffee on the porch. Ben would read through the news on his iPad while his wife opted for crosswords on hers. Curled up at their feet was Harley, the pair's beloved Golden Retriever—their third child.

The back yard always smelled of a combination of fresh, exotic fragrances due to Natalie's natural green thumb and love of unusual flowers. The colors always amazed Ben. They were so bright and vibrant, nothing like anything in any of the neighbors' yards. If it were left to him, the entire backyard would probably look like a jungle with unruly weeds as high as his waist. Nat liked working in the yard. It was one of her favorite pastimes. When she was lucky enough to get her husband to lend a hand, she needed to give him very clear, very specific instructions.

Ben's mind was wondering a bit as he admired the newest rose bushes Natalie had planted along the back walkway leading to the little garden gazebo. There were going to be a lot of moments like this in the near future. Every once in a while he wondered if he really was ready to retire. It's not that he'd been getting pressure from home or anyone else to hand in his papers. He certainly still had the fire in his belly, but there was just something telling him it was time. He'd put in his years of service, he'd made a mark. It was time for some new blood. He smiled thinking about that. At one time, he and Tommy *were* the fresh faces in the department.

It would be nice to sleep more than four or five hours a night, to not worry about getting am emergency call on Christmas or Easter and having to leave the family, to not see that slight hint of fear deep in his wife's eye every time he left for work. As the chief of police, he was an administrator, so not in the same danger as other members of the force, but his penchant for showing up at crime scenes and involving himself in high-risk investigations worried Natalie.

The incident at the hospital the previous evening was the perfect example. It could have turned into a fiasco. But luckily it ended with no one getting hurt. The patient had an "episode," the doctors explained. A paranoid schizophrenic—deeply troubled by the voices he was constantly hearing in his head—grabbed a syringe from the nurse and managed to block the door so neither she nor the orderly with her could leave. Protocol dictated that the police be called. The PCPD's chief negotiator, one of two the department employed, tried unsuccessfully talking the patient into letting the hostages go but had no luck. In the end, the needle wielding man tired himself out and fell asleep, allowing the nurse and orderly to get out of the room safely.

Sergeant Jeremy Romero, the Emergency Responsive Team commander, was prepared with a worst-case scenario plan if they needed to take the patient by force, but Ben wanted to hold off on that option for as long as possible. After talking to the man's doctor and the head of the mental health ward, the chief didn't think the patient was a real danger. Ben didn't want to escalate things by bringing in a full assault team of body-armed clad special force officers. Not that he was trigger shy, his gut just told him this was a situation that could be resolved peacefully. As the case was so often before, he was correct.

On his way home from the standoff at the hospital, Ben called the mayor and left him a message as a courtesy, in case anyone asked him about the incident. The chief was used to the mayor wanting to be kept in the loop on the "big" things, but ever since he'd announced he was running for congress, he wanted to know details about everything. And if it wasn't the mayor asking, it was his brother, Gary Oland, who was really the one calling the shots on his brother's campaign.

There was a small article, four pages into the *Herald-Dispatch*, about the events at the hospital. It was buried in amongst all the other local news. If he hadn't been looking, it's possible he would have missed it all together. That's what Ben liked to see: *nothing* about the Parker City Police on the front page of the paper. No news was good news in the crime fighting business. It meant they were all doing their jobs.

After getting through the top headlines, mostly related to the heated presidential primaries, Ben went right for the sports section. He couldn't wait until the upcoming football season when he would finally have the time to get to some Ravens games. In fact, he and Tommy were talking about buying season tickets so they could go to all the home games.

Natalie brought out two fresh cups of coffee and took her seat on the glider next to him. In the distance, there was the unmistakable wail of a police siren.

Instinctively, Nat put her hand on her husband's knee. She didn't want him jumping up and chasing after it.

"Whatever it is, they can handle it without you," she said softly. "If they need you, someone will call. They always do."

The siren continued, growing louder and louder until it finally stopped… on East Branch Avenue…directly in front of Ben and Natalie's house.

Whatever it was, it was bad enough that they hadn't called. They showed up in person.

Harley was the first on his feet, only beating Ben by a split second.

Walking along the porch that wrapped around from the back of the house to the front—one of Ben's favorite features of his home—he literally ran into his assistant. Out of breath, Drew looked like he was going to be sick. The young officer was pale and sweating. If Ben hadn't heard the siren, he would have thought he ran all the way from the station.

"Drew, what's wrong?"

"Sir...," the corporal began, completely out of breath.

Natalie walked around the corner just in time to see Ben, white as a ghost, throw up over the railing.

Chapter Twenty

Then...

Word of Beverly Baker's murder spread like wildfire. Nothing so grizzly had happened in Parker City for as long as anyone could remember. Even more shocking than the murder itself was the victim. An upstanding, wealthy member of society. Beverly Baker was not some street punk caught up in the middle of a gang fight or a drug addict who fell in with the wrong crowd. What had happened to Beverly Baker was cold-blooded murder. It was unthinkable!

It had barely been a day since the murder and gossip was running rampant. The headline in the morning paper certainly hadn't helped. "Matriarch Murdered!" was printed on the front page of the *Herald-Dispatch* in huge letters over a sensational story with very few details and a lot of editorializing by Roger Benedict.

The evening news out of the local Baltimore television stations had even aired stories on the murder. Images of the Parker Historical Society building behind yellow crime scene tape and police cars with flashing dome lights were splashed all over the TV screens. Much like Benedict's article in the paper, the newscasts didn't have much detail to report other than a prominent member of the community was killed in a horrible fashion.

Naturally, everyone had their own theory about who killed the notorious matriarch of the Baker family. As more and more people heard about the murder, the details became more and more exaggerated with each telling.

No matter where one went that cool spring day, it was the only topic on anyone's mind. The entire county was abuzz with whispers and speculation. The ladies at Sunrise Salon, the very hub of Parker's rumor mill, were not lacking for things to say. Most were shocked and horrified by what happened, but there were a few who wondered why it had taken so long for someone to do in the dragon lady. Sunrise was the place everyone in Beverly's social circle had their hair and nails done, so naturally they were the ladies who thought they knew her best. Her closest friends—at least to her face.

"I have it on good authority," Claire Parker announced to the ladies in the salon, "the police raided Howard Worthington's house yesterday after they found Beverly's body. It seems he's the prime suspect."

Not to be outdone in her own shop, Helen Ray, the salon's proprietress added, "They caught him packing up and getting ready to leave the country."

"Then why was he at the bank this morning?" asked another of the ladies from behind an old copy of *Woman's Day*. "He didn't look like a man on the run."

"The cops are obviously watching him to see if he had an accomplice," Helen concluded.

Beverly's murder, quite simply, had sent the city down a path of wild speculation and conjecture. Whether they had known her or not, people were taking an interest in what had happened. As the young reporter from the *Herald-Dispatch* pointed out to Ben and Tommy outside the crime scene, something interesting had finally happened. Nothing like this ever happened, so it was only natural for everyone to be sucked into the frenzy.

Even students at Tasker River High School, where juvenile imaginations were in overdrive on a regular basis, were coming up with their own horror stories about what happened the previous evening in the creepy old brownstone downtown. No doubt the house would now be haunted by the ghost of the wicked Beverly Baker seeking vengeance on her killer. Soon teens would gather outside the historical society at night and dare one another to go inside and face the evil spirit.

Having been a teenager at one time himself and knowing the way a young boy's mind works, Ben already had that thought and asked for an officer to be posted at the historical society so no one could try and get in and disturb anything until they were ready to release the crime scene.

Throughout the day, the teachers did their best to keep the students on task, but in the end, there was only so much they could do. When the entire city was distracted by such a surreal incident, why wouldn't the students react the same way? By the end of the day, the teachers were just happy to be able to keep the kids in their seats.

Tasker River High was the largest high school in the county, and its student body was rapidly growing. When enrollment numbers finally reached a tipping point, the county school board was forced to approve a long awaited second high school for the city. Ground had been broken the previous fall and construction was well underway, but it would still be another full school year before students would be able to step foot into Charles Carroll High on the opposite side of the city.

Regardless of the warnings from faculty members who instructed the students to go straight home after school—there was a killer out there, after all—the teens believed themselves to be invincible, so no one paid much attention. After the final bell, the kids still took their time going home, many stopping for an afternoon snack. Rax, Hardee's, McDonald's, and Dairy Queen were all side-by-side on the street only a few blocks from the school. The fast food corridor was always busy after school let out, students filling the restaurants and parking lots doing all the things teenagers always do to let off steam after a day of math, literature, foreign languages, and science.

Like every school filled with pre- and post-pubescent adolescents, cliques formed a natural social order. The jocks hung out with the jocks, the nerds with the other nerds, and, of course, there were the hot girls who ruled the school, the Lipstick Gang.

And Linda Carlson was their leader. President of the senior class, head cheerleader, and editor of the yearbook, she was involved in practically every activity imaginable. All the while maintaining a 4.0 average and holding the regional cross-country title.

Academics and extracurriculars aside, she was the alpha. Orbiting around the auburn beauty were her best friends—Penny, whose father, Bernard B. Moss III, was the owner and publisher of the *Herald-Dispatch*; Ann Marie Tildon, the mayor's niece; and Tammy Greyson, a transfer from Philadelphia whose father was a lawyer now working for the new Reagan Administration in Washington. These were the girls at the top of the high school hierarchy.

The young ladies were in their usual booth with their usual after-school indulgence. Fries and diet sodas in front of each, separate conversations were going on at once. One of which was about the upcoming senior prom. A topic on all the minds of the upperclassman.

Penny and Ann Marie were the decoration committee co-chairs and had taken it upon themselves to make the dance the most grand and elaborate affair the high school had ever seen. It would come as no surprise to anyone that the two picked the colors of the decorations to match their own dresses—pastel coral and ivory.

"It's a shame you broke up with Greg," Ann Marie was saying to Linda, munching on a handful of fries and speaking at her usual mile-a-minute pace. "Who're you going to go to the dance with now? I guess you could always let J.D. take you. Have you seen his new car? Or maybe Big Ron? Dennis, from Mr. Thorne's class, told me that Jimmy Fenton, who's in his first period class, and friends with Big Ron, said he was asking about you. What about Gary O.?"

"Greg's brother?" Linda asked, raising an eyebrow.

"Oops. I forgot."

"They're twins, Annie! How could you forget they were brothers?" Penny said in complete disbelief. How could she be friends with such an airhead, she often wondered.

"Maybe Linda's new mystery man can take her to the dance," Tammy chimed in, changing the focus of the conversation back to where it began.

Rolling her eyes, Linda finished the French fry she was eating and said, "You know he can't do that. He's..."

"...an *older* man," Penny said, mocking her friend. "You should still bring someone. It's not like there aren't a hundred guys drooling over you. Just close your eyes and point. For once, ditzy over here might have a good idea.

I hear J.D. has a pretty big—"

"Penny! I'm not doing that. I don't want…" Linda caught herself before she said his name, then continued, "…*him* to see me with someone else."

Penny had proven time and time again she wasn't afraid to say whatever was on her mind. "I'm doing an older guy, too, but I'm still going to the prom with Todd. He just better not be expecting anything. He's lucky enough just to get to walk into the gym with me. But I'll probably let him feel me up afterwards."

"Since when did you start seeing *an older man?*" Ann Marie began to pry as only a girlfriend could.

"That's none of your business. You think Linda's the only slut here?"

"Excuse me!" Linda turned so fast she almost knocked over her soda. "I'm not a slut!"

Linda's outburst came at one of those unfortunate moments when the other conversations in the place had begun to die down, so everyone in the fast food joint was now staring at her.

"Mind your own damn business, you pervs!" Penny yelled. Turning back to her friend, she said, "You seem really tense. I guess Mr. Mystery Man isn't doing his job. Maybe you should've stuck with Greg. At least he knew what to do to make your eyes roll back in your head."

"Stop it, Penny," Ann Marie said, blushing. She always got uncomfortable when they were talking about sex. Plus, to make it more awkward, Greg was her cousin!

"For Christ's sake, you need to get laid. Move. I have to go to the ladies," Penny said, pushing Tammy out of the booth. "Don't talk about me while I'm gone."

"She's such a bitch," Linda said, before Penny was out of earshot. Not that she really meant it, and Penny knew that. Just like she didn't mean Linda was a slut. It was just their way with each other.

"You don't think they're going to cancel the prom because of what happened to Ms. Baker, do you?" Ann Marie asked innocently enough.

"They better not," Tammy said, more forceful than she expected. "I didn't know the woman, so why should her getting killed stop me from going to my senior prom? Who cares if some old bitch got knocked off?"

"My dad knew her and didn't really like her," Linda started saying, "but no one deserves what happened to her."

"I heard she was strangled so hard her head almost came off," Ann Marie added.

"Who told you that?"

"I heard Dr. Hoffman telling Miss Chambers in the hall outside the library this afternoon."

"How would he know?"

"He's the principal. He's supposed to know these things."

Linda and Tammy just stared at their doe-eyed friend, wondering how she was able to function on a daily basis. She was so naive.

The silence was broken when Penny bounced back from the ladies' room. "What'd I miss?"

"Just Annie being Annie," Tammy said once again moving so Penny could get back into the booth.

"I told you. She's a spaz, she needs to get some. What's our plan for tonight?" Penny asked, taking a handful of fries from Tammy's plate. "Can someone pass the ketchup?"

Sliding the bottle across the table, Linda was more than happy to share her plans for the evening. "I'm heading home to get ready for a date."

"The mystery man?" Penny asked, rolling her eyes.

"Yes, as a matter of fact. But remember, I'm spending the night at your place, Tammy. Now if you'll all excuse me, I have to go get ready. I'll check ya later."

Chapter Twenty-One

Attracting attention no matter what she did or where she went, most eyes were on Linda as she left Hardee's. And she loved it. Unlike most of her peers, she knew the life she had become accustomed to in high school wasn't going to last forever. In just a couple of months she would be graduating, valedictorian naturally, and everything was going to change. That's why she'd decided to make the most of her popularity now, because who knew what would happen when she got to college?

That was one of the reasons she'd broken up with Greg Oland. Sure, they'd had a good time together the last couple of years. And Penny was right, he knew how to make her wiggle between the sheets. But he was still very immature. Not like her "mystery *man*." He had it all and for everything Greg was able to make her feel in bed, he took her to a whole new level. He had the experience and was more than willing to share.

She was thinking about him the whole way home. How he'd hold her hand, brush the hair out of her eyes, nibble on her earlobe, look right into her eyes when he was inside her. Linda felt flush, realizing she was getting turned on just thinking about him. Unfortunately, she hadn't come out of her daydream in enough time to stop at the stop sign at the entrance to her neighborhood. Luckily, there hadn't been any cars coming and the little old lady on the sidewalk was far enough away she hadn't been in any danger.

Linda pulled her little Triumph convertible, a gift from her father, into the empty driveway. Her parents were going to be at the Kennedy Center in Washington, seeing the tour of some Broadway show. It was her mother's idea, not her father's. He had no interest in the performing arts. It was like pulling teeth to get him to even come see her in the yearly school play. With them out of the house, she didn't need to worry about explaining where she was going. A note on the refrigerator door saying, "Spending the night at Tammy's" was all she needed.

Running straight up to her bedroom, Linda tossed her book bag and purse on the bed and began to get undressed. Before getting in the shower, she stopped to look at herself in the mirror. It was no wonder she always caught guys checking her out; she had a great body. Toned legs, flat stomach, a rock-hard butt, and perky little breasts. That's all guys cared about, wasn't it? None of the *boys* in school could give a crap that she had a 4.0 average and an IQ of 118, meaning she fell into the superior intelligence category. They saw her emerald green eyes and pouty lips, her tight body and just wanted to jump her bones.

In the shower, Linda soaped up and rinsed off. Normally she might linger a bit under the hot water, letting the steam turn the bathroom into a makeshift sauna, but she wanted to leave for her rendezvous sooner rather than later. For some reason, she had a feeling about that night. Something big was going to happen, and it made her feel all giggly and excited.

Once she was out of the shower, she went to work on her makeup. Eyeliner, eye shadow, blush, and lipstick were the tools she used to paint her masterpiece. The previous summer she worked behind the makeup counter at Montgomery Ward, picking up a lot of tips. She found it difficult at times showing women she didn't think should ever leave their houses how to do makeup. In Linda's opinion, there was just no help for some people.

For the evening's outing, she settled on her favorite bellbottoms and a bandana shirt that would have given her father a coronary if he saw her. Sure, it was going to be a little chilly, it was still only the beginning of spring after all, but she wasn't too worried about staying warm. He knew how to get her blood pumping.

The sun had only just begun to set when Linda hopped back in her car and left for her date. She was so caught up in the anticipation of the evening that she didn't see the car parked two doors down pull out and follow her.

Chapter Twenty-Two

Now...

Corporal Drew Collins received the worst telephone call of his life moments before running out of the chief's office and sprinting the entire way to his car. The reserved parking space in the private lot and department issued fleet car were supposed to be perks of being the chief's assistant. In reality, they were more like consolations for being on call all day, every day. After Drew spoke with Colonel Dempsey of the Parker County Sheriff's Department, who told him that Tommy Mason had been found murdered in his home, he knew that wasn't something he could tell his boss over the phone. He needed to tell him face-to-face. As painful as it would be, it was news that had to be delivered in person.

During the short drive—made even shorter by the lights and siren—from the PCPD to Ben's house, all Drew could think of was how he was going to tell his boss his best friend was dead. Sheriff Tom Mason was a larger-than-life figure in Parker County. The thought of someone breaking into his house and killing him was unthinkable to Drew. And if *he* was having this difficult of a time accepting the news, and he'd only known the sheriff in passing for the last few years, how was the chief going to react?

The minute Ben saw Drew, he knew something was wrong. He could read it all over the young man's face. The corporal looked as though he was in serious physical pain. Ben couldn't for the life of him think what could have happened. Never in a million years would he have guessed what Drew finally worked up the courage to tell him.

After hearing the heart wrenching news, Ben wanted to get to Tommy's house as quickly as possible. Drew, always the one looking out for his boss, didn't think the chief should be alone, so offered to drive. His car could go just as fast, and at least there would be someone there with him. The offer fell on deaf ears, however, as Ben was already in his car and pulling out of the driveway, leaving Drew no choice but to follow behind.

They were nothing but two shiny white streaks racing along the interstate. Both vehicles broke every speed limit as they raced west out of Parker City. The flashing lights and wailing sirens helped to keep the other drivers on the road out of their way. The chief's Interceptor reached ninety miles-an-hour a number of times on its way to Middleboro. The drive, which Ben had made countless times, would normally take fifteen to twenty minutes from his house to Tommy's, depending on the traffic. Seven minutes after climbing into his car, he was almost at the Middleboro town limit.

Everything was gray and fuzzy. At first, he didn't think he'd heard Drew correctly when he said, "Sir, I'm sorry, but Sheriff Mason is dead." He'd needed the out-of-breath officer to repeat himself. Even then, the words hardly made sense. Everything after that happened in a haze. He thought he remembered saying something to Natalie and hearing Harley barking in the distance as he ran for the car, but wasn't certain.

His mind was racing, thinking about everything and nothing all at the same time. Both of his cell phones were ringing, their electronic chirping a distant annoyance at the moment. The digital screen on his dash indicated that Drew and Natalie were alternatingly trying to reach him. He knew he should answer, but he just couldn't bring himself to say anything yet.

Keeping up with him the entire way, Drew was right behind him. He could see the corporal talking into the air, no doubt on the phone with the deputy chief at the department, filling him in on what was happening or maybe he was on with Natalie. He was a good kid, Ben thought. He'd take care of things and make the calls that needed to be made.

Tommy lived in a little neighborhood just beyond the Welcome to Middleboro sign that greeted those coming from Parker City and points east on Route 70. Passing that point, the sign being nothing more than a blur in his rear-view mirror, Ben saw a line of sheriff's department vehicles lined up along the street.

Even with the recent increase in its population and the continued interest from those looking to build new homes in the area, Middleboro was still a relatively small town and therefore did not have its own police force. Instead, it was under the jurisdiction of the sheriff's department, like a number of the smaller municipalities in Parker County.

Coming to a screeching halt at the yellow crime scene tape that stretched across the street, Ben jumped out of the car and, as was his habit, immediately went to adjust his tie. That's when he realized he'd left so fast he hadn't grabbed his tie or hat. There was a good chance he didn't have his wallet with him either. He'd give himself a ticket for driving without a license later.

The uniform of the sheriff's department was a stark contrast to the gray and blue of the Parker City Police. The sea of tan reminded Ben he was out of his jurisdiction and had no authority here, but Heaven help anyone who tried to get in his way.

Before he'd even closed the door to his car, Drew was at his side, taking off his own tie to give to his boss.

"Thanks, Drew, but a tie isn't going to make a difference."

"Sir, just remember, these aren't our guys. We're well beyond the PCPD's jurisdiction."

"I know, Drew. You need to…"

"Call Commander Channing and update him. Already done. He's taking care of everything at HQ. "

"And…"

"Call your wife. I've spoken to her too. I also called your sister. She said she'd head over to your house to be with Mrs. Winters so she isn't alone."

Ben knew the kid would take care of everything.

Ducking under the yellow police tape, like he'd done at so many scenes before, only one sheriff's deputy approached him. It was clear he didn't recognize the chief, otherwise he wouldn't have tried to throw himself in front of the oncoming steam engine that was Benjamin Winters. His relationship with the sheriff was well known and documented, so there was no reason to think he wouldn't be showing up at the crime scene. At least the uniform should have been a clue that the two weren't just a pair of average Joes off the street.

"I need to speak with whoever the commanding officer is here," Ben said before the lumpy deputy could manage to get a word out.

Struggling to keep up with the city police officers' pace, the chubby sheriff shouted, "You need to turn around. This isn't Parker City. You're out of your jurisdiction."

Drew spun on his heels and intercepted the deputy so Ben could continue without anyone nipping at his heels. The police chief got to the driveway as a tall, blond, leather-skinned looking deputy with a goatee stepped out the front door. Had Ben not already known, he would have easily been able to recognize this was the man in charge. He carried himself in a different manner than the other deputies; much more alert, keeping an eye on everything happening around him. That and he was wearing an officer's uniform with a gold eagle on his collar, signifying his rank. Colonel Ryan Dempsey was an Army Vet, a former Maryland State Police Trooper, and Tommy's top deputy. The following Monday morning, he was also to be sworn in as Parker County's new sheriff.

Ben and Dempsey were friendly acquaintances, but not friends. They primarily knew each other through the joint efforts of their departments. As Chief of the Parker City Police, Ben had been on the search committee to find Tommy's replacement. While a number of those appointed to the committee by the county executive wanted to bring in someone from outside Parker, he had fought to promote Dempsey to the top job. Ben had his diplomatic moments and in the end convinced enough of the other search committee members to recommend Dempsey for the county's top law enforcement post.

"Chief, I'm so sorry," Dempsey said, extending his hand and shaking Ben's. "Tom was a good friend to me, but I didn't know him like you did. I can't even begin to imagine how you're feeling. We're all still trying to get our bearings on this one."

"What happened?"

"Ben, you don't need to be here. We can handle this. This is top priority. Everything else is on hold right now. I have all our resources on it. I promise you."

"He was my partner, Ryan. He was my friend."

"That's *why* you can't be here, Chief Winters." His words hung in the air.

Ben stared into Dempsey's hard green eyes. He knew the incoming sheriff was right. He would have told someone in his position the exact same thing. He didn't blame him, he knew he was just trying to do his job and maintain the control and integrity of the scene. But he wasn't backing down. There was nothing and no one keeping him from getting in that house.

"I need to know what happened," Ben said, controlling the urge to sidestep the guy altogether and push his way into the house.

Dempsey's inner struggle was clear. Everything he'd been taught and trained to do said to keep the chief out. This was a matter for the sheriff's department, and he wouldn't let just anyone walk in and start asking questions. The problem was, this was Ben Winters. This wasn't just *anyone*. His reputation alone was enough for any agency to *want* his assistance on a case. Especially one of this nature—the obvious murder of a top law enforcement official.

After what seemed like an eternity of silence, Dempsey finally said, "I got a call while I was at the courthouse meeting with the state's attorney. The sheriff was supposed to sit in on one final crime stat meeting first thing this morning. He never showed. That wasn't like him. He hated those meetings, but he never missed them. But since today was his last day, no one really thought that much about it.

"Then when Tom didn't show up to his nine-thirty with me and no one could get him on the phone, I sent a car 'round to check the house and see if he was here. The deputy saw Tom's vehicle parked in the garage, but got no answer when she knocked on the door. She did a circle 'round the house and saw the back door open. This is what she found inside."

Dempsey stepped aside, following Ben into the house.

Chapter Twenty-Three

Then...

Saint Joseph's Episcopal Church sat across the street, looking east over the thirty acres making up Jefferson Park. One of the oldest churches in the city, the congregation was formed in the mid-1700s, though it wasn't until 1766 that the first Saint Joseph's Church was actually constructed. The original building survived for close to one hundred years through a number of repairs and minor renovations. Finally, in 1860, the church was razed and a neo-gothic structure of brick and carved stone rose in its place. As the Civil War was getting ready to erupt, it was a particularly prosperous time in Parker, so no expense was spared.

For a time, it was the tallest building in the city with its bell tower piercing the sky, pointing to the heavens. The tower boasted one of the most magnificent views of Jefferson Park and the surrounding city. On a clear day, the scene stretched for miles on end. In recent years, however, very few were allowed to ascend to the bell tower. Having recently celebrated its 120th birthday, the structure had aged to a point that no longer made it safe for excessive traffic up and down the steep, rickety wooden staircase leading to the tower.

It wasn't only the bell tower that had fallen into disrepair. A number of areas had deteriorated beyond the help any contractor could provide. During a Sunday morning service, a beam anchoring one of the six wrought-iron chandeliers that hung in the sanctuary cracked, punching a hole in the ceiling and causing the chandelier to fall ten feet before catching. No one was hurt, but it was the straw that broke the camel's back. The church council convened and agreed the entire building needed to be renovated, even if only to make it safe to continue to worship.

It was a heady undertaking, raising the amount of money needed to modernize the structure. With so much effort already going into trying to restore the downtown after the flood, finding the needed funds was slow going, even with a number of the area's wealthiest individuals being members of the church. Saint Joseph's sat outside the flood zone, so survived the onslaught of the torrential rains, but could not fight the hands of time.

Construction scaffolding now completely surrounded the church at the corner of 3rd Street and General's Way. The building was nothing more than a shell. Inside was a vast empty space with nothing more than temporary support structures to keep the entire building from collapsing in on itself. The interior was to be completely rebuilt. The project was much like what had been done to the White House during Harry Truman's presidency when the historic house was gutted and rebuilt from the inside.

A chain-link fence was erected around the property in an effort to keep anyone from trespassing and getting hurt wandering around the construction site. The deterrent did little to keep people from getting into the site in the evenings. People found ways into the construction site—a gate left unlocked accidentally, a hole in the chain link. Where there was a will, there was always a way.

Linda Carlson in particular had taken a liking to sneaking onto the property to meet her mystery man. It wasn't just enough for her that he was older, but meeting somewhere they weren't supposed to be made it all the more dangerous and exhilarating. She couldn't help herself, it was like a drug. There was a time she would never have imagined herself sneaking around like this...or sleeping with one of her teachers.

Leaving her car a few blocks away by the park, Linda walked to Saint Joseph's and found the loose piece of fencing in its usual place. How no one had fixed that yet was beyond her. She was just glad they hadn't. Pulling the wire aside, she ducked through the opening as she'd done so many times in the last couple of weeks. Before she was through to the other side, a piece of the metal fence grabbed her thin top, giving it a tear as she pulled free. Swearing under her breath, she rolled the piece of fencing back into place so it wouldn't look like it had been disturbed to anyone passing by.

Linda didn't know if she'd beaten her lover there or not, but she couldn't wait to see him. That day in class, she'd wanted him so bad. The thought of how she felt when she was with him and what she was going to do to him when they were alone had completely distracted her. Of course, she had to play it cool. Absolutely no one could know she was involved with her English Lit teacher. He could lose his job and maybe even be arrested. It wouldn't matter that they loved each other. No one in a stuck up town like Parker would ever understand.

The glow from the distant street lamps was the only thing lighting her way as she quickly crossed the grounds to the church. With every step, her heart beat a little faster in her chest. Every time she was with him, it was like the first time, which she'd told him it was, even though that was an outright lie. She figured he might know that, but still played along. She just couldn't control herself around Mr. Miles. More importantly, she didn't want to.

The construction crew may not have been able to safeguard the site and keep people from getting through the fence, but they were able to secure the entrances to the church. With one exception. A large door made from wide planks of white oak banded together with iron straps rested precariously over an opening leading into one of the transepts. The door was the only remaining piece of the original Saint Joseph's Church. It was nothing short of a miracle it had survived in such good condition for over two hundred years. The church council referred to it as their very own religious relic.

Because of its weight, Linda was only able to shift the door enough to squeeze through, ignoring the loud crack that came from one of the oak planks. She was more successful this time, not catching any of her clothing on the rough wood. Once inside, she was engulfed in silence. With the windows in the sanctuary boarded up for their protection with giant sheets of plywood, darkness filled the space except for random spots of moonlight dribbling in through the holes in the roof.

A chill ran down Linda's spine, goosebumps popping up on her bare arms and shoulders. Maybe she should have brought a jacket with her.

She'd be alright. He'd be there to keep her warm soon enough.

Good things come to those who wait, she thought to herself, hearing the familiar creaking sound coming from the old wooden door as it was pushed aside.

Chapter Twenty-Four

Watching Linda trot out of her house wearing that tiny shirt and tight jeans made his blood pump faster. He didn't think that was possible, but she had that effect on him. From the first moment he'd laid eyes on her, he'd been head over heels in love. Just watching her excited him. Every move she made was elegant and sexy as hell. How he ached for her.

Stop it!

The voice was whispering to him again.

Stop drooling over the tramp. She's a whore.

He knew the voice was right, but he couldn't help himself. The stiffness in his pants was a natural reaction of which he had no control.

Following Linda's little white convertible through the street was an exhilarating game of cat and mouse. He knew where she was going and could have just waited there for her, but this was more fun.

Easing his own car into a space a few spots behind hers, he waited until she was halfway down the block before he got out. As he'd done a number of times, he stayed in the shadows following Linda toward Saint Joseph's. Since construction had begun, he'd been to the church on a number of occasions, with and without Linda Carlson.

The day had been a blur, everyone talking about Beverly Baker's gruesome murder. He'd known he was doing the world a favor by getting rid of the dragon lady, but he'd never thought it would stir up such a fuss. In the grand scheme of things, she was a nobody, so why did people care so much?

After getting home that night, after his time with Beverly, he'd gone right to bed and slept better than he had for as long as he could remember. He woke up completely refreshed and ready for the day. Even the voice, which never stopped telling him what to do, seemed to be appeased. It hadn't said one thing to him during breakfast. He wondered how he'd feel tomorrow morning.

Using the same hole in the fence she used to get into the construction site, he pulled the chain link out of the way, darting through the opening it left. Linda hadn't been too careful, he thought, seeing a piece of material that looked like it matched her shirt stuck to one of the jagged wires.

The site was quiet and empty, as he knew it would be. That's why it was the perfect place to meet someone. It was easy for a couple to be alone here, spooky as it was. But the solitude provided a very intimate setting.

It was interesting how what could be creepy to one person was romantic to another. A church like St. Joseph's, wrapped in its cloak of scaffolding and gutted of its interior, was the perfect backdrop for a bad horror movie. Tonight, however, it was the setting of a secret tryst between lovers.

Not wanting to leave any footprints that could end up being traced back to him, he used Linda's steps to mask his own. Adjusting his gait to match hers, he carefully followed the path she'd left in the dirt.

Pushing the old wooden door aside, it creaked and popped like it always did. Linda shouldn't be concerned with the noise. She was here to meet someone, after all.

Her voice was soft and sweet, drifting through the darkness. "Joe? Is that you, baby? Hey, I just realized. I'm meeting a guy named Joe at Saint Joe's!"

He couldn't help but roll his eyes at the inane comment.

Stupid slut.

Through the shadows he could make out Linda's figure lingering by one of the scaffoldings erected inside the former sanctuary.

"I haven't been able to stop thinking about you, baby."

"I've been thinking about you too," he said, just loud enough for her to hear.

"Then why don't you come over here and give me a big kiss?"

The same feeling he'd felt the other night at the historical society was coming back to him. The adrenaline was beginning to surge through his body once again. Seeing her—his victim, his prey—standing alone in the darkness of the hollowed out church was energizing. He was thoroughly beginning to enjoy this feeling. The voice was right. These evening adventures were thrilling.

"What are you waiting for, baby? Get over here," Linda ordered in her sexiest voice. "I need someone to keep me warm."

It wasn't until he was only a few feet away that she realized something wasn't right. Even in the dark, he could tell Linda's body had suddenly tensed. She was no longer in a playful mood. Her defenses were quickly raised. As he took another step closer, Linda took a step backward. She was now fully aware something was very wrong.

Now!

In a split second, he lunged at her. The sudden movement startled Linda, causing her to stumble backwards, tripping over a stack of lumber. In an instant, he was on top of her. Lying on the ground with the wind knocked out of her, there was nothing Linda could do to defend herself.

Struggling to push him off, she felt hands all over her. They felt like they were coming from every direction. Linda was trying everything she could to fight her way free. But there was no way for her to get any leverage. He was too strong. She was pinned down. Trapped.

A momentary flash of light from somewhere outside was just enough to allow her to see his face. Just for an instant. What she saw was horrifying. She'd never seen anyone look like this before. His eyes were on fire. She'd never seen so much rage.

There were no words to describe the abject terror she was feeling. She had no idea what was happening or why.

A blow to her stomach caused an explosion of pain more intense than she'd ever felt before. The muscles throughout her body began to spasm. Waves of nausea swept over her. A second surge of pain almost knocked her unconscious as the next punch connected with the side of her face.

Wracked with pain, she tried to scream, but it was like a nightmare. When she opened her mouth, nothing came out. Could this all be a dream? Maybe she was curled up safe at home with the posters of Wesley Eure and Shaun Cassidy looking down on her from her bedroom ceiling. Every time she opened her eyes, she hoped to see the teen heartthrobs looking back at her like they did every morning. Instead, all she saw was a dark figure holding her down.

The weight of her attacker on her chest was making it difficult to breathe. Gasping, there was finally a moment of relief as he rolled off and flipped her over onto her stomach. Grabbing her hair and yanking, Linda was pulled onto her knees, her jeans tearing as they caught on a sharp piece of lumber. It was all happening too fast.

For a moment she was free, able to crawl forward. But she might as well have been in the bell tower. The ringing in her ears was so loud it was making her sick to her stomach. Not that the pain in her stomach was helping matters. It was already difficult to see in the dark, but as her eye began to swell shut, seeing became virtually impossible.

With every ounce of her being, she wanted to jump up and run, but her arms felt like they were being weighed down by barbells and she was still having a hard time catching her breath. All she wanted was to wake up and this be a bad dream. But it only got worse.

He grabbed her hair again and pulled her head back, exposing her neck.

She didn't think she could be any more scared until she felt the course braids of a rope being wrapped tightly around her throat. Clawing at the cord in a full panic, Linda watched the shadows in front of her eyes disappear and everything go completely black.

Chapter Twenty-Five

Now...

In his almost forty years on the job, Ben had seen every type of crime scene one could possibly imagine. Each told its own story. But the one thing they all had in common was the underlying sense of sadness and loss. There was never a happy crime scene. Whether it was a burglary or an instance of domestic violence, a drug bust or a homicide, police officers were the ones who saw the worst of humanity.

It wasn't like in the movies. That was always the first thing Ben would tell new recruits in the academy. Policing was hard. Not glamorous. It took hard work, integrity, and courage. There were always going to be bad days. But they were the ones that made the goods days that much better.

Even now, Ben still felt that initial surge of adrenaline when he crossed the yellow tape and stepped into a crime scene. More often than not, what the forensic team found at the scene would be all the authorities needed to solve the case. It was rare to find a criminal as smart as the ones on television that left no clues of any kind. The type of criminal that left entire police forces dumbfounded as they continued their crime sprees unhindered didn't really exist. In the case of murderers, most weren't all that smart, at least in Ben's experience. He thought most killers were pretty stupid. They always left something behind because the majority of murders weren't premeditated or part of some larger criminal conspiracy. They were heat of the moment events. When you don't plan for something in the first place, there is no way to account for everything that can, and will, go wrong. Not to mention how to cover it all up after the fact.

Random murder sprees like those of Jack the Ripper and the Zodiac Killer weren't common. Victims usually knew their killers, which could be helpful in giving the police somewhere to start. Having an initial list of suspects was a good thing for any investigation.

The murder of a police officer was different. Wearing the badge, one could have a long list of enemies, any of whom could want you dead. A few suspects helped the police by narrowing their investigation. Too many suspects could take too long to go through and require more manpower than was available.

Ben knew all of this. But no matter how well trained an officer was, when the crime scene was your best friend's house, nothing could prepare you. Emotions took the place of reason. The heart trumped logic every time. Which is exactly why a police officer should never work a case with which they were so closely connected.

Looking around the familiar living room, Ben knew manpower wasn't going to be a problem. He wondered if there were any sheriff's deputies anywhere else in Parker County or if they were all outside. It certainly looked that way. Too many eager bodies could also be a problem, the chief worried. It could lead to people stepping on each other's toes and falling all over one another, literally and figuratively.

Colonel Dempsey, the man now in charge of the Parker County Sheriff's Department earlier than expected, stuck his fingers in his mouth and let out a shrill whistle to get everyone's attention. The sound pierced the air, instantly cutting through the drone of numerous conversations mixing together to create a dull roar. The room fell silent instantly.

"Clear the house," he ordered. "The chief and I need five minutes."

Ryan Dempsey was taller than Ben by a good number of inches and about twenty years his junior. After closing the door behind the last forensic photographer, the acting-sheriff not only appeared to shrink before the chief's eyes but age well beyond his years. This was not how he wanted to start his tenure, and the shock was clearly taking its toll.

"Ben, it's pretty bad. Everyone in the department wants in on this." He paused, looking out the big picture window at the army of deputies on the front lawn. "Tom wasn't just the boss, he was our friend. I realize it's not the same as he was with you, but we're going to find whoever did this. I promise you. I hope you understand why I can't let you be involved. I'm already breaking protocol just letting you in here. Under the circumstances, though..."

Everything Dempsey was saying became background noise when Ben saw the reddish-brown stain on the sofa. It hadn't felt real until that moment. Someone had broken into Tommy's house and killed him.

Tracing the path of blood along the floor from the living room to the kitchen, Ben braced himself for what he was about to see.

"Are you sure you want to go in there?" Dempsey asked, already knowing the answer.

Taking a deep breath, Ben began reaching for the doorframe to steady himself. Realizing he wasn't wearing gloves, he quickly pulled his hand away. He wasn't going to be the one responsible for contaminating the crime scene. Though he was certain his prints were going to be found all over the house. He'd been there twice the previous week alone—the first time to drop off an early copy of a report on Parker City's crime stats and then a few days later with Natalie for dinner.

In the kitchen, Ben found Tommy's body lying on the floor, covered by a bloodstained white sheet.

There was too much blood for him to have been shot. Looking to Dempsey for an explanation, the colonel said, "He was stabbed in the stomach. Twice. Pretty deep, according to the initial examination. We have the knife, though. It was found on the floor over there. It's already on the way to the lab."

Kneeling beside the body, Ben crossed himself and said a quick prayer before slowly pulling back the sheet. Involuntarily, he gasped when he saw Tommy's pale face with a streak of dried blood running down his cheek. Hands trembling and a sick feeling in his stomach, Ben started to pull the sheet back into place, then stopped when he saw the marks on the neck. A thin, dark bruise circled Tommy's throat.

"He was strangled?" Ben asked, not taking his eyes off the brutal mark.

"They found traces of nylon fibers. It looks like they came from the cord to the blinds over the kitchen window. It was by the back door. It went with the knife over to forensics. We'll know for certain after the lab runs its tests, but it's the working theory."

Tommy Mason had been stabbed, then strangled to death. Tommy Mason had been strangled to death the same day he started talking about a decades old murder case involving a killer who strangled his victims. Tommy Mason had been strangled to death after telling his former partner there was something about that case he wanted to talk about.

It was like Dempsey was reading his mind when he said, "I don't believe in coincidence, Chief. If I was going to kill a man like Tom Mason, it would be with a gun, not a rope. You don't strangle a big guy like this unless you're trying to send a message. Do you think this has something to do with the Spring Strangler case?"

Ben hated that name. However, there was no doubt in his mind Tommy's murder was related. His answer was "I have no idea."

Chapter Twenty-Six

Watching his boss exit the house with Colonel Dempsey on his heels, the chief's mood was clear. His face was ashen and drawn, and though barely perceptible, his hands were shaking. Under no circumstance was Drew going to let him out of his sight. Let alone drive himself anywhere, home or to the office. He was in no state to be behind the wheel, and after putting up a half-hearted fight, Ben gave in and tossed Drew the keys. They'd arrange for someone to pick up Drew's car when they got back to the station.

The young officer was good company in any situation. When Ben needed a sounding board, someone to bounce ideas off, Drew was more than willing to share his thoughts and opinions. A more youthful perspective often proved very valuable. However, when Ben needed the quiet to think and collect his thoughts, his assistant didn't open his mouth. Turning into a mighty gatekeeper, he would do whatever necessary to keep his boss from being disturbed.

The car ride from Middleboro to the office was filled with twenty minutes of painful silence. Drew stayed focused on the road, hitting the ignore icon on the dashboard screen every time a call was trying to come through. Ben sat in the passenger seat next to him, eyes closed, hands still trembling.

Drew pulled the chief's unmarked cruiser into its usual spot and shut off the engine. Ben made no attempt to get out of the car. He wasn't moving. Just sitting, staring out the window. He still hadn't said one word since leaving the sheriff's house.

"Sir, it would probably be better if I took you home. No one expects you to come in today. I've already spoken with the division chiefs. And Commander Channing said he can handle things for as long as necessary. Clearing your schedule won't be a problem. I'll take care of—"

"I need to be involved in the investigation, Drew," Ben said, cutting him off. "I just don't know how I'm going to do it. It's completely out of our jurisdiction and Dempsey, as polite as he could be, made it clear that he wanted me to stay away."

Ben's mind was racing. He knew this had to do with the murders in '81. He knew he had no legitimate way to investigate the case without pissing people off and possibly breaking a few laws. And he knew he needed to find a way around that.

"I have plenty of friends in the sheriff's department," Drew offered. "I can have them pass me anything important so you can keep up with the case."

"Drew, I don't want you getting mixed up in this. But I appreciate the offer. I really do."

Regardless of what the chief said, Drew was still going to talk to his contacts and keep an eye on the direction in which the investigation was going. If there was a killer on the loose in the county—Parker City being smack-dab in the middle of that county—the chief of police had every right to stay informed. At least that was going to be his justification.

After a few deep breaths, Ben finally stepped out of the car and started for the building's rear entrance. Drew kept pace at his side. Officers were coming and going, each giving the chief a nod or quick salute as they passed. A handful stopped to express their condolences. By now, everyone who wore a badge knew what had happened to Sheriff Mason. After the first report went out, the police scanner lit up. From the state troopers assigned to Parker County to every municipal law enforcement agency, everyone in uniform had heard the horrific news. And everyone in the PCPD knew how close he was with the chief.

Whenever a member of the law enforcement community was killed, it was a loss for all of them. They were brothers and sisters in arms. But when an officer loses a partner, it was another kind of loss. If you weren't a police officer, there was no way to explain or truly understand.

Standing next to the door wearing a pair of khakis and a beat-up old leather jacket was a ghost from Ben's past. His face bore noticeably more wrinkles and his hair was now silver, but there was no mistaking him. Leaning against the wall with that same cocky smile he always wore was Roger Benedict. He still looked like a cheap knock-off of Tom Cruise.

There was no way to avoid him, Ben thought without breaking his stride. Drew, on the other hand, was instantly wary of the man casually standing around what was supposed to be a restricted area. With the stream of officers and department personnel coming and going, someone should have asked what business he had there. A man loitering outside the police department should have sent up red flags.

Drew was the first to speak. "Can we help you with something, sir?"

"Ben Winters, how long has it been?" Benedict asked, ignoring the junior officer.

"Not long enough, Benedict. Why are you here? Last I heard, you were in New York."

"Keeping tabs on me, Chief? I thought you would've heard. I'm the new editor of the *Herald-Dispatch*."

"You're back in Parker?"

"Roger Benedict?" Drew asked. "You left a message last night saying you wanted to set up a meeting with the chief."

"That I did, Skippy. Is now a bad time? You really look surprised. Didn't Tommy-boy tell you? I spoke to him a couple days ago and let him know I was back in town. Sorry to hear about what happened to him, by the way."

The words were a kick in the gut.

Ben really should have let Tommy shoot the reporter outside the historical society back in 1981.

"You talked to Tommy? He knew you were back?" Ben asked, wondering why his former partner hadn't mentioned the conversation, or if that's *why* Tommy wanted to talk.

"I thought I'd help my crime reporter out. Can I get a quote from you about the sheriff's murder? Do you think the Strangler has returned to haunt you?"

Roger Benedict was the one who first dubbed the killer the "Spring Strangler" back when he was covering the murders. As with any catchy nickname, it stuck. Ben hated when the press gave killers names like the BTK Killer or the Night Stalker. It glorified them and turned them into celebrities.

"What do you mean? Why would you think this has anything to do with a case from over thirty years ago?"

The newspaper man raised an eyebrow. "Well, the sheriff was strangled, wasn't he?"

It was one thing for someone in the press to know the county's sheriff had been murdered. Anyone monitoring the police bands could have found that out. But no one had released any information about the cause of death. Dempsey had sworn he wasn't going to give out any details yet. He recognized the ramifications of releasing the fact the sheriff had been strangled and the conclusion to which people would jump. How did Benedict know already? Ben had only known for a couple of hours himself.

"Mr. Benedict," Drew said, stepping between the two men, "I think you need to go. Chief Winters has no comment at this time."

Benedict made a move to sidestep Drew just as the door opened and two uniformed officers exited on the way to their squad car. Sizing up the situation in an instant, both could tell something wasn't right. The tension between the three men standing in the parking lot was palpable.

Instinctively, the first officer, the more senior of the two—a corporal like Collins—placed one hand on Benedict's arm as the other went to his service weapon. His partner stepped up next to Drew, increasing the barrier between the man and their chief.

"Do we have a problem here?" the first officer asked, looking to his boss.

"Everything's fine," Benedict said, backing up. "I'm the editor of the *Herald-Dispatch*. I was just saying hello to an old acquaintance that I haven't seen for a while. That's all. Your chief and I go way back."

The officers were still waiting for instructions before standing down.

"It's okay, guys," Ben finally answered, breaking a momentary silence. "Mr. Benedict was just leaving. In fact, why don't you escort him back to the newspaper? I'm sure he has work to do."

Chapter Twenty-Seven

Then...

As Jimmy Peterson, or "Big Jim" as his friends called him, heaved himself out of his pickup truck, his work boots crunched the crisp frozen dirt. It had been another cold spring night, leaving a layer of frost on everything, including the dirty around the construction site.

"I don't understand why we have to start so early when it's so cold," Hector Gomez said, exiting from the other side of the cab.

"We start this early," Big Jim answered, "because that's what the boss says. Just be thankful it isn't summer yet. Working in the heat is going to be miserable. If this summer's anything like last summer, we're gonna be toast."

Hector grabbed his metal lunch pail and followed Big Jim toward the scaffolding-wrapped church they'd been working on for so long. There were some days that seemed like nothing got done. He was afraid this was going to be one of those days.

"Are you going to be at Ken's this weekend?" Big Jim asked, taking a key ring from his pocket and fumbling around until he found the one he was looking for. As he listened to Hector hem and haw about why he may or may not show up at their friend's cook out, Jim unlocked the main gate to the construction site. As the assistant foreman, he had a set of keys to open all the doors and gates on the site. One of his many jobs each day to open everything up before any of the other construction workers arrived in the morning.

Five minutes into Hector's answer about his plans for the weekend, Jim cut him off and said, "Man, I was just asking if you were going to be there. It was a simple yes or no question."

"Obviously someone got up on the wrong side of the bed this morning."

"I didn't get up on the wrong side of the bed, you just haven't shut up since I picked you up. And in all that time your lips have been flappin,' you haven't actually said a damn thing."

"That hurts, man. That really hurts," Hector said, clutching his chest, pretending to feel his heart breaking.

Jim stared at his friend without saying a word. Finally saying, "You're gonna need to find another ride home if you keep talkin' like this, dude."

With a laugh, Hector followed Big Jim around to the back of the site behind the church. It was going to take both of them to move the big wooden door blocking the guys' main entrance and exit point into the old building.

Rounding the corner, they saw that the door was partially open already. Someone had moved it just enough that it looked like a person could squeeze through.

"Damn kids!" Big Jim said in frustration. "If we get in there and have to clean up some party shit, I'm gonna be pissed."

After he and Hector pushed the door open all the way, Jim went to turn on the power to the work lights which had been set up throughout the cavernous space. With all of the windows boarded up, there was very little natural light in the building. As the high powered work lamps began to light up, he was pleasantly surprised to see everything pretty much looked like it had when they left the previous day. Construction material and tools lay in piles in the various areas where work was currently being done.

From outside, voices of some of the other construction workers could be heard as they began to filter into the construction site.

Big Jim was turning to head back outside when Hector grabbed his arm.

"What's that?" he asked, pointing halfway down into the empty church. "By that lumber."

Squinting, Jim saw what looked like a pile of rags someone had left on the ground. "I don't know. Clothes, maybe?"

"Nah," Hector said, taking a few steps toward the heap lying in the dirt. "That looks…that looks like…"

Jim had already turned to leave, but when Hector stopped talking mid-sentence, he stopped and looked back. Hector was standing over the pile with an expression of his face Jim didn't understand. He actually thought his friend might be crying. It wasn't until Hector dropped to his knees and crossed himself like the good Catholic Jim knew he was that the construction foreman knew something was wrong.

Chapter Twenty-Eight

The sun had barely had a chance to make it over the horizon before everything went sideways at Saint Joseph's. The call was made to the PCPD just as soon as Big Jim could get his hefty legs to carry him to the construction trailer where he could find the nearest telephone. Out of breath, gasping for air, the big man had a difficult time trying to explain to the officer on the other end of the line what they'd found. As he was reporting the discovery, Hector and another construction worker were keeping the rest of the crew from entering the church.

For the last day and a half, Ben and Tommy had been crisscrossing the city, talking with everyone who had been at the historical society's board meeting the night Beverly Baker was murdered. Each person they spoke with pretty much said the same thing—Beverly was a horrible person; she made everyone's life miserable; no, they hadn't seen or heard anything out of the ordinary that night. The detectives didn't have much to go on.

Before leaving the night before, Ben squeezed a chalk board into the office so he and Tommy could make notes and organize their work on the investigation.

Not having left the station until almost one in the morning, Ben was only able to get a couple hours of sleep. He was back at his desk before six. It was made very clear to him that solving Beverly Baker's murder was the department's top priority, so rest and personal time was to be kept to the barest minimum. His and his partner's jobs were definitely on the line.

To his credit, Tommy also came in early. He arrived only a few minutes after Ben, a bag of donuts in hand. By seven o'clock, they'd gone over everything from the day before, making sure they hadn't forgotten anything, and started to plot out the course for the investigation that day. They were hoping to have the autopsy report before lunchtime.

Tommy was in the break room brewing a new pot of coffee, the second of the morning, when Ben's phone rang. It was Shirley from Dispatch reporting the call of a body found at Saint Joe's.

Ben sat staring at the receiver in his hand for a good thirty seconds, the wheels in his head spinning out of control. The look on his face must have said it all because when Tommy returned with fresh mugs of coffee, he knew immediately something was wrong. Quickly filling his partner in on the call he just received, the two headed out the door.

The drive from the station to Saint Joseph's Episcopal Church didn't take more than a few minutes. Just long enough for Tommy to finish off the last cigarette in the pack before opening another. Ben focused on the road and what passed for morning traffic in downtown Parker as his partner blew smoke out the window. Neither said a word.

Arriving at the church, the scene was very different from two days ago. There was no chaos, no crowd gathered to see what was happening. Other than their own, there was only one other squad car.

Of all people, it was Buck LuCoco who waddled over to them. The officer's usual arrogant and condescending demeanor was nowhere to be seen. LuCoco seemed uneasy, almost nervous.

Mopping his sweat-soaked brow with a graying handkerchief, he said, "I'm really not sure what we have here. I mean, we've got a young girl's body but…it looks like she was…um…"

Ben knew LuCoco could be difficult to talk to and get information from, but that was because he was usually trying not to be helpful. This time it was something different.

"Buck, what's wrong?"

"Look it, I'm not the coroner, I don't know how they figure things out for sure, but it looks like…it looks like this girl was strangled."

Two murders in as many days in Parker City was already too much to think about. Two murders where the victims were both strangled? That didn't take a detective to figure out there may be a connection. Whether there was evidence tying the two cases together, that was a different story.

LuCoco led Ben and Tommy into the church through a door that was propped open by a pair of cinder blocks. He explained that was the way the construction workers entered and exited the building during the day. After being shown the body by the assistant foreman when he first arrived on the scene, Ben was surprised to find LuCoco actually did something right by ordering the crew off the site. That explained the group of irritated men in hard hats lingering in a clump on the sidewalk.

The young girl was lying on her back, much like the way they found Beverly Baker. Looking around at the tools and building materials scattered about, the dirt and debris from the internal demolition of the church, and the mess created by the reconstruction of the interior, neither Ben nor Tommy could imagine how they were going to find any useful clues as to what happened. There were footprints everywhere. Rust stains looked like blood. Tools out in the open could have been handled by anyone. The crime scene unit was going to have their hands full.

Ben's heart was thundering in his chest as he looked down at the delicate young woman lying at his feet. The lump in his throat prevented him from saying anything at that moment.

Tommy on the other hand didn't have the same problem. "Sonofabitch! She looks like a kid! She's a teenager at most! Ben, this is…"

"I know," Ben said, holding up his hand. "I know. I'll take a quick look. You go call in the cavalry. We're going to need everyone."

As Tommy went to radio for additional units, Ben made a cursory inspection of the victim. Bruising on her face indicated a severe blow and the ligature marks around her neck proved LuCoco's assumption was right. She'd been strangled with a massive amount of pressure, judging by the deep impressions left on her throat.

There was a key difference between the first murder and this one, however. Beverly Baker was strangled with bare hands. This girl was strangled with some sort of rope. The ribbing left behind on her neck was clear to the naked eye, despite the discolored and badly bruised skin. Why had he—still assuming it was a *he*—changed his method of strangling his victims? Ben wrote the question in his notebook.

Killing someone by strangling them was personal.

There was also a certain amount of uncontrolled rage needed to murder in this fashion. Literally to be so physically close to a person when you kill them isn't something of which everyone is capable. Ben was thankful for that incapability and the fact that the vast majority of people couldn't commit murder of any kind, let alone in such a disturbing manner.

Ben continued comparing the two crime scenes, noting that neither victim appeared to have been sexually assaulted. The coroner's report would have to verify that, but both women were fully clothed when they were found.

The clear difference in the victims' ages was something that struck Ben as important. Another note went in his book.

By the time Tommy returned, Ben's mind was racing. In the distance, police sirens could be heard approaching the church.

"Two murders, Ben. I think it's safe to say Stanley's going to want to talk to you."

Ignoring the fact the chief was never happy, this was going to make him downright apoplectic. No doubt everyone in the PCPD chain of command was going to weigh in, as well as the mayor.

The problem was going to be figuring out if the two murders were actually related. Ben's gut told him they were, even if the MOs were slightly different. Beverly Baker was an older, established member of society killed in an office. The victim currently in front of him was a teenager, at most, killed in the middle of a construction site. They were the same, but different. It was a detective's worst nightmare.

Chapter Twenty-Nine

Officer LuCoco was leaning on the hood of his patrol car when Ben and Tommy finally emerged from the church after spending time talking to the State Police CSU technicians. Evidence collection was going painfully slow inside, but the victim had at least been identified. A purse was found near a stack of lumber and along with the usual items a teenage girl carried was Linda Carlson's driver's license and school ID.

What hadn't been found was any sort of rope that could have caused the ligature marks on the victim's neck. There were plenty of cables and other material to tie and bind things together, but nothing with a braid. Whatever the killer had used, he'd taken it with him. But had he also brought it with him in the first place? That would be a clear indication of premeditation.

The coroner's van was pulling up as Ben and Tommy passed LuCoco, who gave them a nod like he would to any other officer. Maybe they'd turned a corner with him. He might have realized what two murders in the city in a span of three days could mean. When the cards were on the table, police officers stuck together and had each other's backs.

It was no surprise when Ben checked in with the station that Lieutenant Dennis had left word that he wanted to see him immediately. The station was exactly where they were heading when they saw, standing at the corner watching all the activity at Saint Joseph's, none other than Roger Benedict.

"You!" Tommy shouted, running across the street toward the reporter. "What the hell are you doing here?"

Benedict raised his hands innocently, press badge in one of them. "I'm just covering a story. A second murder? I couldn't ask for a better headline."

"How'd you hear about this? Where're you getting your information?"

"Detective Mason, I told you. There's a little birdie keeping me informed."

Ben caught up to his partner just as it looked like he was going to take a swing at the journalist. It was a look he'd seen a number of times. Luckily, he was able to stop Tommy from making a big mistake and turning a bad situation into a worse one.

"Detective *Sergeant*," Benedict said, greeting him in his most patronizing tone. "Good to see you. Care to comment on the fact two women have been strangled in Parker City in the last forty-eight hours?"

There were only two explanations for how this guy could know the second victim had been strangled since the only people who should know at the moment were wearing badges. Either he had a source inside the department who wanted to see sensational headlines splashed all over the front page of the paper or—an even more terrifying thought—the man standing in front of them was the murderer. Or was somehow involved.

"I don't have any comment at the moment, Mr. Benedict," Ben said as calmly as possible. "And I would caution you not to write anything until official information is released."

"Of course not. We wouldn't want to start a panic. It would be terrible for the city if women felt they were being hunted by a crazed serial killer." It was the tone in his voice rather than the words he uttered that sent a chill down Ben's spine. "How could any of them feel safe walking the streets knowing the Spring Strangler was on the loose?"

"The what?!" Tommy exploded.

"The killer needs a name. What do you think? Spring Strangler. I'm a sucker for alliteration."

"You're treading on thin ice, asshole," Tommy snapped.

"Detectives, I'm not trying to cause any trouble. I'm just doing my job. What if we make a deal? I give you something, you give me something. A little tit-for-tat, so-to-speak."

Turning his partner away from the reporter and toward their car, Ben said over his shoulder, "No comment."

Raising his voice so everyone on the street in earshot could hear, Benedict said, "Here's a freebee for you. Linda Carlson was Greg Oland's girlfriend. Greg Oland, the mayor's son."

Chapter Thirty

For the second time, not only did Roger Benedict know before anyone else that a woman had been killed—strangled—he knew *who* the victim was. That wasn't sitting well with Ben, but he was desperately trying to keep his personal feelings about the reporter in check. Benedict could very well be the killer, but there was no actual proof. Tommy wanted to slap the cuffs on the slimeball, drag him down to the station, and sweat a confession out of him under the hot lights of the interrogation room. Even though that's not how it actually worked, Ben was warming up to the idea.

Leaving Saint Joseph's, they were afraid Benedict might have the audacity to show up on the Carlsons' doorstep and try to get a comment for his story and, in the process, be the one to break it to Linda's parents that she'd been killed. Arriving at the house, they instead found Captain Brent with the family. The chief sent him to inform the Carlsons of what had happened. Linda's mother was verging on hysterical and her father could barely speak. It was heartbreaking. Easily the worst part of Ben and Tommy's job, seeing a family devastated like this.

Brent sent the detectives back to work, saying he would stay with the Carlsons for a little while longer. They could be interviewed later, after they'd had some time to process everything and calm down. So it was back to the PCPD.

The meeting with Lieutenant Dennis went as well as could be expected. On behalf of the chief, he made it clear this case needed to be closed quickly. Everyone appeared to be on the same page, though. The thinking was that the same person committed both murders. No one had any evidence to support the theory, just their guts. But sometimes that was all they had to work with.

Ben spent a good portion of the afternoon writing his report on the Linda Carlson murder scene. Then he compared it to the one he wrote the day before about Beverly Baker's. He was looking for any and all similarities, but wasn't coming up with much. Anything that did appear to be similar between the two cases was noted on the chalkboard.

If he could just find *something* to connect the two murders, it would give them somewhere to begin. Ben read and reread the reports. Then he put them aside and looked at the initial findings from the State Police at the historical society.

"Anything?" Tommy asked from the doorway.

For his part, while Ben was doing the paperwork, Tommy had hit the streets. He'd spent time checking in with some of the more unsavory individuals with whom he was acquainted. If anyone had heard anything about the Baker or Carlson murders, these particular people weren't going to be willing to talk at the station.

Unfortunately, like Ben, he found himself without any leads.

Parker's underworld having yielded nothing, he decided to circle back to the list of respectable names who had served with Beverly Baker on the board of the historical society and cross reference them with Linda Carlson to see if there were any common threads.

In a small city like Parker, Tommy found plenty. Everyone knew everyone else in some way. Professor Epstein from Hammermill College was a frequent guest speaker at Tasker River High and would have lectured in one of Linda's history classes. Bruce Maitland and one of Linda's friends' father were partners in a law firm. There were overlaps like that for almost all the members of the Parker Historical Society. The only one completely in the clear was Dorothy Elizabeth Parker who, at 81, had been confined to bed after hurting her knee playing tennis the afternoon following Beverly's murder.

Sitting in their office, staring at the ceiling, neither wanted to admit it, but Benedict had given them their only solid lead. Greg Oland. If nothing else, it was a place to start with the Linda Carlson investigation. A boyfriend was as good a place as any to begin.

Chapter Thirty-One

Neither Ben nor Tommy thought it was a good idea to let anyone know they were going to need to speak with the mayor's son. Chief Stanley had been furious when they wanted to interview the president of a bank, so who knows what his reaction would be if they told him they were about to question the son of the mayor.

"So, are we thinking Greg Oland could have been involved with Beverly Baker's murder *and* Linda Carlson's?" Tommy asked from the passenger seat, between drags on his cigarette.

"I have no idea what I'm thinking right now," Ben admitted. "Other than strangling as the cause of death in both cases, I don't see any immediate connections. So, for the moment, we work the Carlson case separately."

Tommy exhaled a long stream of smoke. "Are you sure you don't want one of these?" he asked, motioning to the half-empty pack of cigarettes on the dashboard. "They help me clear my head."

"I'm good. Thanks."

"They're good for stress, too. And buddy, I hate to tell you, you look stressed."

"Shut up."

The Olands, Parker City's first family, lived in a majestic Victorian mansion overlooking Jefferson Park, in one of the most exclusive older neighborhoods in the city. A three-story plum colored home with a wraparound porch and turret made it look like a life-sized doll house.

The original founding families of the city had built their homes next to each other on Grandview Avenue, passing them down from generation to generation. Though Charlie Oland was not a descendant of one of these great families, his wife, Mary Ann Tildon, was. It had been her family's money that helped launch Charlie's political career.

It was a story told time and time again. A handsome, charismatic young man full of great ambition and little means meets an attractive young woman with little ambition and great means. Mary Ann had been instantly taken by Charles Francis Oland. He was everything she had been raised to desire in a husband. Even though Charlie didn't come from an Ivy League family, the Tildons welcomed him with open arms, as well as an open checkbook when he first ran for a seat on the city council.

Easing the rickety squad car to the curb in front of the row of stately manors, the gears gave a final ear-piercing squeal as Ben shifted into park. As Ben reached for the door handle, he caught a glimpse of thick black smoke billowing from the car's tailpipe in the rear-view mirror.

"How much longer 'til we get our new car?" Tommy asked, walking through the lingering exhaust fumes.

"I have a feeling it's going to depend on whether we close this case or not," Ben answered, following his partner up the path to the front door.

To both of their surprise, it was the mayor himself who answered the door. Charlie Oland was a politician straight out of Hollywood central casting; complete with the thickest head of perfectly coiffed hair that never moved, a square jaw that would put Superman's to shame, and a smile that could melt a woman's heart. When he worked a room, he made every person with whom he spoke feel like they were the only person there. Even if it was only during a thirty second handshake. If he could make good on his promises of rebuilding and revitalizing Parker City's downtown, there was no telling how high his star would rise.

Ben and Tommy frequently saw the mayor in action. He'd spoken at a number of department events since taking office and was extremely close to the chief. As mayor, he'd also proven he was a friend to those who wore a badge. The detectives hoped that goodwill towards the police would offset the inconvenience of their showing up unannounced at his home.

It was a known fact within the various municipal departments that the mayor worked long hours at City Hall, so it was a surprise to find him home at four-thirty in the afternoon. Maybe just a brief stop before heading off to an afternoon meeting or evening event, Ben thought, as he was still wearing his suit and tie.

"Can I help you, gentlemen?" Oland asked through his famous thousand-watt smile.

"Sorry to bother you at home, Mr. Mayor, but I'm Detective Winters. This is my partner, Detective Mason," he said, both producing their badges. "We were hoping to have a few words with your son, Greg."

The mayor's smile faded a few hundred watts as the corners of his eyes tightened and his perfectly chiseled jaw clenched ever so slightly. They were close to imperceptible, but both detectives witnessed the subtle reactions.

"I…um…of course, please come in, Detectives. It's Ben and Tom, right?"

To be able to know their first names was impressive. Either he was really good at remembering the name of every person he ever met, or it was because they were the PCPD's only two detectives. Since they were something of a pet project of his, it stood to reason he would know their names.

"May I ask why you want to speak to my son? Chief Stanley assured me the entire police force was focused on Beverly Baker's case. Does this have something to do with the investigation? I'm not trying to be difficult. Just trying to understand."

Tommy's own charm kicked in. "I don't know if you are aware, but this morning a young lady, Linda Carlson, was found murdered at Saint Joe's. I'm terribly sorry, sir. We believe you may have known her. We were informed that Greg and Linda were dating and we're looking to talk with her friends."

The mayor didn't immediately respond. He stood in the doorway blinking as if what Tommy had just said didn't make any sense. As the news settled in, he raised his hand to cover his mouth as he slowly began shaking his head. "That's terrible. Linda was such a sweet girl. You don't think Greg had anything to do with this, do you? I can assure you…"

"We're not saying that at all, Mr. Mayor. It's just a matter of covering all the bases," Tommy said, quickly defusing a situation that could have gotten very tense. "We're just trying to learn as much about Miss Carlson as possible."

Satisfied that it really was nothing more than a fact-finding visit, Charlie Oland showed the two detectives through the foyer, passed what Ben could only guess was the music room because of the grand piano and cello, to a sitting room that looked out over a lush flower garden. The floral theme carried into the room with sofas covered in rose patterned upholstery and large paintings of country gardens hung on the walls. The décor seemed a little too feminine for the masculine mayor.

"If you gentlemen would make yourselves comfortable, I'll go get Greg."

After the pair of sliding doors closed, Tommy looked around the room and shook his head. A froufrou sitting room like this was not a concept he could grasp. He would be the first to admit he really didn't understand how the other half lived. Every night he hung up his holster in a trailer in a mobile home park just outside the city. It was nothing like the Victorian mansion, but it was all he needed and he loved it.

Ben, on the other hand, appreciated the relaxed feel of the room. It reminded him of his grandmother's house. Like Tommy, his home was modest, a small one-bedroom apartment in a converted brownstone. But he could still appreciate the finer things.

It wasn't long before the doors slid open again and the entire Oland family entered. Mary Ann Oland, formerly Tildon, was an elegant, beautiful woman with porcelain skin and bright red hair. She had an air of old money about her. Taking a seat opposite the detectives, she sat with her back straight as a board as the mayor perched next to her on the arm of the sofa.

Following behind them was Greg Oland…and a second Greg Oland. Ben and Tommy did a double take as two identical teen boys walked into the sitting room.

Chapter Thirty-Two

For the briefest of moments, Ben had forgotten that the mayor had twin sons. He'd only heard about them, never seen them. So wasn't aware they were *identical* twins.

Seeing the surprise on the detectives' faces, the mayor introduced the pair, "Gentlemen, these are our sons, Gregory and Gary. As you can see, they're identical twins."

Ben stood and walked toward the boys, the first extending his hand, saying, "Hello, sir. I'm Greg."

"And I'm Gary," the second said without making any move toward the visitors.

They were tall like their father, but both on the medium to skinny side. If it wasn't for the different hairstyles, one wouldn't be able to tell them apart. Greg's eyes seemed softer though, with a friendly sparkle. Gary's were darker and cold, more brooding. As a seventeen-year-old, anything could have put him in that kind of mood. Ben wasn't taking any offense.

Even though he'd known twins before, he'd never seen a pair that looked so much alike. It was unsettling. He wondered if the two ever played tricks on anyone, switching identities and pretending to be the other. Judging by their mother's firm stare, he didn't think a prank like that would be looked on too highly.

Greg sat down next to his mother while his twin hovered in the corner, clearly wondering why he needed to be there. At that age, everything and anything was an imposition. There were probably a hundred other things the boy wanted to be off doing, but his parents obviously wanted to present a united front. That was perfectly all right with Ben. Knowing Greg had a brother, he was going to want to speak with him as well.

"We weren't together anymore," Greg said, the first time Ben referred to Linda as his girlfriend. "She broke up with me."

"She was a slut," his brother blurted out.

"Gary! Watch your language," Mary Ann snapped. Had he been standing closer, Ben thought she might slap him.

"Oh, please." Gary rolled his eyes. "It's not my fault she'd boink any guy around. Rumor is she was doing it with an old guy. I guess she's tired of guys her own age."

"Stop it, Gary." Greg was obviously uncomfortable. "You don't need to say those things about her."

There was something odd about the brothers' dynamic with one another. Was Gary defending his brother or insulting him? Having three of his own brothers, Tommy was sitting quietly trying to figure it out. Just by their body language, it was clear that Gary was the more dominant. His anger and frustration seemed to get the better of him, while Greg was slightly more reserved and thoughtful. He never answered a question without thinking about it first.

"Linda wasn't a bad person," Greg said, as if he was pleading for someone to believe him. "She didn't deserve to be killed."

There was a loud scoff from the corner that everyone tried to ignore.

Leaning forward on the sofa and locking the mayor's son with his warmest gaze, Tommy asked, "Can you think of anyone that would want to hurt Linda? Did she have anyone at school that was giving her a problem?"

"Are you kidding me? Linda was a first-class bitch." Gary was now standing behind his brother, red in the face. "She's the one who made people's lives miserable. Her and those slut friends of hers. They're all useless."

"Okay, Gary, enough, I shouldn't have brought you in here. You need to go. I'm sorry, Detectives," the mayor apologized.

Gary's clear hatred of Linda was puzzling. If Linda had dumped Greg for an older man, he should have been the one that was upset. Not his brother.

Not like that.

Twenty minutes later, Charlie Oland was showing Ben and Tommy out. After Gary was excused, the conversation remained civil, and the detectives were able to collect the background information for which they were looking. Linda Carlson was popular and seemed to be involved in every extracurricular activity Tasker River High had to offer. According to Greg, everyone liked her and she made it a point to get along with everyone. It felt like he was trying a little too hard to make Linda out to be a saint. But Ben would rather keep the boy talking.

She and Greg had dated for a little over a year but recently broke up. Greg admitted it was because of another guy, and he too had heard that he was older. He even alluded to the fact it might be one of their teachers. Needless to say, that sent his parents through the roof. Neither could bear the idea of a teacher taking advantage of one of his teenage students. Greg tried to explain that was just a rumor, but Ben and Tommy knew they were going to need to look into it, nonetheless. The bell had been rung.

The trickiest question Ben had to ask was where the teen was the previous evening. He didn't want it to sound like they considered him a suspect, but he needed to know. Greg said that he and his brother had gone to the video arcade after school to blow off steam, then come home to watch television. And do their homework, Mary Ann Oland added rather awkwardly.

Before he concluded the interview, because of the similarities in the two murders, Ben asked Greg if he'd known Beverly Baker.

"From parties and different things dad took me too," he answered in a weak voice.

"She and I worked together on a number of issues and served on various boards together," the mayor offered. "Parker City isn't all that big. A lot of the same people do all the work when it comes to charities and groups around town. Mary Ann even served on the historical society board with her a few years back."

"She was a terrible woman," the mayor's wife said without shame. "I believe her goal in life was to make everyone miserable. I, for one, am not sorry she won't be around anymore."

"Mary Ann, please. Show some respect." Charlie Oland looked shocked and embarrassed.

"Don't, Charles. You made a deal with that she-devil a long time ago. Between her coercive influence and my family's money, you got the job you wanted. There was nothing in that deal that said I had to like her."

The tension that disappeared when Gary left returned three-fold with Mary Ann Oland's outburst. Her feelings toward Beverly seemed to be right in line with everyone else's, including Howard Worthington. The mayor, on the other hand, either liked her or more likely, knew she was someone he needed in his corner as mayor. Politics made strange bedfellows.

On the way back to the front door, Ben had a chance to get a better look at the house. It was immaculately decorated with antiques and artwork, Oriental rugs, and possibly his favorite piece, a full-sized suit of armor outside Charlie Oland's study right off the foyer. He wasn't sure how he missed it on the way in; or the curtains and fabric swatches of every color lying on the floor in a giant heap. Rope tie backs with gigantic tassels on the end stuck out from under the material, while curtain rods leaned precariously against the wall. A stack of paint cans was piled next to them.

"It looks like you're doing some redecorating," Tommy said, pointing to all the materials on the floor.

Shaking his head, the mayor said, "My wife is constantly redoing one room or another. This week it's the living room. Next week will probably be the dining room. It's never ending. Every time she looks at one of those home decorating magazines she gets a new idea."

Reaching for the door handle, Oland stopped, turning back to Ben and Tommy. His tone became more serious. "Detectives, I just want to apologize again for Gary. You know how teenage boys can be sometimes. He's usually the quiet one to be perfectly honest with you. And Mary Ann, well, there was always something of a rivalry between her and Beverly when they were growing up. Some grudges just last longer than others."

For all the pomp and circumstance that came with the man's job and the larger-than-life character Charlie Oland presented to the general public, Ben now saw him as just a man with a family with flaws just like everyone else.

"Thank you for your time, sir. If we have any other questions, Detective Mason or I will be in touch. For right now, I think we have what we need."

Usually, when someone is murdered, the police investigating the crime look at the people closest to the victim first. A boyfriend or jealous ex is always a good place to start. In this instance, though, Greg wasn't coming off as the killing type. Ben and Tommy arrived hoping this interview would rule Greg Oland out as a suspect. For the most part, it did. The troubling part was, they were now leaving wondering if they should be taking a closer look at his twin brother Gary.

They were getting nowhere.

After speaking with the Olands, they found no clear connection between Beverly Baker and Linda Carlson. They did learn that Linda might have been having an affair with one of her teachers, though. Stopping by the high school and making some delicate inquiries would need to be the next step.

Chapter Thirty-Three

Now...

Ben spent most of the weekend holed up in his den. The last time he'd spent two whole days at home was when he'd come down with the flu a few years earlier. Even then, Natalie practically tied him to the bed to keep him from leaving the house. Missing work was unthinkable. He just wasn't someone who could stay down.

But after what had happened, Ben was in no mood to face anyone or anything. The pain of losing Tommy was proving to be too strong.

It still didn't seem entirely real. How could Tommy be gone? The thought of him not being there to pick up the phone left a knot in Ben's throat.

Harley remained curled up next to Ben the entire time, except for a couple of trips outside to the bathroom. He only left his post then because Natalie lured him away with left over strips of steak. It didn't matter where his master was sitting—at his old rolltop desk in the corner of the room or in his recliner—the Golden Retriever was never more than a step away. As a dog loved all his life and raised as if he was one of the children, he knew when his master was hurting. So Harley stayed dutifully by Ben, partly for comfort and partly for protection.

Though he was still keeping up with the most essential of his duties as chief of the Parker City Police Department, his deputy chief had stepped in and taken over for the last few days. Ben needed time to himself, which meant Drew's skills as a gatekeeper were being put to the test. Since news of Tommy's death broke—quickly becoming national news—it was hard to find someone who *wasn't* trying to get in touch with Ben.

In the old days, there would be a stack of little message slips piled up next to the telephone. One for each call Ben received and needed to return. The constant advances in technology changed that. Now each of those messages was waiting for him in the inbox of his email along with notes Drew included for each call.When last Ben checked, there were over a hundred messages for him. Only a handful of those Drew had flagged as necessary for him to address sooner rather than later. The vast majority of the others were calls expressing sympathy.

Ben wasn't ready to return any of the calls, but that didn't stop him from scrolling through the list on his phone. As he was looking at the names of those who'd called, a notification popped up on the screen. Drew red flagged this one.

It read: *Director Rigley just called the office. I told him you were working from home. He said he would call you there.*

No sooner had Ben finished reading the message, the house line began ringing. There were only a few people who had the Winters' home telephone number. FBI Director Alan Rigley was one of them.

"Ben, I don't even know what to say," the director said when he answered the phone. "I'm sorry I couldn't call earlier. I've got the typical federal bullshit for you…anything you need to solve the case, the Bureau is at your disposal and all that. But seriously, between friends, man, *anything* you need, you call me. You know I've got certain…resources…I can make available. This one's personal. I have a lot of strings I can pull. Just say the word and I'll start yanking."

"Thanks, Alan. You know this isn't my case, though. You need to offer those resources to Sheriff Dempsey."

"That just doesn't sound right, does it? Sheriff Dempsey. He's next on my call list."

For two men that usually laughed their way through conversations with one another, the call was very somber and rightfully so. At one time, Tommy

Mason, Alan Rigley, and Ben Winters had been very close. They weren't the three musketeers or anything like that, but as close as three high-ranking law enforcement officials could be. Even so, Alan Rigley knew his relationship with his fallen friend was nothing close to Ben's. But he wanted to make sure Ben knew he was there officially and unofficially.

Ben knew all he needed to do was ask, and Alan would send an army of federal agents to Parker and come up with a reason to assert jurisdiction over Tommy's case. Then he'd find a way to put Ben on the FBI's payroll and tap him to lead the investigation. But Ben couldn't do it—as much as he wanted to. There were rules and procedures for a reason. He just hoped Dempsey would take the director up on his offer of federal resources.

A few hours after talking to Alan, Ben was still in his den. He'd spent a good deal of time looking at all the photos on the wall. Tommy was in half of them. The memories came flooding back like old movies he hadn't seen in years. Holidays, family vacations, their lives had been so intertwined. Ben's heart just hurt.

When the mantle clock in the living room chimed midnight, Ben was propped in the corner of the sofa with Harley's head on his lap, watching a rerun of *Ocean's Eleven.* Not the George Clooney-Brad Pitt remake; the original 1960 film with Frank Sinatra and his Rat Pack gang.

He'd sent Natalie to bed, saying he was just going to watch a few more minutes of the movie, then sent Drew a message letting him know he'd be coming back to work in the morning. Both had continually been checking on him, Nat in person and Drew via phone, text, and email.

Natalie had been giving him space but kept a watchful eye. Saturday and Sunday night she'd made two of his favorite meals, her homemade lasagna and chicken parmesan, forcing him to join her in the dining room, not letting him become a total recluse.

Just as he was getting ready to shut off the television and head to bed, his cell phone chirped the tone he'd assigned to Drew. It was two o'clock in the morning according to the display on his phone screen. He needs to get a life, Ben thought. Though he knew full well he couldn't manage without the young, energetic, and intuitive corporal who'd helped to make his job so much easier in recent years.

The email read: *I know you said not to, but I did. I'm not sorry at all. Go ahead and fire me if you want.*

There was a document attached, labeled 'TM/Initial.Doc.'

Opening the file, Ben saw it was a copy of the initial crime scene report from Tommy's house. Drew's friends, whoever they were in the halls of power, had slipped him a copy of the Crime Scene Unit's first draft of the report. That's what his email was referring to, the conversation when Ben told him not to pull any strings or get involved.

The chief would have to admonish him in the morning for disobeying a direct order. That admonishment would be arriving in the form of a salted caramel mocha Frappuccino, Drew's favorite. Just for good measure—to show how serious he was—Ben would throw in a piece of the double chocolate cake Nat made for dessert. Something the young officer was never shy of saying how much he enjoyed. Drew was a good guy and was going to go far.

Taking a deep breath, Ben started scanning the file as best he could on his phone. Finally giving in to his age and admitting his eyesight wasn't what it used to be, he turned on his laptop and logged in to the PCPD network so he could pull up a full screen of the attachment.

He'd read so many crime scene reports over the years that they had stopped phasing him, but this one was different. He was having a hard time keeping his emotions in check. There was no way to distance himself from this case. But to read the report and pick out the important facts, he needed to compartmentalize and focus on the words and keep the feelings out of it.

With the glow from the computer screen provided the only light in the room, Ben began reading through the report.

It all appeared to be pretty standard. There was a note that the autopsy revealed Tommy had died of manual strangulation, with the investigators at the scene connecting the cause of death to the nylon cord from the blinds in the kitchen. Small fibers pulled from the neck wound confirmed the assumption. Unfortunately, the only DNA found on the cord belonged to Tommy. The candle that was used to strike the sheriff in the head was found next to the body and came up negative for DNA and fingerprints. The bloody knife found at the scene was clearly the weapon used to stab Tommy. With the amount of blood at the scene, the medical examiner doubted whether Tommy would have survived regardless of being strangled. The two stab wounds would most likely have proved fatal. Forensic tests run on the knife revealed the presence of two types of blood.

Ben read that line in the report again.

There were two types of blood found on the knife?

Ben's heart began to beat a little faster.

Unfortunately, the report went on the say, there was no DNA match. The mystery blood didn't match anything in any of the databases through which it had been run.

Had Tommy injured his killer? There's no way he would've gone down without a fight, Ben thought.

Several partial prints were found on the knife. All of which belonged to Tommy. But it had two types of blood on the blade! The conclusion was Tommy managed to turn the attacker's own weapon against him.

For the first time in three days, Ben smiled, thinking about how his friend had helped provide the investigation with a very important piece of evidence and possibly the key to solving his own murder.

Chapter Thirty-Four

Monday morning, Corporal Drew Collins was waiting outside Ben's house bright and early. With him, another young officer and an unmarked fleet cruiser ready to ferry Ben on his way. Before heading to the station, the chief's presence had been requested in the mayor's office. That meant the first stop of the day would be the Ivory Tower, the new—even though it was approaching ten years old—City Hall. The current Mayor Oland had asked for a private meeting, making Ben feel like he was being called to the principal's office.

"I really didn't need a car, Drew. I could have driven myself."

"Sir, I'm just trying to make your day as easy as possible."

"I know and I appreciate it," Ben said, tossing his briefcase into the backseat. "About your email last night," he continued, ducking into the car, handing his assistant a Tupperware with a piece of gooey chocolate cake, "this is for you as a punishment for disobeying my direct order. Don't ever do it again."

"You're the boss," Drew answered, closing the door with a smile.

Between the house on East Branch and City Hall, Ben read through some reports from the office and checked his email for the fourth time that morning. He was trying to stay as focused on work as possible. After his appointment with the mayor, he had a meeting with his division chiefs. It was the regular Monday morning executive meeting. He'd been asked several times if he wanted to cancel, but declined. His personal tragedy could not interfere with the running of the PCPD. Some would think Ben should take some more time before going back to work. Others would know that Tommy would be furious if Ben missed a day at work because of him. Ironic, considering Tommy was the one always saying Ben worked too hard.

City Hall was just beginning to show signs of life when Ben arrived. Freshly polished, the morning sun bouncing off the marble floor in the lobby nearly blinded anyone walking through the main entrance. The mayor's personal assistant, a small middle-aged woman with distinct Asian features, was waiting for Ben. With a tight smile and an extended hand tipped with bright red fingernails, she greeted him and escorted the chief through the lobby to the elevators. He'd been to the building on countless occasions and couldn't for the life of him remember the last time he was met by anyone at the front door. What was this meeting going to be about?

The short trip from the lobby to the fifth floor was taken in complete silence. Ben's natural instinct would have been to make small talk, but he knew Aimi Pritchard was not the type who took to idle chatter. Her reputation as the mayor's ironfisted enforcer was well known. She was a no-nonsense office administrator.

The Charles F. Oland Building was a glistening example of a modern government center. A sleek design, almost futuristic furnishings, and a layout determined by the latest workplace efficiency studies made the place cold and uninviting. Ben never felt comfortable there. It was nothing like the old City Hall. Very symbolic of the way Parker City had changed.

Ushering the chief into the mayor's reception area, Mrs. Pritchard asked if she could get him anything like a half-caf latte or a raspberry scone? Ben remembered a time when plain old coffee was all that was offered at morning meetings. Politely declining, he took a seat as the mayor's "bouncer" went to announce his arrival.

The minute she opened the frosted glass door to the inner office, the extraordinary soundproofing became apparent. In the second it took for her to open the door, it went from complete silence to hearing the mayor yell, "…was completely necessary! I did what…"

The assistant's entrance brought the mayor's outburst to an immediate and abrupt halt.

"Sir," Aimi said from the doorway, "Chief Winters is here."

A handsome man barely in his fifties, what people nowadays were calling a silver fox, appeared from inside the office. He didn't have the same physical stature as his father, the former mayor, but Greg Oland had all his charm and then some. It was a sharp contrast to the quiet boy to whom Ben was first introduced over thirty years earlier. He might not have looked as imposing as his father, but he could still command a room.

"Chief, please come in," the mayor said, welcoming him with a smile.

Turning more somber once they were in his office, the mayor put his hand on Ben's shoulder and said, "I just want to say again how sorry I am, Ben. Sheriff Mason was an extraordinary man."

"Thank you, Mr. Mayor. He was just that. And a good friend, a very good friend."

Oland opened his mouth to say something else, but the words Ben heard next came from behind him. "Are there any leads?"

Ben turned to see the mayor's identical twin, Gary, seated at the small conference table in the corner, flipping through a large binder emblazoned with the mayor's congressional campaign logo on the cover. The man was always hiding in the shadows, Ben thought.

Even though it was well known that Greg Oland's campaign had raised a huge amount of money and he'd hired a team of top-notch professional political operatives to advise him, his brother was clearly the one calling the shots. It's the way it seemed to be with the two boys. Greg was always the one out in front, charming, cheerful, ready to lend a hand and get involved with whatever he could. Gary was the power behind the throne. He was the one guarding the family and its fortune. All the while, not only working to increase its influence, but his own power as well.

The mayor's life was an open book, having spent a good deal of it in the public eye as an elected official. Gary, on the other hand, worked in the backrooms and corridors of power, making things happen. He was always more comfortable twisting arms than shaking hands like his brother.

"Gary doesn't mean to be so abrupt," the mayor said apologetically. There's the Greg Oland Ben first met back in 1981, much more mild and defensive. "But, with the primary coming up, and a crime of this nature happening in the district, the campaign needs to know what's going on. We don't want to be caught off guard by anything."

"Especially if this has anything to do with what happened back in '81," Gary added, staring at the chief over his reading glasses.

Leaning against his desk, the mayor realized he'd never offered Ben a seat. Apologizing and gesturing for him to sit on one of the uncomfortable looking metal ergonomic guest chairs, the mayor continued.

"Ben, first, if there is anything I can do, or if the city can help move the investigation along, please, just tell me. I know how close you and Tom were. I want to help."

"The case is in the hands of the Sheriff's Department. It's outside my jurisdiction. I don't want to get in their way or cause—"

"But you'd like to take over the case yourself," Gary interjected. Ben wasn't sure if it was a question or a statement. "You have to have talked to someone in the sheriff's office by now. What have they told you?"

Ben liked the mayor as well as he liked any of the mayors he'd served under. He did not like his brother, however. He never had. So there was no way he was going to tell him anything about the investigation, even though he was technically not supposed to know anything himself.

Shaking his head, he answered the way he felt was best. With a lie.

"I don't have any information. I don't think Colonel…," he caught himself, then continued, "*Sheriff* Dempsey would tell me anything even if I asked. And he shouldn't. I would do the same if I were in his shoes. We have jurisdictional lines for a reason."

This would usually be when Ben launched into his lengthy lecture about the importance of respecting and need for boundaries and not interfering with other agencies' investigations. But today it would have been half-hearted at best. Ben desperately wanted to be involved but needed to show he could follow the rules.

Puzzling was the fact Ben still wasn't one hundred percent clear about what the purpose of this meeting was. He just knew the Oland brothers didn't look too pleased. Could Tommy's murder really affect the mayor's congressional campaign that much? Were they genuinely concerned? Ben couldn't tell, but he wasn't going to be the one to share any information, especially since it was information he wasn't supposed to have in the first place.

After one more failed attempt to find out what, if anything, Ben knew about the investigation the mayor's brother, very conspicuously, motioned to his twin to wrap it up. Greg Oland politely brought the meeting to its conclusion and escorted Ben out to the reception area.

Closing the door behind him and lowering his voice when they were in the outer office, the mayor said to Ben, "I'm sorry about Tom. And I'm sorry about calling you in here this morning. And while I'm at it, I'm sorry about Gary. The campaign is concerned about what happened. No one wants the press to start digging up the Strangler case again. Gary, in particular, doesn't want to rehash the past. It wouldn't look good for anyone."

Ben hated politics.

Through a tight, forced smile, Ben said, "I understand, Mr. Mayor. You have to cover all the bases."

And your ass, Ben thought.

Chapter Thirty-Five

While Ben was at the station going through the coroner's report on Beverly Baker, checking and double checking the details of her autopsy, Tommy and a couple of patrolmen were at the Carlson residence to see if they could find anything useful in Linda's things.

Upon returning, Tommy produced a stack of letters and notes from her friends. All of which appeared pretty standard and innocuous at first read. The real prize in the search of Linda's things came in the form of her diary. If you ever wanted to see into the head of a teenage girl, you read her diary.

Thumbing through the pages, Tommy was making notes as he read. Nothing was jumping out at him. The entries were the typical thoughts and feelings of a girl in high school. She had good days and bad. One day she hated her best friend Penny, the next day she was her favorite person in the world. After a while, Tommy started to get a headache reading through Linda's musings.

The sections about Greg Oland were downright boring. They started out like one would have expected. She definitely had the hots for him in the beginning, but their high school romance cooled off pretty quickly. Tommy remembered his days in high school. His and his girlfriend's extracurricular activities were downright X-rated. As a guy, he wouldn't have been caught dead keeping a diary, but the memories were etched into his brain.

Linda kept things going with Greg until a few months earlier when she started writing about a new "man" in her life. She wrote about how smart and mature he was, how forbidden their love was, how her parents would kill her if they found out about him. There was no name, though. Had he missed it? Tommy flipped back and forth, rereading the most recent entries. She hadn't even used his initials. There wasn't anything pointing to him being one of her teachers either.

Rubbing his eyes, Tommy tossed the diary on his partner's desk.

"I'll trade you. I can't read anymore teenage philosophizing. Let me see the autopsy."

Taking his turn, Ben found the same things as Tommy. There was a mystery man they needed to talk to but had no idea who he was. Hopefully, one of Linda's friends would know. They'd visit Tasker High in the morning. They needed to have a chat with Penny Moss, Linda's best friend, as well as Anna Marie Tildon and Tammy Grayson, the other two who were featured most prominently in the diary. If anyone was going to know who Linda was secretly seeing, it would be her girlfriends.

A solid lead was what they needed, something to point them in the right direction. Something that would start to unwind the tangle of questions. If only it were like in the movies. This would be when a little piece of paper with the mystery man's name, address, and telephone number fell out of the diary onto the floor.

Ben turned back to the first entry that mentioned this new man in Linda's life and started rereading the pages that were dated up until the day before her murder. Flipping the last page over, he thought he saw something scribbled on the back cover of the journal itself. Changing the angle of the book and holding it up to the desk lamp, he was able to see a telephone number written in pencil on the dark brown jacket.

"Did you see this?" he asked Tommy, reaching for the phone. "There's a phone number here."

"Where? I didn't see anything."

Ben pointed to the barely visible handwriting on the inside of the back cover as he dialed the number. The phone rang once, then again, then continued ringing. He was just about to place the receiver back on its cradle when he heard a gruff voice on the other end answer.

"Hello?"

"Hello. This is Detective Sergeant Ben Winters with the Parker City Police Department. To whom am I speaking?"

There was a hesitant pause before, "I'm Leo…Leo Sutton. I'm the janitor."

"The janitor?"

"You're calling the teachers' lounge."

"The teachers' lounge?" Ben shot a look at his partner.

There was another brief pause, then the janitor answered, "Yeah. At Tasker High."

Chapter Thirty-Six

Tasker River High was the largest of the schools in the Parker County School System. Its students ran the spectrum, coming from both lower-income families living in the more rundown sections of the city to children of some of the wealthiest families. In the county, it was the gold standard of schools. In the state, it was considered a top tier school. A constantly higher graduation rate and number of students going on to college made it the highest achieving public school in Western Maryland.

Built in the '50s, the school was a massive cement structure. It was a two story gray block in the middle of several acres surrounded by a chain-link fence with no frills or fancy decorations. It could have easily been mistaken for a prison if a passerby didn't know any better. The overall campus was a different story. Education was important inside. But outside, an emphasis on sports was everywhere. After twenty-five years, the campus now included fields for soccer and baseball, a state-of-the-art high school football stadium also used for track and field events, and a separate aquatics building for swim meets.

Both Ben and Tommy were alums of Tasker River. But back in their day, they didn't have any fancy sports facilities. That hadn't stopped the Tasker Trappers from being the state football champions two years in a row.

Climbing the steps and walking through the front doors, as both had done for four years of their early lives, the two detectives realized everything looked and smelled exactly like it had when they were in school. Dark brown and mustard yellow lockers clashed with the floor that was a shade of green Ben had never seen outside the halls of Tasker River High. The same institutional smell at the police station lingered in the hallways here too. It must have been something in the paint they used in every municipal building ever constructed.

The atmosphere in the school was somber, to say the least. Small groups of students huddled together up and down the halls, talking to one another in hushed voices, eyes fixed on the floor, many wiping away tears. The student body was clearly devastated after learning about Linda Carlson's murder. Not that death and murder weren't things they were confronted with every day in film and television. But this was different. It was real. Someone they knew and saw every day in school was killed in a horribly vicious manner. And like with Beverly Baker's murder before, the rumors that were spreading were becoming more and more exaggerated.

Ben wasn't too old to remember how difficult being a teenager was, or seemed to be at the time. But to have one of their classmates die, let alone be brutally murdered, was unimaginable. Making it worse, as if that was possible, was the fact the whole thing was splashed all over the front page of the paper.

That morning at the station there was nowhere on the second floor where the chief could not be heard screaming when he saw the story in the *Herald-Dispatch*. The headline, in big bold letters read, "Spring Strangler Strikes Again???" Three question marks. As if the editor of the paper wanted there to be any doubt that the same person had killed both victims.

As angry as Chief Stanley had been, it paled in comparison to the fury growing inside Ben and his partner. If they could have dragged Roger Benedict into the station, locked him in a cell, and thrown away the key, that would have been the nicest thing they thought to do to him. Tommy made some suggestions about what they could do, but Ben kept reminding him they were the good guys and most of his ideas crossed some serious lines.

After discussing Benedict's unexplained knowledge of both Beverly Baker and Linda Carlson's crime scenes with Lieutenant Dennis, he said he would have a couple of officers pick the reporter up at the newspaper and bring him in for questioning. His access to inside information warranted a chat.

All three of the officers knew he wasn't going to give up his source, no doubt claiming the sanctity of the press, but that didn't mean they couldn't give him a hard time and just make his life miserable for a few hours.

With Benedict being sweated at the station—one potential suspect being accounted for—Ben and Tommy headed to Tasker River High to speak with Linda's friends. The detectives were met in the school's office by the principal, Dr. Frank Hoffman. He was a short, round man whose face was showing the signs of a lifetime dealing with teenagers. Other than gray hair and more wrinkles, he looked just like he did when Ben and Tommy were students. He even smelled the same. It was the unmistakable combination of cigarette smoke and Brute cologne. Even Hoffman's clothes were the same, an ugly sweater vest under a worn tweed jacket. Ben used to wonder if Dr. Hoffman owned anything other than tweed. Apparently, he didn't.

"Thomas Mason and Benjamin Winters." The nasally voice in no way fit the principal's hefty physical stature.

"That's Detectives Mason and Winters, Mister…I mean, Doctor Hoffman," Tommy replied in his typically charming, smartass way.

"Of course. My apologies." Hoffman adjusted the glasses sitting on the edge of his nose as he looked the men up and down. "You two have done Tasker High School proud by becoming police officers."

"Detectives," Tommy corrected, again with a smile.

"Yes, I'm sorry. It's just that…"

Letting the man who was now perspiring profusely off the hook, Ben said, "It's alright, Dr. Hoffman. I'm sure it's not a good day for you or any of the students here."

A wave of appreciation washed over the administrator's face.

Ben wanted to put him at ease. The more relaxed and open people were, the easier it was going to be to get the information they needed to catch whoever had decided to prey on Parker City.

Showing the detectives into his office, Ben and Tommy silently noted how nothing at all had changed since the last time they'd been called to the principal's office to be reprimanded for a prank they pulled on their science teacher. The orange rug brought back memories Tommy had tried very hard to forget.

"Dr. Hoffman," Ben began, flipping open his notebook. "Did you know Linda Carlson?"

The principal ran a hand over his forehead, using it instead of a handkerchief to wipe away the beads of sweat lining his brow. "As well as I know any of the students, really. She was very popular. I do know that. And involved in so many activities. She was part of a number of the school's clubs. And a very good student."

"Was there anyone who might have had a problem with Linda?"

"Detective, you remember what high school was like. All the students think they're ready to be called adults, but really they're still children. And children are not very nice. Especially to each other. I guess it's possible Linda might have let her popularity go to her head and upset someone." Hoffman paused, then added, "She might not have even known she upset someone. Adolescents are adolescents after all."

Neither Ben nor Tommy could disagree with that, but it still felt like the principal was holding something back.

Leaning forward in his chair, Tommy asked, "Is there any reason you can think that Linda Carlson would have had the telephone number to the teachers' lounge written in her journal?"

Another cascade of sweat began pouring down the nervous man's forehead.

"Students aren't supposed to have that number," Hoffman said, surprisingly emphatic. "Teachers know they are not supposed to share that information."

The detectives still needed to get a better feel for who Linda was and the types of activities she was involved in. As well as the people with whom she associated.

The principal pointed out that the girl's social life was public knowledge around the school. Everyone's was. That's just the way it was in high school—secrets could not be kept secret for long. Everyone knew Linda dated the mayor's son. Dr. Hoffman noted that social gossip like that would have been impossible to keep quiet. As it was when the two broke up. Why they broke up, however, the principal couldn't say.

"There's no reason Linda would have the telephone number to the teacher's lounge?" Ben asked, circling back just to make certain that point had been covered, and to set up his next question.

Taking a moment to think before he spoke, the principal mopped his thick brow. He finally said, "It's possible one of the teachers gave it to her. But as I said, they aren't supposed to give that number to students. I can tell you that. I make sure to tell the teachers not to give the students the telephone number to the teachers' lounge. I can't think of a reason one would give out that number."

Allowing the answer to hang in the air for a moment, Ben then asked, "Have you heard any…*social gossip* about Linda possibly having a romantic relationship with one of her teachers."

The principal's eyes looked as though they were going to pop out of their sockets. The beads of sweat on his forehead turned into geysers as his face flushed. He was so taken aback by the question he couldn't even speak.

Neither Ben nor Tommy could tell if his over animated reaction was all an act or if the idea of one of his teachers having an affair with one of his students truly sent his mind spinning.

"That's…that's impossible," he stammered before being struck by a coughing fit. Fighting through the wheezing, he managed to say, "That's unthinkable. Outrageous! Who told you that?" The angrier he got, the harder he coughed.

After giving Dr. Hoffman a moment to catch his breath, Tommy said, "It's just a rumor that came up through our investigation."

"Well, you can forget that rumor, *Detectives*. None of the teachers at Tasker River High would cross that line. It's unthinkable. It's outrageous! *Outrageous!*"

Chapter Thirty-Seven

It took some time for Dr. Hoffman's complexion to return to its usual pinkish hue. Longer for him to be able to breathe again without suffering a coughing fit. When he'd finally regained his composure, he asked one of the secretaries to send for the friends of Linda's with whom the detectives wished to speak.

Penny Moss, Ann Marie Tildon, and Tammy Grayson were all gathered in Miss Kirkpatrick's classroom. A history teacher, her room was decorated with posters of the United States Constitution and Bill of Rights, timelines of major historic events in the country's past, and copies of important speeches like Lincoln's Gettysburg Address and Franklin Roosevelt's inaugural speech in which he declared, "We have nothing to fear but fear itself." One entire wall was covered with portraits of all forty U.S. presidents.

Miss Kirkpatrick was seated behind her desk at the far end of the room. She looked like she was grading papers but was obviously keeping an eye on the girls. Ben couldn't help but notice how attractive the young teacher was. She barely looked much older than the students he was here to speak with. Not that he looked that old himself. When he was still just a patrol officer in the department, the other guys used to joke that he wasn't old enough to shave, but he could carry a gun. Admittedly, he wasn't like Tommy. He could get away with only shaving once a week.

Focusing on the matter at hand, Ben put the teacher out of his mind and began sizing up the three teens.

These girls were the most popular on campus, at least according to the principal, and Linda had been their queen bee. Looking at them now though, sitting together, huddled in the empty classroom, Ben couldn't help but think how small and frail they appeared. The truth was, they *were* still children.

One didn't need to be a detective to figure out the girls had been crying. The bloodshot eyes and streaks of mascara running down their cheeks gave that away. Even though the tears had stopped and they were now trying to put on a brave front, each had her own tick, a physical manifestation of the stress, fear, and anger she was dealing with internally. Ben recognized each one, taking a seat across from the girls. A person's body language could say just as much as words. Sometimes more.

Penny was trying to play the part of a tough girl who didn't have any feelings about what was going on. The continual twirling of her long curly blonde hair around her finger told another story and betrayed her real anxiety. Ann Marie definitely wasn't handling the situation well and didn't care who knew. She just sat with her arms wrapped around herself, eyes fixed on some distant point out the window. The third girl, Tammy, kept taking her glasses on and off, never feeling comfortable with or without them.

Ben did everything he could to put the girls at ease and ignore the fact Dr. Hoffman was hovering behind them. The detectives would rather have spoken with the girls alone, but the principal would have none of that.

Tommy began the interview using the softest tone he could. These girls didn't expect to wake up one morning and find out one of their best friends had been murdered. They needed to be handled with care and some understanding of what they were going through. Extracting information from adults was hard enough, so trying to get answers that could be helpful from devastated teenagers could end up being next to impossible.

The questions the detectives had were the same they'd been asking everyone. Was there anyone in Linda's life that might have wanted to hurt her? It was no surprise that Penny, Ann Marie, and Tammy all swore up and down that *everyone* loved Linda. The only person that might have a problem with her was Greg Oland because of their breakup. Penny tossed that idea out, not needing much coaxing.

Ben was beginning to rethink his first impression of the young Miss Moss.

She might be tougher than he was willing to give her credit for. There was a steeliness behind her eyes, maybe even outright defiance. Definitely an attitude. Penny Moss was making it clear without actually saying it, she was now in charge. The queen is dead, long live the queen, Ben thought to himself. When there was an opening in the social ranks, there was always someone ready to fill the void.

Penny had given the detectives the perfect segue, however.

Being as careful and conscious of his words as possible, Tommy leaned forward and asked, "Do any of you know if Linda had started spending time with an older man?"

Tammy and Ann Marie went white in the face. Penny flushed. It appeared the question hit a collective nerve.

Both Tammy and Ann Marie began shaking their heads.

"Linda would never date an older man," Tammy said, taking her glasses off, laying them on the table, then putting them right back on. "She wasn't like that."

Ann Marie didn't say anything but nodded vigorously in agreement.

Penny sat stone faced.

Ben jumped in. "You see, it's just that we were told that Linda had recently started seeing an older man. We were led to believe he might even be a teacher here at Tasker River."

"Who told you that?" Penny snapped. "Was it that pecker Greg Oland?"

"We've come across something in Linda's diary that could back up what we were told."

"You read her diary!" Penny slammed her hands on the table.

"We needed to see if there was anything in the diary that Linda had written that could help us with the case."

"What did she say about us in there?" Penny was becoming extremely agitated.

Sensing Penny might say or do something she would regret, Tammy put her hand on her friend's shoulder and said, "Detective, Linda never told us she was dating a teacher. If it was Greg that told you that, it's just because he was mad that Linda broke up with him."

A large part of Ben wanted to believe that, but something was telling him otherwise. Whether Linda's friends were just trying to protect her reputation, or they truly didn't know she was seeing someone, let alone one of their teachers, he knew they weren't going to tell him anymore than they already had.

Ben scribbled a few notes as Tommy finished up the interview with some basic questions about the last time they'd seen Linda; what kind of mood she was in, where each of them was the night of the murder?

When they were satisfied they'd gotten all the information they needed, Ben thanked the girls for talking to them and told the principal he could take them back to their classes. As Ben and Tommy were getting ready to leave, Miss Kirkpatrick, who until then had been sitting at her desk trying to look like she wasn't paying attention to what was being discussed, asked if she could speak to them for a moment.

"Of course," Ben answered with a smile. "I'm Detective Sergeant Ben Winters and this is my partner, Detective Mason. And you are?"

"Natalie Kirkpatrick. I'm one of the history teachers. I couldn't help but overhear, did you say you think Linda was having an affair with one of the teachers here at the school?"

Tommy shot Ben a look. There was something in her voice that sounded like she wasn't surprised.

"I can't say that I know anything about that, but there is one teacher that all the girls have a crush on. Joseph Miles. He's new this year and teaches English literature. I hear the students whispering about him all the time."

"And do you have some reason to believe he would get involved with a student?" Tommy asked.

"I don't know. He's young and very charming. You know how teenage girls can be. Reading romantic stories can give them ideas."

"But what about Miles?" Tommy pressed. "Would he cross that line?"

"Detectives," she said, becoming quiet, "I don't want to believe any teacher would take advantage of one of their students, but when I'm around Mr. Miles, I just have a very uneasy feeling. I'm sure it's nothing. I shouldn't have even mentioned it."

"Miss Kirkpatrick, thank you for talking to us," Ben said with a genuinely warm smile. "Every bit of information helps. If you think of anything else, please don't hesitate to call me at the station."

After thanking her again, the detectives left to find Joseph Miles.

Walking down the hall, under his breath, Tommy started singing, "Ben and Miss Kirkpatrick sitting in a tree…"

Chapter Thirty-Eight

To say that Dr. Hoffman was not pleased was an understatement. He did not like the idea of Ben and Tommy looking into the possibility of Linda Carlson having a romantic relationship with one of her teachers. The principal said he wanted to keep his staff out of it, but Ben got the distinct feeling he just didn't want them talking to Miles specifically. Did Hoffman know something about the lit teacher he was trying to conceal? Or was he, understandably, just uncomfortable having the police on his campus in general?

Begrudgingly, Ben was given Miles's classroom number and the two detectives found themselves walking down the hall once again. This time, they had company. They were in the middle of a class change, surrounded by students rushing from classroom to locker to classroom. The ringing of the bell was like someone turning on a spigot. The students rushed out of their classrooms and through the hall like waves of water.

"I don't miss this," Tommy said over the roar of voices bouncing off the metal lockers.

Ben didn't say anything. He was lost in his thoughts, trying to make sense of everything. There were two people they could tie to Linda Carlson: Greg Oland and possibly Joseph Miles. However, Greg didn't appear to have any motive to kill Beverly Baker. Could they tie the teacher to Beverly somehow? That was if they were still working under the assumption both women were killed by the same person.

When they reached room number 131, where Miles taught the students about the works of Austen, Brontë, and Miller, they found the door locked.

Ben was about to knock when Tommy grabbed his hand, stopping him only a split second before his knuckles made contact with the frosted glass pane in the door.

"Do you hear that?" Tommy asked.

Listening, Ben could hear raised voices on the other side of the door. Whoever it was, they were having an argument.

This time, before Ben could knock, the door flew open and Penny Moss literally ran into him as she charged out of the room.

"Penny? Are you alright?" Ben asked, catching the girl by the shoulders. There may have been a stream of tears running down her cheeks, but judging by the look in her eyes, they were clearly tears of anger, even rage. There was a fire burning behind her bright green eyes. Shaking loose and pushing passed Ben without saying a word, the teen stormed down the hall. The sea of students parting before her.

Next through the door was a young man in a wrinkled button-down shirt and plaid tie. As he ran into Ben, his glasses flew off. Reflexively, Tommy reached out and caught them in mid-air.

"Excuse me," the man said. "I'm just…"

"We're looking for Mr. Miles," Tommy interrupted, handing the glasses back to their owner. "Is he in there?"

Taking the glasses and slipping them into his shirt pocket, he answered, "*I'm* Mr. Miles. Joseph Miles."

First Miss Kirkpatrick, now Mr. Miles. How young were these new teachers, Tommy wondered. Both could have passed for students themselves. Not that he and Ben were all that old, but that was different. They didn't *look* that young. Did they?

Ben flashed his badge and introduced himself and his partner. The teacher looked surprised, then confused, then concerned. The range of emotions swept across his face in seconds.

"We have some questions for you about your relationship with Linda Carlson," Tommy said, shouldering his way through the door into the classroom. "Let's talk in here."

Following Joseph Miles into the room, Ben got a better look at the guy.

He could understand why the teacher might have so many admirers among the female students. He had piercing blue eyes, a day's worth of stubble on his chin and cheeks, and a full head of thick, wavy brown hair. He didn't look like any teacher Ben ever had. This guy looked like a rebel, another reason the girls would like him.

"How can I help you, gentlemen?" The teacher had regained his composure and was all smiles, trying to sound as charming and amiable as possible. "I think you said something about Linda Carlson?"

"First of all," Ben said, taking control of the interview, "was there a reason Penny Moss just ran out of here so upset?"

"Her friend was killed. It makes sense she would be upset, doesn't it?"

"And the locked door?" Tommy threw in.

"Faulty lock. It happens from time to time. The building's pretty old. I've been asking the janitor to fix it for weeks."

Ben was starting not to like Mr. Miles. He was too cool. Too quick with his answers. All very blasé. His attitude rubbed him the wrong way.

"Why would she come to you?" Ben continued.

"I tell all of my students my door is always open to them. Except when that lock's acting up, of course." His attempt at humor went over like a lead balloon.

"Do you really think this is the time for jokes, Mr. Miles?"

"Of course not. I'm sorry." There was a tense pause before he went on. "I'm here for my students. Whatever they need. If they need to talk, to yell, to cry. They all know they can come here."

"Especially the girls, right?" Tommy asked, leveling his gaze at the young academic.

"I'm not sure what you mean, Detective."

Tommy was more than happy to explain. "You see, Mr. Miles, during our investigation of Linda Carlson's murder, we've come across some information that she was seeing an *older man*, as everyone has been saying. Possibly one of her teachers here at the high school. We also talked to someone who said that that teacher might be you."

The teacher's reaction was not what one would expect. He didn't immediately jump to his feet and protest the accusations. Instead, he remained seated, raised an eyebrow and shook his head.

"Young girls can have crushes on male authority figures. It's as simple as that, Detectives. I'm very open with my students and encourage them to talk to me when they have problems. If one or two of them takes that the wrong way..." He shrugged. "I certainly don't encourage any of it. I'm sure both of you have had your own admirers...being police officers...wearing a badge..."

Ben, who was normally calm and collected, was trying hard not to lose his patience. It appeared Mr. Miles had an answer for everything. He didn't like the idea that this teacher could have taken advantage of one of his students. Then to see another one running out of his classroom in tears sent up all sorts of red flags.

The conversation between Tommy and Joseph Miles continued as Ben sat quietly, listening to his partner go around and around with the silver-tongued educator. It was a verbal sparring match on a championship level.

When Tommy finished with his questions, he closed his notebook and looked to Ben, who knew just by the look on his partner's face that Joseph Miles was now a definite suspect in the murder of Linda Carlson. But Ben had one final question.

"Mr. Miles, did you know Beverly Baker?"

Before answering, he tilted his head, trying to understand the reason for the question.

"I..." Miles paused for a moment, finally registering the question's implication. "I helped her with a project for the historical society a couple of months ago."

Chapter Thirty-Nine

The idea of Linda having an affair with Mr. Miles never even crossed Penny's mind. She knew Linda was seeing someone she wouldn't talk about, which would make sense if he was a teacher. But Linda wasn't like that. She might have been cool in most people's eyes, but Penny thought she could still be pretty square. For her to be sleeping with Mr. Miles…with Joseph…*her* Joseph…Penny thought she was the only woman in Joseph's life. At least that's what he'd told her.

To find out that he'd been screwing her best friend at the same time he was sleeping with her set off emotions inside Penny she'd never felt before. Emotions she didn't even know she had. What made everything one hundred times worse is that she learned about the betrayal from two police detectives. Then when she confronted her—now ex—lover, his denial was half-hearted at best. He was a lying, cheating, manipulative ass and Linda was nothing more than a slut. She deserved what happened to her.

After storming out of Miles's classroom, she cut school for the rest of the day. There was no way she was going to be able to sit through biology or civics class. On a good day, she could barely pay attention. She didn't want to see or talk to anyone the rest of the day. All she wanted was to hide in her bedroom.

One minute she was in tears, the next she wanted to hit someone over and over again until her knuckles bled. She just wanted someone else to feel as badly as she was feeling. To hurt as badly; to feel like their stomach had been ripped out of them and stomped on. She felt like she was being torn apart from the inside.

Sitting on her bed, staring at the wall—covered with posters of Van Halen, The Police, and a dozen other rock groups—Penny wanted to scream. Then, realizing there was no one else in the house, that's exactly what she did. She knew getting involved with a teacher was wrong but couldn't help it. Joseph Miles was so smart and charming. He always understood how she was feeling. Now she finds out the man she thought she was going to spend the rest of her life with was banging her *and* her best friend. Then another thought struck her. What if there were even more?

It hadn't even registered yet that the police thought he could be involved with Linda's murder. Penny was too focused on the betrayal she felt than the danger in which she could have been. Had she been asked if she thought Miles could kill someone, her answer would have been absolutely not. He was a kind, caring, romantic person. He'd read her poetry and taught her about wine. Then again, she wouldn't have thought he was boning more than one of his students. Obviously, she didn't know him as well as she thought.

Joseph Miles had used his position to take advantage of her, she decided.

Still riding the emotional rollercoaster, Penny's hatred began to ease, leaving her with the longing to see him again. How could she want to yell and scream at him, tear his eyes out, and kick him in the balls, but still love him?

Feeling the urge to throw up, Penny ran into the bathroom where she spent a good part of the next hour sobbing while she clung to the toilet. When she couldn't cry any more, she pulled herself up and caught a glimpse of herself in the mirror. She looked a mess. Mascara streaks ran down her cheeks, unstopped except by the puffy bags under her eyes. Her lipstick was so badly smeared she looked like a clown. Running hot water in the sink, she washed away all the makeup. The water burned. By the time she finished scrubbing away the artificial pastel colors, her skin was raw. The steaming water had turned her pale skin a bright pink. She didn't care. She was alone in the house. No one was going to see her.

That's when she realized how quiet the house was.

Penny's father, the owner of the *Herald-Dispatch*, was away on business. He was always away on business. She rarely ever saw him anymore. Especially since he'd recently bought up a number of small community newspapers in Pennsylvania and was "expanding the Moss news empire," as he would say. Penny's mother, stepmother actually, was on a week-long shopping trip to New York City with some of her friends. Her stepbrother, who was only a year younger and one grade behind her in school, was on some overnight field trip in the Catoctin Mountains with his science class or something. Penny never listened when he told her what he was doing. In school, she avoided him at all costs. With everyone gone, she had the house all to herself.

Normally, she'd call Linda and the girls to come over and hang out, but that wasn't going to happen. Instead, she picked up the hot pink phone on her nightstand and dialed a number she wasn't sure she should. After three rings, the voice of Joseph Miles came on the line. It was his new telephone answering machine.

As instructed, Penny waited for the beep then said, "Joseph, it's me. I'm so sorry. I'm so sorry. I believe you. I know you love me and I love you. I know you weren't doing anything with Linda. Those cops are just looking for someone to blame. I'm all alone tonight...no one's home. When you listen to this, please come over. I want to see you. Or call me...I'll come to your place...or you could come here. Please. I miss you. I love you so much."

Gently hanging up the phone, a flood of tears erupted, leaving Penny sobbing uncontrollably once again.

Chapter Forty

Now...

Bright yellow police tape warning everyone to stay out crisscrossed the front door of Tommy's house in Middleboro. Seeing that sight, something he had seen at countless crime scenes over the years, made Ben's heart ache. He still felt sick to his stomach every time he thought about Tommy.

He couldn't even count how many times that day he'd caught himself asking if there was something he could have done. If he'd asked Tommy to go to the hospital with him, would that have made a difference? What if the two had gone out to dinner that night? Would Tommy still be alive?

Deep down, Ben knew the answer.

The sheriff's department was ruling out a robbery gone wrong. There was no evidence pointing in that direction. Even though parts of the house had clearly been ransacked, nothing in the house had actually been taken. Add to that the way Tommy was killed, it didn't fit with him interrupting a burglar.

Tommy had been a target.

After all the years on the job, Ben knew to trust his gut. Right now, his gut was telling him this was somehow related to the murders from 1981. After nearly forty years, Tommy said he needed to talk to him about the old case and less than twelve hours later he was killed in his home. He said he'd had a conversation with someone, Ben thought back to the last time he'd talked to Tommy.

Who could he have been talking to? There weren't that many people left around who were involved in the case. Chief Stanley died of a heart attack several years after the case was closed. Captain Brent, who'd gone on to become the Maryland State Superintendent of Police in the '90s, passed away just a few years ago after a prolonged battle with cancer. The same year Stanley died, their lieutenant left the Parker City Police and moved west, joining the Las Vegas PD. The last thing Ben heard, he was now happily living out his golden years in a Vegas retirement community.

Tommy also said he'd come across some old papers. If these papers were important, Ben knew there was only one place Tommy would have put them. Not in his safe at the Sheriff's Department, not in the one in his home office. Those places would be too obvious and the first place someone would look.

According to the report Drew obtained from his friend, Tommy's study had been tossed. Somebody was obviously looking for something. The safe, a relatively cheap fireproof lockbox, had been pried open and riffled through. Unfortunately, there was really no way to know if anything had been taken or if whoever had gone through the house found what they were looking for. But all Tommy ever kept in there was his passport, his insurance policies, the deed to the house, and a few other financial documents. Ben had confirmed that with the new sheriff. All of those items were still in the safe when Dempsey's deputies catalogued the room and its content.

If Tommy had lived within the limits of Parker City, thereby putting the house in Ben's jurisdiction, he would have been able to go into the house and find what he was looking for without a problem. Being that the case belonged to the county's sheriff, he was going to need to break into Tommy's house. Not necessarily "break in" per se since he did have a key. But he was still going to have to cross the tape that clearly told people to stay out, which in itself was a crime.

Parking Natalie's car a few streets over, Ben walked around the block twice to see if anyone was watching the house. If someone saw him, he just looked like an old guy out for an evening walk. A baseball cap, Orioles jacket, and jeans were his disguise. It was a very common look for a cool spring evening.

Making his third pass by the brick rancher, he was both relieved and angry that a deputy hadn't been stationed outside the house. With no official police presence, it would be easier for him to get in and out. This being a high profile case, someone should have been assigned to watch the house. At least for the first few days after the murder to make sure no one broke in or tampered with the scene. As he was about to do.

Ben was well aware of the irony of the situation.

Getting into the house proved to be as easy as crossing the front lawn without being seen, unlocking the door, ducking under the tape, and slipping inside. It took all of thirty seconds.

The house was dark and quiet and completely still.

Using the miniature flashlight on Nat's key chain, which was much brighter than he'd expected, Ben scanned the living room. Everything looked exactly like it always did when he visited. Except for the blood trail leading into the kitchen. Seeing it was like a kick in the stomach.

Ben knew the forensic team had combed through every inch of the house. The county's Crime Scene Unit held one of the highest accreditations in the region, so anything there was to find that could help lead them to Tommy's killer had been tagged and bagged, and was now being processed.

Even though Ben was already technically breaking the law by just being there, he wanted to disturb as little as possible. He was still a police chief, after all, so he had brought a pair of latex gloves so not to leave any more fingerprints and disposable shoe covers for his feet.

Making his way down the hall, Ben passed Tommy's office. Papers covered the floor and desktop, whose drawers had been emptied of their content. File folders were tossed here and there, while pictures on the wall were hanging at odd angles, having been moved to see if anything was behind them.

It made sense that someone would think the late sheriff kept important papers related to investigations and other high-level matters in his study. That's where most people kept their important documents. However, Ben knew his friend and knew that what he was looking for was in the closet in the guest room across the hall.

Sliding Tommy's old police uniforms to one side and a couple of hanging garment bags to the other, Ben found a stack of boxes marked 'records and cassettes.' Sitting on the top of one of the stacks was an old Pioneer stereo system, or at least parts of one. The thing was pretty well beaten up. Tommy bought it back in the '80s and could never part with it. Even though the thing stopped working decades earlier, he refused to get rid of the outdated and broken down machine.

Pulling a loose screw from the side, Ben carefully lifted the turntable off its base, revealing a hollowed out casing. All the electronics and audio pieces had been removed long ago. In their place was an accordion file folder. It really was the perfect hiding place. Ben had a similar hidden-in-plain-sight type of compartment at his house, too. It might seem a little too cloak and dagger to some, but some documents were too important to be kept in the conventional safe places.

Not wanting to waste any time, Ben grabbed the folder, replaced the turntable, and then the clothes to where they had first been hanging. Everything looked just like it had before.

It took all of five minutes to get in and out of the house with what he hoped would shed light on why Tommy had been killed. Tossing the files on the passenger seat next to him, he put the car in gear and headed for the Parker City Police Department. He wanted to go through all the papers in the safety of his office, in a building with a large number of people, all loyal to him, and most of whom were carrying guns.

As he eased the car into the traffic on I-70 heading toward Parker City, he said a little prayer that the gods of law and order would forgive him for disturbing a crime scene. But it was for a good cause, he promised them.

Chapter Forty-One

Tommy's files were spread out across the table in the chief's executive conference room at the PCPD. Simply labeled "1981," the folder contained what appeared to be every note and piece of paper Tommy had collected regarding the case. One section contained official documents—copies of the police reports, crime scene photos, as well as the autopsies of each victim. Another pocket was stuffed with newspaper clippings on the case from as far away as Chicago, with lines from different stories highlighted. All of the articles from the *Herald-Dispatch*, written by Roger Benedict, were paper clipped together separately.

There was another set of articles from the time that seemed unconnected while still being somewhat relevant. One about the Parker County Historical Society and its planned events for the year, a featured spread from the *Herald-Dispatch*'s Home & Garden section about the renovated manor homes including the Olands' and Mosses' recently redecorated mansions, and a profile of Dr. Franklin Hoffman published just after his forced retirement following the events of the school year.

There were two folders full of background information and official government records. One for Roger Benedict, the other for Joseph Miles. Tommy compiled complete dossiers on both men. Everything from where they went to school, where they had lived and worked, all the way down to lists of speeding tickets each had received was included. Somehow, Tommy even managed to get his hands on a copy of Benedict's transcripts from Boston University. If it had been anyone other than his former partner, Ben would have thought the files had been put together by a professional stalker.

There was also an article about a murder case outside of Philadelphia where the victim had been strangled. The only reason it caught Ben's attention was because the piece was written by none other than Roger Benedict and published in the *Philadelphia Inquirer* only a few months after he'd left Parker City to take a job with the paper in the City of Brotherly Love. Coincidence, Ben wondered, knowing that was the same question his friend must have asked when he added the newspaper article to the file.

It seemed that after working in Philadelphia the reporter moved to Miami, then San Francisco, then New York City, bouncing from one paper to the next as an investigative journalist. Most recently, before returning to Parker City, he'd been an online editor for the *New York Post.* According to a handwritten note, Tommy learned from a source at the city paper that Benedict had been fired, but management was keeping the reason quiet.

So that's why the slime ball left a job with a big paper in a big city to come back and take over as editor of the *Herald-Dispatch*, a paper that was, by all accounts, struggling to stay afloat.

The file on Joseph Miles was much thinner. He'd never left Parker City after all, not that he'd had the chance. Tommy had collected a number of articles from psychology journals relating to student-teacher sexual relationships. One author went so far as to say sexual attraction between a student and teacher is inevitable. Ben found the whole topic disturbing, just as he did thirty-plus years earlier.

Miles and Benedict had been at the top of the list of suspects, so it stood to reason Tommy would have continued to collect information on them. Neither of the detectives were ever truly satisfied with the outcome of the case. Too many questions remained unanswered in their minds, but the brass wanted the whole ordeal put to rest, so as the young and inexperienced investigators they were, they followed orders and closed the book on the Spring Strangler case.

There were other dossiers in the file, including one for each of the Mayors Oland, Charles and Gregory, as well as Howard Worthington, and even Buck LuCoco, the fat old sergeant who retired to Florida, where he spent his remaining years fishing before passing away "quietly in his sleep." LuCoco's obituary was included along with a hand written note by Tommy that read "Died in bed with a hooker."

It was not uncommon for a detective to have that one case that stuck with him. Ben knew a number of retired detectives that still worked on cold cases they'd never been able to solve. But what he was looking at now was closer to an obsession. His friend and former partner never told him that he'd kept working on the case even though, officially, it was closed.

The amount of information and documents he'd collected was staggering. It's true that Ben kept his own copy of the official case file tucked away in his desk, but it was nothing compared to what was now taking up the entire conference table.

Something in the file was important, and Tommy had wanted Ben to see it. Was it something new? Or was it something that finally connected all the dots? What did he find? The chief kept asking himself the question over and over. Each time becoming more and more frustrated with himself that he couldn't find the answer. It had to be staring him in the face. But after going through the entire file twice, he still didn't see anything that sent up any mental red flags.

He'd been at it for hours, poring over every piece of paper in Tommy's file. It wasn't until he finished the second pot of coffee that Ben realized how late it was. Or how early, depending on how one looked at it. The old grandfather clock in his office next door was chiming two o'clock. He'd remembered looking at his watch and seeing that it was midnight and saying he was just going to read for fifteen more minutes, then head home. Two hours later, realizing how tired he was, he admitted he wasn't going to be able to figure anything out tonight. He'd start fresh in the morning. He might even have Drew take a look at the files. A fresh set of eyes was always helpful.

Locking his office door behind him, Ben cursed Tommy for not having just told him at the retirement party what he'd found. If it was that important, why not talk about it right then and there? Walking down the grand staircase of the old City Hall, the chief wondered if Tommy had told him about whatever it was he'd figured out, would his friend still be alive?

Chapter Forty-Two

Then...

Penny Moss had cried herself to sleep after calling and leaving two more messages on Joseph Miles's answer machine. The tough girl image she put on was just that, an image. The truth was, it was nothing more than a façade. She was just a confused, insecure teenager like all the rest at Tasker River High.

The shadows dancing on the wall, caused by the street lamps outside, startled her as she shook the cobwebs out of her head. Looking around her room through a pair of puffy eyes, she tried to figure out how long she'd been asleep. According to the little pink alarm clock on her nightstand, it was almost ten o'clock.

She realized the pain in her stomach had nothing to do with her yearning to talk to the man she loved, but everything to do with the fact she hadn't eaten anything since breakfast. She was starving.

Her mind still fuzzy, it took her a few moments to gain her bearings.

The sun having disappeared hours ago and no one home to start a fire in the Elizabethan-style fireplace her stepmother insisted on having installed in the living room, or to turn on the recently rebuilt furnace—a leftover from when the house was built just after the turn of the century—the chill in the air made her shiver. The hardwood floor in the hallway felt like a sheet of ice under her bare feet. Thankfully the carpeting on the stairs helped to remedy the situation.

Passing by her father's study on her way to the kitchen, she noticed his briefcase lying on his desk and the antique lamp, another purchase of her stepmother's, lighting the room. Apparently, her father had returned from his business trip at some point and hadn't even bothered to look for her. It would have been nice for him to show some concern for her considering her best friend had just been killed. Looking out the window, she saw his car wasn't in the driveway, so he had just come and gone. Typical, she thought, flipping the lights on in the kitchen.

A half carton of milk, a jar of grape jelly, and a few Tupperware with leftovers from God knows when was all she found in the refrigerator. As for the cupboard, it might as well have belonged to Old Mother Hubbard. A dusty can of black beans and a half-empty box of baking powder sat together on a shelf.

This is just sad, Penny thought to herself. It looked like she was going to have no choice but to drink her dinner. The best part of having absentee parents was that they didn't care enough to lock the liquor cabinet.

A tumbler from the kitchen and a bottle of a sweet California Merlot would just have to do. Curling up on the couch with the bottle of wine, she settled in to watch *Knots Landing* and drink away her sorrow.

By the end of the hour-long drama, the merlot bottle was almost empty and Penny was pretty numb. Bleary eyed and emotionally drained, she practically rolled off the couch. Steadying herself as best she could, it took some time to stumble her way from the living room back through the kitchen.

Haphazardly tossing the empty wine bottle into the sink, Penny shivered as a gust of cold air blew through the kitchen, rattling the brass pots and pans hanging over the stove. Looking around, Penny didn't remember the window being open when she came through earlier.

"I hate this old house," she said, slamming the window closed, scratching the palm of her hand on the broken latch that had popped open. Already unsteady, the force of her action made her stumble backward a few steps.

Mumbling and cursing her way through the kitchen, Penny staggered up the stairs, not noticing the figure lingering in the shadows of the darkened dining room.

Chapter Forty-Three

The Victorian mansion on Orchard Park Avenue where the Moss family lived was one of the largest houses in the city. Built a hundred years earlier, the fact the house was still standing after all that time was a testament to the craftsmanship of a bygone era. The most striking feature was the stone portico that had been added to the house by an elderly Bernard Parker Moss during the height of the Great Depression. Relatively speaking, it had been a minor construction project, but one that put a good number of struggling Parker City residents to work. Some applauded him for his effort to help those hit hardest by the collapse of the U.S. economy, while other in the community decried him for spending the amount of money he was on increasing the size of his already ostentatious home. There was no way he could have won, no matter what he did.

It was still easy to get into a house built in the 1800s, no matter how much work had been done on it in recent years. Old wooden window frames and worn latches were an intruder's friend. A quick blow to pop the lock, and that's how he'd been able to get into the kitchen.

He'd been watching the house for a couple of hours, so knew Penny was the only one home. Her father, the powerful newspaper magnate, made something of a surprise appearance, running in and out. He might have been inside for ten minutes, but from what he understood of Mr. Moss, that was his average time at home these days. The man was more concerned with his growing news company than what was happening in his daughter's life.

Watching Penny stumble through the kitchen with an empty wine bottle in her hand swinging back and forth made him smile. She always put on an air of indifference, trying to get people to believe she was tough. Some people would say she was just a girl seeking attention. He thought she was a bitch. At least that's what the voice was telling him. Just like Beverly Baker and Linda Carlson. They ruined people's lives and deserved to be punished. No one else was willing to do what needed to be done.

It's up to you.

The voice was becoming more out of control. Linda was supposed to be the end of it, but then seeing how Penny reacted in school, it proved she was just as bad. The world was going to be a better place without any of them.

The sound of Penny slamming the window closed quickly brought him back to the moment and out of his thoughts. He heard her swear as she scratched her hand. Like a lion in the wild stalking his prey, he thought he could almost smell the fresh blood. Tightening his grip on the cord in his hand, he watched as she began to climb the stairs.

It was clear the wine was affecting her. Mumbling the entire way to the top of the stairs, she swayed back and forth with each step.

Pathetic. She deserves this.

Feeling the voice push him from the shadows, the killer bolted up the stairs after Penny. Taking them two at a time, he reached her at the top of the steps. Wrapping the braided cord around her neck, he pulled so hard her feet lifted off the carpeted floor. Completely intoxicated, and as tiny as she was, there was no way for Penny to put up a fight. She struggled for a moment, clawing at the ligature around her throat. Trying to pry it away, she quickly lost her strength. Before her body gave up entirely, she managed to lift her legs enough to kick the wall, pushing her and her attacker backwards.

Slamming into the corner of the wall, he almost went tumbling down the stairs. The anger inside of him exploded. Never having let go, he pulled the cord so tight he expected Penny's head to come off. With the final bit of air choked out of her, Penny's body went completely limp. Unwrapping the cord from around her neck, he watched as she crumpled to the floor, eyes wide open, staring up at him. With a shove of his foot, Penny's body rolled down the steps, coming to rest on the cold linoleum floor in the kitchen.

Sweet dreams, Penny.

Chapter Forty-Four

Ben was startled awake by the sound of cannon fire outside his bedroom window. Shooting straight up in bed, he couldn't remember where he'd left his service weapon…or what his name was for that matter. He'd been in such a deep sleep, he couldn't clear the fog from his mind. Another volley of shots quickly cleared his head. At some point in the middle of the night, a thunderstorm had rolled in. The rain beating against the window confirmed there was no actual battle raging outside.

He'd only been asleep for a couple of hours. It had been another late night at the office and he knew it was going to stay that way until the case was closed. He'd spend hours at his desk pouring over the notes he'd made at the crime scenes, hoping something would click. When he'd made no major breakthroughs by one a.m., he finally called it quits for the night. He wasn't getting anywhere and needed some sleep. Solving the case was already proving to be a challenge. If he needed to start fighting exhaustion as well, there was no way he'd be able to catch the killer.

After staring at the ceiling for what seemed like forever, Ben knew he wasn't going to be able to fall back asleep any time soon. Instead of staying in bed tossing and turning, doing nothing more than frustrating himself, he decided to head to the kitchen and make some coffee. If he wasn't going to be able to get anymore sleep, he'd just get a jumpstart on what would no doubt be another busy day.

The young detective rented a small one-bedroom apartment in a converted townhouse near Jefferson Park. Having an apartment on the top floor of the four story building gave him a decent view. Park City could be so beautiful on a nice day when the sky was blue, and the sun was shining bright. On a gray, wet day like today, it was going to be pretty miserable.

Overall, the apartment wasn't much, but it was all Ben needed. The bedroom fit a full-size bed, dresser, and tiny nightstand. Most of his clothes were hung in the hall closet across from the bathroom, which had just enough room for a toilet, small pedestal sink, and a combination bathtub-shower. Standing in the center of the bathroom, with his arms outstretched, Ben could easily touch the walls on both sides. The living room served more as a home office than a place for him to unwind or entertain guests; while the kitchen, tucked away in a corner behind a table and two chairs, barely saw any use. Be it ever so humble, there was no place like home.

For the amount of time he spent there, Ben was perfectly happy. The rent was decent, there was always hot water, and he liked the landlord. She was a sweet little old lady named Mrs. Blackwell that lived on the first floor and knew everyone in the neighborhood. Whenever a holiday rolled around, Ben would find a plate of appropriately decorated cookies outside his door with a note from Mrs. B.

Even after that first cup of coffee, Ben was still feeling the lack of sleep hitting him hard. As the thunder outside subsided, he found himself dozing off, sitting on the sofa. Happily giving in, when Ben woke the second time that morning after another couple of hours of sleep, he felt much better.

After going through his morning routine, he'd arrived at the station long before his seven-thirty meeting with the chief, Captain Brent, and Lieutenant Dennis. For the chief to be in the office that early, it showed the severity of the situation. Two women had been killed in three days—brutally murdered. And the prime suspect was a teacher who appeared to have been having inappropriate relations with a student. Ben couldn't see how it could get any worse.

At the appointed time, Ben entered Chief Stanley's office to find everyone already assembled, along with Mayor Charlie Oland. It didn't surprise the detective that the mayor decided to take a personal interest in the case. After all, at the end of the day, the buck stopped with him. If he couldn't protect the people of Parker City, he'd be thrown out of office in the next election, and whoever took his place would no doubt fire Edgar Stanley, whether he was an institution or not. Ben hated the fact that politics always had a part to play in things.

The chief was hunched behind his desk as the mayor wore a path in the carpet, pacing back and forth. Brent and Dennis were seated quietly at the small round conference table by the door. Without saying a word, his cigar clenched tightly in his teeth, Stanley used his chin to direct Ben into one of the two guest chairs opposite his desk.

Detective Sergeant Ben Winters was clearly the one in the hot seat.

Stanley looked like a rhinoceros ready to charge. His eyes were black, narrow, and focused on Ben. "I was against this whole detective squad from the beginning, but Charlie insisted. So? What're we getting for it? Two women killed. Do you have any leads? Is there anyone you like for these murders?"

The man's voice was low and gravely. No doubt from years of smoking cigars. His tone and his words were cutting. He couldn't help himself, Ben thought. He just needed to remind everyone one more time he never wanted detectives in the department. The old ways were the best ways as far as he was concerned.

Before Ben could respond, the mayor jumped into the fray.

"No one here is blaming you for anything. I want to make that clear," he said, shooting a pointed look at the police chief. "I, for one, want to hear directly from you where this investigation stands. I realize it's only been a couple of days, but what can you tell us at this point?"

Ever the diplomat, Charlie Oland wanted to diffuse as much tension as possible. Yet, he didn't seem too worried about angering the chief by putting him in his place. Ben appreciated his support. Even if it was somewhat self-serving.

Not knowing exactly what was going to be asked at this meeting, Ben brought all the reports and files on the case he and Tommy had put together so far. Lieutenant Dennis also had copies that he gave to the mayor and chief.

Starting at the beginning, Ben walked everyone through the case. Captain Brent, who had been keeping close tabs on the case, asked a few questions to clarify some points, not necessarily for himself but for the mayor and the chief's benefit. By the end of his briefing, Ben could see that everyone was leaning towards Joseph Miles being the killer. He wasn't sure if it was the evidence, what little there was, that was most convincing or just the fact he was a teacher sleeping with a student…allegedly.

Wanting to make sure he covered everything, Ben explained why the reporter Roger Benedict was also a strong suspect—possibly even more than Miles.

The chief would have none of it, though. He wanted the teacher brought in for questioning. Stanley made himself very clear in no uncertain terms. If Ben was unwilling to bring the teacher in, he'd have someone else do it and both members of the detective squad could kiss their badges goodbye.

As Ben was about to suggest having a further conversation with Benedict as well, there was a knock on the door.

"What is it?" the chief barked, angry at the interruption.

The chief's secretary opened the door and stepped aside, allowing Tommy into the office. Ben's partner was carrying a folder with the state coroner's seal on the front.

"I'm sorry to interrupt," Tommy said, handing the file to Ben. "I thought you'd want to see this right away. It's Linda Carlson's autopsy report."

Naturally, Ben wanted to see the official autopsy. Unless it revealed something earth shattering, though, there was no reason to interrupt the meeting.

Scanning the report, Ben's eyes widened when he reached the specific line his partner had circled with a red pen.

Chapter Forty-Five

There was complete silence after Ben informed everyone gathered in the chief's office that the coroner had determined Linda Carlson had been pregnant at the time of her death.

The sound of a pin dropping and hitting the floor would have echoed off the walls.

It was there in black and white. The teen had been pregnant. Ben reread the section of the report, then handed the file over to the chief.

After reading it for himself, in one motion, Stanley slammed the folder on his desk and jumped to his feet. The surge in upward momentum from his hefty frame sent his chair wheeling off behind him, smacking into the wall.

"That explains it. The girl told Miles she was pregnant, and he killed her."

"That doesn't explain why Beverly Baker was killed though," Tommy pointed out, trying his hardest not to sound like a smartass.

The chief narrowed his gaze and looked like he was about to launch over his desk and throttle Tommy. Before there was any bloodshed, Ben stepped between his partner and the chief. He was afraid the desk might not be enough to keep his boss from charging.

Linda Carlson being pregnant would give Joseph Miles motive to cover up his affair. But Tommy was right. How did Beverly Baker tie into it?

The mayor looked like he was going to be sick. Ben completely understood the feeling. They didn't seem to be getting any real traction on this case. Sure it was still early in the investigation, all things considered, but the mayor and the chief wanted the case closed and unless they caught a break that pointed them in a different direction, Joseph Miles was clearly their number one suspect.

As much as Ben and Tommy both wanted the killer to be Roger Benedict, neither having a problem with the thought of him locked up for the rest of his life, they both had to admit the information that was coming together did point to the young school teacher being the murderer. At least of Linda Carlson.

Stanley was about to say something when the meeting was once again interrupted by the door opening and his secretary rushing in ahead of a red-faced, out of breath Buck LuCoco. As always, his uniform was wrinkled yet stretched near its tearing point over his massive stomach. Ben could never understand how that was possible. Apparently, wherever he'd come from, he'd run the entire distance.

"There's been another murder," he wheezed, clinging to the doorframe for support.

Chapter Forty-Six

Now...

"So, let me understand." Drew paused to finish off the morning's third cup of coffee. "Even though the case was solved, Sheriff Mason continued to investigate as if it were still ongoing?"

"I didn't say the case was *solved*," Ben corrected. "It was *closed*...at least as far as everyone was concerned. There's a difference. Neither Tommy nor I ever felt satisfied with the outcome. But there was a lot of pressure to close the case. Especially after the third murder. The mayor, the chief, the press, everyone was coming down on us to find the killer. You can't even begin to imagine what it was like.

"Parker City had never gone through anything like this. There was a killer on the loose. Three women in four days were strangled—two teens and one of the richest women in the city. It didn't seem like anyone was safe. Well, that's what the papers were saying."

"Just think if it was today," Drew suggested, "with Facebook, Twitter, the twenty-four hour news cycle, and every news outlet just trying to be more sensational than the next. You just have to look at some of those crime blogs. They turn some of the littlest incidents into the crime of the century."

Ben sighed. "It was a terrible time. We needed to find the killer and do it as fast as possible."

"So, when you found someone that looked good for it," Drew said, slowly turning over the pages from one of the files for the umpteenth time, "you closed the case. When you did, the murders stopped. Everyone assumed you got the guy. Even though there didn't seem to be any solid connection between Beverly Baker's death and the other two."

"Correct," Ben said, sitting forward.

Drew thought for a moment, then picked up the folder with the information on Roger Benedict. "Then there was Benedict, who magically appeared at each crime scene and seemed to have knowledge that no one else did. The murders also stopped when he left town."

"Benedict was who Tommy and I liked for the murders, but when the whole thing with Joseph Miles blew up, the brass decided we had our man. Truth-be-told, we didn't have any concrete evidence pointing to Benedict. It was just a gut thing."

The pair had been going through Tommy's files all morning. By the time Ben arrived back at the office after only a few hours of sleep, he found Drew already at his desk. The corporal was reading through old newspaper articles he found online from the time of the murders.

Reporting had been much different back then. For the most part, there just wasn't as much of it. Murders like this today would have created such a sensation there'd be stories about it from coast-to-coast. Back then it just wasn't like that, and Parker City was far from the forefront when it came to places people cared about. The majority of what Drew was able to find came from the *Herald-Dispatch*.

Ben wanted a fresh set of eyes to go through his former partner's files, and he didn't trust anyone more than Drew. He was sharp and proved himself to be resourceful. After his retirement, Ben had already made the necessary arrangements so Drew could be transferred to the Criminal Investigation Division if he wanted. His skills should not be put to waste, and Ben had great hopes for the heights he could reach.

Drew started at the beginning and went page by page, news clipping by news clipping, file folder by file folder. When he came across something that he found interesting or brought a question to mind, he scribbled a note down on his scratch pad. By the time he'd finished reviewing all the material, he had pages of notes.

As Drew began working his way through his notes, Ben felt like he'd just taken the witness stand. The kid was good. He methodically took Ben through the case; first trying to connect all the dots, then trying to tear them apart again. Drew Collins, prosecutor, was on full display.

It was lunchtime before they came to the end of Drew's cross examination. Both men were mentally exhausted, but the younger officer was now completely caught up on everything that happened in 1981.

"Joseph Miles is the definition of a predator. How many girls was he sleeping with in the end?" Drew asked, looking at a copy of the teacher's school ID He could understand why the young teen girls fell for him. He was extremely good looking and a sympathetic authority figure. He was only a few years older, so naturally could empathize with how they were feeling.

"Four," Ben said.

"Pervert. But killing two of his victims to keep them quiet makes perfect sense. I don't understand why he killed Beverly Baker though."

"Exactly. He *knew* Beverly. But back then, everyone *knew* everyone else in Parker. And we never had a chance to ask him about it."

Chapter Forty-Seven

Hours passed in a matter of minutes as the pair went through the old case file. They'd completely lost track of time. Before either of them knew it, the antique 18th Century mahogany Longcase Clock in the corner chimed two, letting them know the afternoon was well underway. Realizing they'd missed lunch, Ben offered to run out and grab some sandwiches from the grill across the street. He felt he owed Drew for taking him away from his actual work that morning. His assistant's desk usually had more paperwork on it than his own. Plus, he could use some fresh air.

Opting to take the more private back staircase to avoid running into anyone who might try to waylay his journey to the sandwich shop, Ben stepped onto the sidewalk and was instantly bathed in the crisp spring air. Coupled with the brilliant sun and bright blue sky, the chief actually felt his muscles relax for the briefest of moments. Normally, this was the kind of day he loved. He'd spend hours walking around the city's streets, stopping and talking to people, popping into shops to visit with the merchants. There was too much on his mind for that today.

Wearing a simple pair of khakis and a polo shirt instead of his uniform, along with a baseball cap and sunglasses, he was able to fly under the radar. Looking just like any other guy on the street, Ben made it around the block to the restaurant without drawing any attention to himself.

Downstairs Deli & Grill wasn't anything fancy, but the food that came out of its kitchen was dynamite. If you didn't know about the place, chances are you would walk right passed the front entrance. There was only a simple sign with an arrow pointing down a set of cement steps to the eatery which was actually below a popular downtown men's clothing store that had been around since the '60s.

Ben was a regular at Downstairs, usually stopping in for lunch a couple of times a week at least. During the lunch rush, the small space was always filled with customers, but at two-thirty in the afternoon, only a couple of tables were occupied. The crowd would reappear for dinner and then stick around until the bar closed at midnight.

Pulling up a seat at the bar, Jackie, one of the regular waitresses, greeted him. Ben had no need for a menu. He knew it forward and backward.

"Drew not picking up lunch today?" she asked.

"No. I told him I'd make the lunch run. I needed to get out of the office for a few minutes."

"Alright then. What'll it be, Chief?"

Ben alternated between the Downstairs Super Club and a double bacon cheeseburger known as the Mega-Meat Monster. Today was definitely a monster burger day. The grease and fat was not going to be good for his arteries, but he was craving the extra thick strips of bacon. For Drew, he ordered a meatball sub with extra cheese. While he was waiting, he asked for a Coke and seriously thought about telling Jackie to put some rum in it. His better angels prevailed, though. He was officially on duty, after all.

If he hadn't been afraid of looking like a passed out drunk, he'd have put his head down on the bar and closed his eyes for a few minutes. The last few days full of stress and little sleep were catching up with him. He was far too old to be staying up as late as he'd been. Then to turn right around and head back to the office after only a few hours of sleep were seriously wearing him down. Resting his chin on his hands, he began to nod off until a voice snatched him back from that place between being awake and asleep.

"Ben? You're not looking too good?"

The voice was unmistakable—a deep, rich baritone that could easily be heard in a room filled with a thousand people and no microphone.

Ben opened his eyes to find Charlie Oland sitting next to him. Now, well into his eighties, the former mayor's age was apparent. The once full, thick head of hair had disappeared, leaving only a thin layer of gray strands in its place. His skin, no longer perpetually tanned and smooth, was severely creased and sagged ever so slightly around the jaw line. For all the signs of his age, though, he was still an imposing figure and had no difficulty commanding a room.

"Hello, Mr. Mayor," the chief said, rubbing his eyes.

"We've known each other for almost forty years, Ben. You can call me Charlie. Besides, I haven't been the mayor for a very long time." His voice was deep and gravely, like so many who smoked like chimneys in the '70s and '80s, only to give it up in the '90s.

"To a lot of people, you'll always be Parker City's mayor."

"I don't know if that's necessarily a good thing."

"It depends on who you ask, I guess." Ben smiled.

"My boy's the mayor now. I'm just trying to stay out of his way. It's his city to run."

"But you still give him advice."

"Every chance I get. Whether he wants it or not," the former mayor said with that thousand-watt smile Ben knew so well.

As the smile slowly disappeared, his mood became more somber.

"Ben, I'm sorry about Tommy. I've wanted to talk to you since I heard the news, but I figured you'd want some time. He was a good man. He could be a real pain in the ass sometimes, but he was a good cop. You two did a hell of a job for Parker. Almost dragged the PCPD into the 20th Century all by yourselves…with a little help from me, of course."

It was odd. Ben sensed a sadness in the former mayor's voice. Tommy was never close with Charlie Oland. He was suspicious of all politicians. Maybe it was part Tommy's death and part nostalgia for a time long gone when things were different.

"Have you heard anything about the case? Are there any suspects?" Charlie Oland asked, sounding genuinely concerned.

"I'm not part of the investigation. I don't know anything more than you."

"I'm sure there've been some questions raised because of the way he was… because of how he died."

No doubt caused by the extreme fatigue he was feeling, before Ben realized what he was doing, he said, "It's strange because that afternoon Tommy said he wanted to talk about the Strangler case. Said there was something he needed to tell me."

Seeing the expression on the former mayor's face, Ben instantly regretted having said anything. Oland's pursed lips and raised eyebrow gave away his curiosity and concern.

Before either man could say another word, the bartender appeared with two grease-stained bags of food. "I'll put these on your tab, Chief."

"Thanks, Jackie."

As Ben stood to leave, Charlie Oland took his elbow. "If there's anything I can do—anything you need—just let me know. I still have some friends in this town."

"I appreciate that. I really do. But as far as the case is concerned, like I said, it's out of my hands."

"I mean personally, Ben. I know how close the two of you were. And there's only a few of us dinosaurs left in this town who still remember what it was like back in the day."

The former mayor was right, Ben thought as he headed back to the station. There weren't that many people left from the early days when he and Tommy first joined the force. Most of the people living in Parker City now had only moved to the area in the past ten years or so. A lot of Parker's history was being forgotten.

Charlie Oland watched the door close behind the police chief, leaving him alone at the bar, nervously tapping his fingers on the dark mahogany surface. A number of thoughts were filling his mind all at the same time. After digging his cell phone out of his pocket, he quickly scrolled through his contact list before shooting off a quick text message.

I need to talk to you tonight.

Chapter Forty-Eight

Grandview Avenue hadn't changed significantly over the last several decades. Its magnificent manor homes still boasted spectacular views of Jefferson Park and some of the most expensive real estate in the city. Charlie and Mary Ann Oland still lived in the grand Victorian that they had when he was mayor and the twins were growing up. Even in their old age, neither saw any reason to give up the family home and downsize. They were both happy to have more space than they knew what to do with.

Still popular figures in the community, Parker City's former first couple was frequently seen out in the evening at one event or another. Political events, social gatherings, or charity dos, it didn't matter. The two liked to stay involved. Both served on a number of boards, including the Parker Historical Society, of which Mary Ann was the current chair.

On the rare occasions that the couple was home in the evening, after dinner, the former mayor usually made his way out to the porch, which wrapped around three of the house's four sides. From there he would sit and watch people passing by on Grandview or strolling through the park across the street. On a clear night, there was a stunning sunset to the west over the mountains that filled him with such peace and tranquility.

Ever since running into Ben at lunch, however, Charlie Oland had been filled with no such warm, relaxed feelings. In fact, he'd been uneasy for the last few days, ever since Tom Mason's murder was reported. This, in part, was why he was locked away in his study instead of sitting outside in his favorite glider watching the sun drift below the distant mountaintops.

Charlie Oland would never use the term "man cave" but his study was his sanctuary. On any given day, the room looked as though it could have come directly out of a museum. Nothing was ever out of place. Everything meticulously arranged; from the leather-bound books no one had ever actually read to the antique desk set that once belonged to Christopher Cox, the first lieutenant governor of Maryland. Charlie Oland prided himself on the order around him. More so now that he was getting older.

To see the study in its current state, looking as though it had been ransacked, anyone who had been in the room before wouldn't know what to think. Old brown file boxes were haphazardly stacked on the furniture, most of their contents lying in stacks on the floor. The former mayor's desk, usually clear of any and all clutter, was covered with random papers, notes, and envelopes. At some point the desk lamp had been knocked over, causing its light to cast giant, misshapen shadows up the walls onto the ceiling.

In the center of the paper tempest was Charlie Oland himself. He had spent a good part of the evening searching through all of his personal files, looking for something very specific—some *things*, rather. A collection of old letters, which he finally unearthed in a box of personal and private correspondence from his days in City Hall.

Holding the stack of yellowing envelopes in his hand reminded him of a time when people would write letters. They'd take the time to actually sit and put pen to paper and think about what they were writing, instead of typing out a quick email and sending it off through the worldwide web. Or worse yet, text that didn't even use full words but letters that abbreviated entire statements. Charlie Oland never thought he'd be one of those old people that complained about how things changed so much, but he was realizing that's exactly what he'd become.

Pushing all of the papers off his desk onto the floor without a care for the additional mess it was making, he laid the stack of letters in the center of the green leather blotter. Finally picking up the fallen lamp and replacing it on the desk, the former mayor noticed his hands were shaking.

It had been a very long time since he'd thought about these letters. He should have burned them all those years ago. Why he kept them was still a question he couldn't answer. He wasn't a sentimental man, and he certainly wasn't interested in keeping incriminating material close by.

Slowly sliding the first letter from its envelope, he felt as though he was opening Pandora's Box. The hell these letters could have caused, and yet, he kept them all these years. And for an inexplicable reason, he needed to see them again.

The stationary's color, turned slightly by age, was still unmistakable—a pale lavender. A giant letter "B" encircled by a rose sat at the top of the page like a crown. Below it was the impeccable handwriting of Beverly Baker.

No doubt, she had sent hundreds, if not thousands, of handwritten letters and notes to people over the years. She was a woman that always liked to make her thoughts known. But how many of those notes were scented with her signature perfume? He could almost smell it. Strange, the power of the mind, he thought slowly passing the page under his nose.

Forty years ago, he and Beverly Baker had been having an affair. These letters were proof of that indiscretion. They had begun their relationship shortly after he was elected mayor. She was a prominent figure in the city, involved with a number of causes. He was the new mayor. They found themselves working closely together on a variety of projects, and one thing led to another. It wasn't a unique story, certainly not the first time in history this sort of thing happened. But the only time Charlie Oland ever strayed; and it almost ruined him.

Chapter Forty-Nine

Reading through the letters, Charlie Oland was filled with such mixed feelings. He wasn't sure how he'd felt about Beverly. It hadn't been love, he knew that much. It was lust. An animal attraction the two felt toward one another. But he did have feelings for her, and having to hide those after she was killed nearly tore him apart. No one could ever know that they'd been seeing each other. The '80s was a different time. An extramarital affair would have destroyed both his personal and political life.

The memories from that dark period came flooding back in waves. He felt like he couldn't breathe, like he was drowning in the past. He needed some fresh air.

Tossing the last of the letters on the desk with the others, seven in all, he slowly pushed himself up from his chair. A few steps away, with an unsteady hand, he poured himself a large brandy from a decanter situated on a little serving table. A few steps more and he opened the French doors leading out to the side porch.

A gust of bone-chilling air surged through the open doors, sending a shiver down his spine. The brandy helped to warm him once again. Bracing himself, he stepped out into the cold night air. Exhaling, he watched as his breath drifted off into the atmosphere. After several deep breaths, his head was beginning to clear as his lungs burned, filling with crisp spring air.

Draining the last of the brandy from the crystal tumbler, he was turning to head back inside when the sound of footsteps on the old wooden planks of the porch caught his attention. The only light came from the study filtering through the windows, making it difficult to see anything but shadows.

"Who's there?" he called into the dark, thinking it must be nothing more than an old man's imagination.

The former mayor's heart began to beat faster as a figure slowly emerged from the shadows. It took a moment for his eyes to adjust and focus. When they did, he wasn't too happy with who he saw.

"What are you doing sneaking around out here in the dark?"

"You said you wanted to talk," answered the shadow in a cool, calm manner, more chilling than the night air.

"In this house, we use the front door," Charlie Oland said, walking back into the study. "It's too cold out here. We can talk inside."

Anything you say, Mr. Mayor.

Chapter Fifty

Then...

Buck LuCoco's announcement that a third murder had been reported sent a shock wave through the office. Everyone was stunned, each trying his best to make sense of what was happening. Chief Stanley's natural reaction was anger, as shown by his reddening face and clenched fists. The mayor, on the other hand, looked like he might be sick. Their opposite reactions summed up pretty well just how confusing the situation had become.

Every man in the room had, at one point or another over the last several days, had the same thought—this wasn't supposed to happen in a place like Parker City. They weren't ready to handle the kind of crime they felt was reserved for big cities. But here they were. Dealing with the fact three people had now been killed in four days.

Without excusing themselves, Ben and Tommy bolted for the door. Tommy grabbed the report out of LuCoco's hand on the way and was reading it to his partner as they sprinted down the hall. Neither thought this was going to turn into a killing spree. They both figured there was some connection between Beverly Baker and Linda Carlson. They just hadn't found it yet. There was *something* that would explain why a prominent member of the community and a high school teenager were the targets of a brutal murderer. A third victim, if Penny Moss's death was in fact a murder and the work of the same person, could mean things were only going to get worse. And if they couldn't figure out what connected all of these women, they wouldn't have any way to tell if there were more potential victims that could be in danger.

The rain pummeled their cruiser as it sped toward the Moss home. The pellets of water falling from the sky struck the car with such force and ferocity that the sound nearly drowned out the wail of the siren. The storm wasn't showing any signs of letting up, forcing everyone to seek cover indoors. That explained the eerily empty streets the detectives were now racing through. Behind the wheel, even with the windshield wipers swishing back-and-forth at their top speed, Tommy was finding it difficult to see as sheets of water cascaded down the glass in front of him.

Not a single word had been spoken between the two men since they'd gotten in the car. They were both trying to make sense of everything that was happening and wondering what it was going to take to put an end to this nightmare.

Turning onto Orchard Park Way, just down the street, Tommy could see the flashing lights of another Parker City patrol car parked in front of a house that could have quite easily passed for a castle somewhere in the English countryside. Towering over the other houses on the street, the Moss family home was something of legend in Parker City. It was the house where generations of yet another one of Parker's great founding families had lived for over a century.

Tommy eased the cruiser into the driveway and threw it into park. Stepping out of the car, the detectives were instantly drenched from head to toe. Ben knew there was no way they were going to find any clues that might help them outside. The rain had no doubt destroyed any usable evidence the killer might have left behind.

Running for cover, Ben and Tommy reached the front porch where they found the first patrolman on the scene, an Officer Hugh Richards, who was trying to calm an irate Bernard Moss, Penny's father. People handled grief and shock in different ways. Moss, a man used to always being in control and calling the shots, had completely lost control. At first, Ben wasn't sure if he was in a rage or hysterical.

"Things like this aren't supposed to happen to people like us!" he was screaming as the detectives joined the pair.

Neither Ben nor Tommy had ever met Bernard B. Moss, the city's newspaper magnate, but they knew of him by reputation. In general, he wasn't liked very much. He hadn't even bothered to find out who the two new arrivals were before he launched into a tirade aimed in their direction.

Moss was well over six feet tall, but as his verbal assault continued, Ben watched as he seemed to shrink before their eyes like a giant balloon deflating as its hot air was expelled. Finally, the yelling came to an end as Moss began to teeter on his feet. In an instant, the fury was gone, replaced with something completely different.

Officer Richards actually had to take the newspaper man's arm to steady him, as Ben showed his badge and introduced himself.

"Mr. Moss, my name is Ben Winters. This is my partner, Tom Mason. We're detectives with the PCPD. We received a call about a murder. Are you the one who made that call?"

Ben wasn't sure if Moss understood what he was saying. A blank stare settled over his face.

"Mr. Moss, I'm Detective Winters. Someone called and said there had been a murder."

Blinking several times, Moss focused on Ben.

"Sir, can you understand me?" he asked. "I'm a detective with the Parker City Police Department. Did you call and report a crime?"

Quietly, almost inaudible due to the torrential rain, Moss said, "My daughter. I…I found her…I found her in the kitchen. She's dead."

Chapter Fifty-One

Entering the Moss home, a strange sense of unease came over Ben. After the last few days, he was getting used to it, though. The grand entry hall, where he was now standing trying to dry off, ran the length of the house from the front to the rear. At its end was a staircase that wrapped around the hall and up to the second and third floors. In whichever direction he turned, Ben saw ornate sideboards and paintings that no doubt cost more money than he would ever see in his lifetime. Above him, not one but two crystal chandeliers lit the space, casting light down upon an enormous Oriental rug in the center of the floor.

Everything looked so perfect—too perfect, he felt. He got the feeling most of it was just for show.

Ben didn't think it was possible, but the rain was coming down harder. The water hitting the windows sounded like pellets being shot from a thousand BB guns. In the distance, thunder could be heard every few minutes.

Officer Richards had made a sweep of the house when he first arrived. Other than finding the victim in the kitchen, it looked like nothing had been disturbed. After radioing in for assistance, he had secured the scene and was waiting for additional officers to arrive.

Tommy remained in the foyer with Bernard Moss, gently trying to coax out of him whatever information he could, while Richards escorted Ben to the kitchen.

The kitchen, like the rest of the house, was immaculately kept. Brass cookware hanging on display looked as though it had never once been used. Colorful serving dishes lined a shelf on the wall, each with an ever so fine layer of dust. Again, more items just for show, not for function. There was obviously a specific place for everything in this house. Except perhaps, Ben thought, the empty bottle of wine that lay broken in the sink.

Beyond the kitchen, Ben could see a door leading to the dining room. Next to the door was a second set of stairs leading from the kitchen to the floor above. Back when the house was first built, those would have been the stairs the servants used. Mrs. Moss, the wife of the Bernard Parker Moss who had built the Harlequin Theatre, would never allow her house staff to be seen using the main staircase in the grand hall. It was clear the Moss family still had a good deal of money, but times had changed. Gone were the days when the house was tended to by a butler, a cook, and an army of maids.

After taking it all in, Ben's eyes finally drifted to the foot of the stairs where the body of Penny Moss lay. Splayed out in an awkward fashion, her legs twisted to one side while her upper torso turned to the other. One arm rested on her chest, the other stretched out to her side.

Officer Richards was doing his best to keep his eyes focused in a different direction. His reaction was only slightly better than Officer Vernon's when he'd discovered Beverly Baker's body. Murder was so uncommon in Parker City, even the police weren't entirely comfortable around dead bodies.

"Did you touch anything when you first came through? Her arms? Her legs?" Ben asked, crouching down to get a closer look.

"No, sir. I just felt for a pulse."

"Did Mr. Moss touch anything?"

"I, ah, I don't know. I didn't ask."

"What about a housekeeper? Who found her?"

"Mr. Moss did. When he came home this morning. Said he was working late last night. And it's the housekeeper's day off, he said."

"And Mrs. Moss? Where's she?"

"I didn't ask."

"We need to find out if Mr. Moss moved the body in any way when he found her."

There was something very different about the way Penny looked compared to the way Beverly Baker and Linda Carlson's bodies had been found. Looking up the staircase then back down at her, Ben wondered if this could have just been an accident. From the smell, it was clear to him Penny had been drinking. The wine bottle in the sink definitely supported that theory. She could have lost her balance at the top of the steps and tumbled back down.

For an instant Ben allowed himself the sadly refreshing thought this was nothing more than a tragic accident. He was ashamed for actually feeling a slight sense of relief. Regardless of the circumstances, a young girl was still dead.

Brushing aside her hair from where it was covering her face, Ben's stomach clenched as he saw the dark ligature mark around the girl's throat. He was no expert, but to him, it looked identical to the braided pattern they had found on Linda Carlson. This was no accident.

"Shit." Ben turned and looked up to see his partner standing behind him.

"Number three?" Tommy asked.

Exhaling and pushing himself to his feet, Ben nodded. "It looks like it. I thought it might have been an accident, but those marks around her neck…" His voice trailed off as he shook his head.

Tommy jerked his thumb over his shoulder saying, "Chief Stanley and Captain Brent are outside with Moss, along with the lieutenant and a Colonel Something-or-Other from the State Police. It looks like this could be out of our hands pretty soon."

"But for now, it's still our case," Ben said, heading up the stairs. Tommy quickly followed, motioning for the patrolman who'd been standing quietly in the corner to stay with the body.

"I want to see her bedroom," Ben said over his shoulder, looking in every door until he found the bedroom that obviously belonged to a teenage girl.

"Are we looking for anything in particular?"

"The same thing we always look for. Clues."

Tommy paused in the doorway. "Did you really just say that?"

"There has to be something," Ben answered, flipping through the books on her bookcase. "We're missing whatever it is that ties all of these murders together."

"Two high school teenagers and a rich socialite." Tommy sighed as he took a seat at Penny's desk. Like the rest of the room, the desk was a mess. It was cluttered with papers, textbooks, teen magazines, makeup, jewelry; everything one would expect to find in the room of a high school student. Finding nothing of note on the surface, he started opening the drawers, which were so filled with random objects he could hardly open them.

Rummaging through the desk didn't look like it was going to pay off until in the bottom drawer, under several copies of *Teen Beat*, Tommy found Penny Moss's diary. He began skimming the most recent entries. What he read shocked him, and Tommy didn't shock very easily. He couldn't believe how explicit the passages were. But he knew this was what they needed.

"Ben. Read this. She was having an affair with Joseph Miles. A pretty X-rated one according to what she wrote in here."

Chapter Fifty-Two

After the discovery of Penny's diary and the entries in which she revealed—in graphic detail—her activities with Joseph Miles, there was no way the teacher could not be brought in for questioning. It looked like he'd been having an affair with not one, but two of his students. Both of whom were now dead. The only tenuous connection was that of Miles to Beverly Baker. He'd known the first victim and helped with a project for the historical society. But what would his motive have been to kill Beverly? Even if that question still remained unanswered, Joseph Miles was the only thing that tied all three of the victims together.

Reading the diary sent Chief Stanley over the edge. At first, Ben wasn't sure what to expect, watching him read the explicit passages. But as his eyes grew larger and larger with each turn of a page, everyone in the room knew the chief was about to blow.

Throwing the diary to Tommy when he couldn't read any further, Stanley spun around, bringing himself nose-to-nose with the head of his new detective squad. Ben saw the rage burning in the old man's eyes and braced himself. He had the briefest thought that being attacked by a bear would be less painful.

Instead of yelling, as was his trademark, Stanley spoke barely louder than a whisper and said, "I want you to go drag that sonofabitch out of that school by his balls and put him in a cell. If he so much as looks at you funny, you are to use as much force as possible to bring him in. Do I make myself clear? I want him behind bars. We have all we need to arrest that prink."

"Sir," Ben started, knowing they were nowhere near having enough evidence to convict Miles of the murders. "I…"

"You have your orders, *Detective*," Stanley barked, cutting him off before he could say another word. Those were the chief's final words before he stormed off to inform the mayor they were about to make an arrest.

Following the detectives through the house to the front door, Captain Brent, as always, became the voice of reason. He might have appeared to be a shoot first, ask questions later kind of guy, but he was the most levelheaded of the PCPD's command staff. He knew when you needed to be tough, and he knew when you needed to play it cool.

Scratching his chin with his meaty hand, Brent said, "Bring Miles in but don't say too much. Don't give anything away. Let him sweat for a while. See if you can get him to do all the talking. Who knows, he may just give something away."

The detectives nodded and headed for their car. Even with the rain beating down, a crowd of bystanders had gathered. It was to be expected considering there were now almost a dozen police vehicles—city, county, and state—and the Crime Scene Unit's van parked outside the Moss's home on the usually quiet, residential street.

"This is a shit show," Tommy was saying as he was about to slide into his seat. Suddenly, with the rain pouring in the open passenger door, he froze, something across the street catching his eye.

"What is it?" Ben asked as his partner slammed the door and bolted across Orchard Park Avenue. Not toward the group of onlookers hiding under a canopy of umbrellas, but to a single figure standing alone under a large tree away from the crowd.

Through the continuous stream of water cascading down the windshield, it took Ben a second to recognize the reporter. Tommy, now completely drenched, was making a beeline for Roger Benedict.

Ben had two choices. Either he could head straight after his partner or he could take a minute to find the umbrella he knew was somewhere in the car. If he took the time to do that, he was afraid his absence would give Tommy the time to do something he'd end up regretting.

Shaking his head, Ben jumped out of the car and ran across the street. He reached the shelter of the large red oak's branches in just enough time to see Tommy taking a handful of Benedict's shirt and lifting him a couple inches off the ground.

"What do you mean someone called you and told you about Penny Moss?" Tommy was shouting.

"Just what I said, Detective. I got a call. I was told there was another murder."

"By who?" Ben asked, coming up beside his partner. "Who called you? Who told you there was another murder?"

"My boss!" he shouted, whether out of fear or because it was the only way to be heard over the onslaught of rain.

"Bernard Moss? He called you and told you his own daughter was murdered?" Ben asked, not believing someone would do that, even if he was the owner of a newspaper.

Pulling himself free of Tommy's grip, he answered in that condescending tone they had grown to know. "He's a newspaper man. He knows how important this story is. That's why I'm here."

His last comment was directed pointedly at Tommy.

"Care to comment? Was Penny Moss killed by the Spring Strangler? Are you two going to be fired now that three women have been killed?"

Completely out of character, Tommy turned without saying another word and started back to the squad car. It was clear neither Benedict nor Ben expected that reaction.

It was Ben, instead, who lost his temper. Turning on the reporter, he snapped, "I find it very interesting that you showed up at each crime scene knowing details about the murders before anyone else. Care to comment for me on how that's possible, you piece of shit?"

"I'm just that good, Detective-*Sergeant* Winters. Obviously, I'm better at my job than you are at yours."

Chapter Fifty-Three

Ben's patience with the reporter was completely gone. At this point, he couldn't care less about the freedom of the press or the rights of the piss ant journalist hack standing in front of him. Ben gave a sharp whistle to attract the attention of the two patrolmen keeping the bystanders away from the crime scene. As Officer Vernon sloshed his way over to the detective, he was ordered to take Roger Benedict into custody.

"What the hell are you doing?" the reporter snarled as the steel cuffs were placed on his wrists. "I haven't done anything wrong. You can't do this!"

Knowing that Lieutenant Dennis had already had Benedict in for an informal "conversation," Ben knew he was going to have to answer a lot of questions for this, but he didn't give a damn. He wanted the creep locked up for a while and to hell with the problems it was bound to cause. If nothing else, it would make him feel a little better knowing the reporter was stuck behind bars.

"What are the charges?" Benedict demanded to know.

"Obstruction of justice," Ben barked as he grabbed the reporter's arm and dragged him toward Officer Vernon's squad car.

"This is ridiculous! You can't do this to me. I'm here covering a story."

"Are you going to tell me who tipped you off about the other two murders?" Ben half asked, half demanded.

"No!"

Ben slammed Benedict against the side of the police car to make his point. "Are you resisting arrest too? It looks like you're going to have to book him for that too, Pete."

Vernon certainly wasn't going to argue with a superior officer, even if Detective Sergeant Winters wasn't technically his superior. He'd known Ben long enough to know he didn't usually get this angry. If he was arresting this guy, there was a reason.

"You're going to regret this," Benedict growled as he was shoved into the back of the squad car.

Officer Vernon closed the door and tipped his hat to Ben. "I'll take care of this, sir."

Ben looked at Benedict sitting in the back of the patrol car, then looked at Officer Vernon. Running a hand through his soaked hair, he realized he was letting the stress get the better of him. He was better than this. He couldn't let his anger blind him. He needed to stay focused. It was his job to bring the PCPD into the modern era and not follow the old ways of Edgar Stanley and Buck LuCoco.

"Pete," Ben said with a sigh, "Keep him in the car for a couple hours while you're here, then let him go. No charges."

"Are you sure?"

"Yeah. Technically, the only crime he's committed is being an asshole. We can't actually arrest people for that."

When Ben climbed into his own patrol car, Tommy was behind the wheel with the heater on full blast, trying to dry his clothes and not catch pneumonia.

"You arrested him?" Tommy asked, stamping the butt of his cigarette out in the car's ashtray.

"I'm having him detained for a little while," Ben answered. "It's the best I can do."

"You're a good cop, Ben. You're lousy at getting even with someone, but a good cop." With that, Tommy shifted into gear and turned in the direction of Tasker Valley High.

Chapter Fifty-Four

Driving conditions had gone from bad to worse to downright treacherous. If the constant downpour of rain wasn't enough, the cloud cover was so thick with angry black clouds it might as well have been the middle of the night. So much water had fallen in the last few hours, flash flooding was becoming a problem. As Tommy guided the cruiser carefully through the streets toward the high school, they listened to the radio as Dispatch directed assistance to various sites around the city.

"You can't deny that Miles looks good for the two girls," Tommy finally said. "He was sleeping with both of them. He gets one pregnant then the other finds out, so he has to clean up his mess."

"I don't disagree," Ben said. "But that doesn't explain why he killed Beverly Baker."

"No. But after he sees we've got him on the other two, maybe he'll realize he doesn't have a choice but to confess."

"When did you become an optimist?"

"Maybe you're just rubbing off on me. Besides, the state's attorney's the one that will have to deal with the motive. We just need to provide the evidence."

"That's just it. There's no hard evidence connecting him to the murder at the historical society. Or to Penny Moss or Linda Carlson's murders for that matter. It's all circumstantial."

"There's not always a smoking gun. You told me that once. So we go with what we've got. My guess is that once we arrest him, we'll find something in his place that ties all of this up in a nice bow. Circumstantial evidence is more than enough to get us a search warrant."

"I hope you're right because my gut tells me something is off about this."

"What did you have for breakfast?"

Ben gave his partner a puzzled look. "Coffee and a couple donuts."

"There you go. You're hungry. That's why your stomach doesn't feel right."

Ben opened his mouth to respond but couldn't think of anything to say. Closing it, he just shook his head and looked out the window.

"Look, I don't disagree with you," Tommy said. "But this is the most solid lead we've had so far. Maybe we'll get lucky and once we have Miles at the station, he'll slip and say something that makes this all make sense. Let's not forget that regardless of whether he killed anyone, he's still a teacher that was having sex with his students. We've certainly got him on that charge. We just cracked a case we didn't even know about in the first place. That's how good we are."

"There you go, looking on the bright side again."

"While we're at the school arresting this scumbag, maybe you should drop by Miss Kirkpatrick's room and let her know you have the situation under control," Tommy added through that cocky grin of his.

Turning onto the street that would lead straight to the school, they found one of the city's fire engines from the Northside Hose Company partially blocking traffic in front of the Hardee's. The bright red pumper truck was just one of a few pieces of emergency equipment Ben saw in the fast food restaurant's parking lot.

Ben recognized the Maryland State Trooper directing traffic. He rolled his window down as Tommy eased the car to a stop.

"Hey, Mike. What's happening here?"

"Part of the roof collapsed," the trooper said with raining rolling off the brim of his hat. "No one was hurt, but there's a good bit of damage in back. I was getting coffee next door at McDonald's when I saw the fire engines roll in. Did they send you over from the city?"

"No. We've got to go pick someone up," Ben said, shaking his head.

"The Strangler case? You got a suspect? It's all the guys are talking about over at the barracks."

Ben was happy to be interrupted by a PCPD squad car pulling up with its lights flashing. "We'll get out of your way. I'll talk to you later, Mike."

"This is one crappy-ass day," Tommy said as he put his foot on the accelerator.

Chapter Fifty-Five

Ten plus hours of continual rain had turned the football field at Tasker River High into a lake. Most of the other sports fields were under water as well, Ben noticed as they drove to the main entrance of the building. They'd chosen not to arrive with sirens blaring, for two reasons. First, they didn't want to take any chance of tipping Joseph Miles off that they were coming for him. Second, they didn't want to start any sort of panic at the area's largest high school. The more low key they could keep this the better.

Climbing the steps to the front doors, the detectives were surprised to be met by Dr. Hoffman. He must have seen them pull up from his office window.

"Detectives, wha…what can I do for you?" the principal asked, obviously extremely agitated.

Ben wondered if he'd heard about Penny Moss yet. Or if there was another reason he was acting so anxious.

"Dr. Hoffman," Ben began, "I'm sorry to say, but there's been another murder."

The administrator's lips began trembling as a line of sweat formed on his brow.

"Another murder? Who? When? Not another student." He put his hand on the wall to steady himself.

Clearly, Hoffman hadn't heard about Penny Moss yet.

"Penny Moss was found in her home this morning," Ben said quietly. "And we're here to arrest Joseph Miles."

"We'd like to do this as quietly as possible," Tommy added. "But we have evidence that he was sleeping with both of our teenage victims."

The news struck the principal like a blow from a sledgehammer. First the color drained from his face, then his knees buckled. Ben and Tommy each grabbed an arm to help steady him. Once he was leaning against the wall, Dr. Hoffman took out a worn handkerchief and began whipping away the sweat from his face.

"I don't understand," he mumbled. "How could he have done this? This doesn't make any sense."

"Dr. Hoffman, it would probably be better if you sent someone to bring Miles to the office so we don't have to go in and do this in front of the students," Ben said, trying to make this as easy on his former principal as he could.

"But...but I can't," Hoffman answered. "Mr. Miles didn't come in today. We had to get him a substitute."

"He didn't come to school today?" Tommy snapped. "Did you talk to him?"

"No. He just didn't show up. I was going to have to fill out a report and..."

Tommy shot Ben a worried look. Miles could be on the run.

Ben knew exactly what his partner was thinking. "We're going to need Miles' home address."

Chapter Fifty-Six

This time, as they were making their way through the sodden streets, Tommy hit the switch for the lights and siren. The blaring sound could just barely be heard over the rain pounding on the car's roof. More than once, the cruiser's wheels hit slick spots on the pavement, causing Tommy to have to bring the car under control before it hydroplaned off the road. Luckily, most people had given up on going out in the rain, so the streets were empty for that time of day.

Ben had radioed in to Dispatch to send the nearest patrol car to Joseph Miles's address but was told that all available units were dealing with the problems the storm was causing throughout the city. In addition to off-duty officers being brought in, some of the uniforms at the Moss crime scene had been reassigned to handle a number of emergency calls. The department was stretched too thin for everything that was happening.

Mile's apartment was only a few minutes away. Ben would have liked to have some additional back up. When Tommy asked to talk with Shirley, she promised to try and get someone there as soon as possible.

"It pays to have powerful friends," Tommy said with a smile.

"Do you even know Shirley's last name?"

The smile quickly disappeared as Tommy ran through a long list of possible last names that he thought might be Shirley's. He would have sworn he'd known it. But that wasn't the kind of relationship they had.

"Logan," he finally answered.

"Sonofabitch."

"Did I get it right?"

"No. It stopped raining." Ben pointed out the window. "And no, you didn't."

He was right on both counts. The rain had just stopped. It hadn't slowly tapered off. It was as if someone just turned off the spigot. Blessed relief, Ben thought.

"Her last name is Morgan."

"I was close," Tommy said as he turned into Miles's apartment complex.

Chestnut Hill Manor was a garden style apartment complex with four three-story buildings built around a center courtyard. It took Dr. Hoffman several agonizing minutes to find Miles's home information. When he'd finally pulled himself together and handed it over, both Ben and Tommy were familiar with the address.

Miles lived in the north building on the second floor.

Outside apartment 203, the detectives positioned themselves on either side of the door and drew their weapons. Ben's .38 felt heavy in his hand.

Using his fist to hammer on the door, Ben shouted, "Joseph Miles, this is the Parker City Police. Open the door."

Nothing. No response. No sound from inside the apartment.

Ben hit the door again. "Joseph Miles, open up! This is the PCPD."

The door across the hall from Miles's opened and an elderly woman looked out to see what all the commotion was about. Without saying a word, Tommy held up his badge and pointed for her to go back into her apartment. With wide eyes, she turned and closed the door.

"Enough of this," Tommy said. He braced himself, then used his foot as a battering ram to open the door. The thin frame cracked with the force and the door swung open. Tommy entered first, gun trained in front of him, looking for any sign of movement. Ben came in behind, sweeping from side to side.

The apartment wasn't big. A small kitchen and bathroom were off the entry. Ahead was the living room with a balcony that looked out over the center courtyard. There was no sign of Miles. But everything looked like it was in its place. It didn't appear that he'd been grabbing things to try and make a quick getaway. Ben found his wallet sitting on the coffee table along with a set of car keys.

Tommy looked to the closed bedroom door and pointed for Ben to take the lead. Slowly turning the knob, Ben pushed the door open, using the wall as a shield in case Miles was waiting for them in the room with a gun. Again, there was no sound or movement. Ben didn't like this. Had Miles already gotten away?

Ben carefully craned his neck around the doorframe. The room was too dark to see anything. The curtains were drawn over the windows, blocking out what little natural light might have trickled in through the blinds. Leading with his gun, he slowly entered the room and felt along the wall for a light switch.

Finding the switch and flipping it on, the room lit up with enough light to make Ben squint for a moment as his eyes adjusted to the sudden change. Blinking several times, he hoped his eyes were playing tricks on him because there, hanging from one of the exposed beams in the ceiling was Joseph Miles.

Chapter Fifty-Seven

"Please tell me you haven't been here all night," Ben said as he walked into his office and found Drew sitting behind the desk with folders from Tommy's 1981 case file spread out in front of him. Ben didn't mind that his assistant had made himself at home behind his desk, he was more concerned that the young man was getting sucked into something with which it would be better if he wasn't involved.

So consumed by what he'd been reading, Drew was startled when Ben spoke to him from the doorway.

"What? No. I've only been here for about..." He looked at his watch, "...an hour or so."

"It's six-thirty, Drew. When did you go home last night?"

"If I tell you, you're just going to be upset. So, let's just skip over that part. I think I found something."

Ben motioned for Drew to remain in the big leather chair behind the desk, and he took one of the guest chairs.

"Sir, did you see Joseph Miles' autopsy photos?"

"Of course."

"When?"

"Excuse me?"

"When did you see the autopsy photos? There were none in Sheriff Mason's files. His copy of the autopsy report wasn't a complete copy. It was missing the photos."

Ben thought for a moment. "I would have seen them after the autopsy was performed. I must have."

"Are you sure?"

Ben got up and walked around behind his desk. Opening the bottom drawer, he removed his own copy of the Spring Strangler file. It was nowhere near as large as Tommy's. He'd only made copies of the official paperwork and reports. He hadn't collected the news articles and personal histories that his partner had.

Flipping through the pages, he came to the section relating to Miles and his suicide. Pulling out the autopsy report, he realized that he didn't have copies of the photos either.

"I swear I've seen the photos, Drew."

"Well, after reading the written autopsy report yesterday—which, by the way, I feel wasn't too thorough—I wanted to see the actual photos for myself. So I had them pulled from the archives and sent up."

Ben sat back down. He wasn't sure where Drew was going with this, but he was willing to go along for the ride.

The corporal pulled the old black-and-white photos out from under a stack of papers. "First of all, I'm shocked that these even still exist. I thought everything had been digitalized but low and behold, I have here the original photos from 1981."

Drew was talking pretty fast, even for him. It was obvious he thought he'd found something. Ben sat quietly, giving him a chance to get to the point.

"After Miles killed himself," Drew said, using air quotes, "Chief Stanley and Mayor Oland said that's all anyone needed for proof that he was the killer. Guilt and the thought of getting caught drove him to suicide."

"That and there were no other murders after," Ben added.

"Fair enough." Drew shuffled the photos in front of him. "I haven't had much experience with this, so I did a little research this morning and made a few phone calls."

Ben cocked his head. "It's six-thirty, who could you have called this early?"

Drew ignored the question.

"When someone commits suicide by hanging themselves, the marks on the neck basically form a 'V' shape starting under the jaw and going up behind the ears." He drew an imaginary line with his fingers along his own neck.

Nodding in agreement, Ben started wondering how much coffee Drew had drank that morning and where this was all going.

"But," he continued excitedly, "when someone is strangled to death by someone else—like in the case of the three victims in '81—the ligature marks on the neck go around in a circle."

"Right," Ben agreed slowly.

Drew stood and handed the autopsy photos across the desk to his boss.

Ben took the old black and white photos and held them up. He instantly saw what Drew had found. A cold chill ran down his spine. Ben shot to his feet as the realization sunk in.

"There are *both* kinds of marks on Joseph Miles's neck," Ben said.

"Exactly. Which means…"

"Someone strangled him, then hung him up to make it look like suicide."

"Miles wasn't the killer," the two said in unison.

Chapter Fifty-Eight

"I can't believe this," Ben said, pacing back and forth across the office. "How did we miss this?"

"Sir, did you ever actually see the autopsy photos?" Drew asked.

Ben closed his eyes and tried to think back. But after looking at hundreds, if not thousands, of crime scene and autopsy photos over forty years, he couldn't say for certain. He certainly thought he'd seen the photos at the time. He remembered how quickly everything happened after he and Tommy found Miles hanging in his apartment. Chief Stanley and Captain Brent had insisted on closing the case. The mayor was only too happy that he could report to the press that there would be no more killings. It was all a blur.

"Drew, I don't know if I ever saw these photos." Ben slumped down in the chair. How could he have missed something like this? "I guess it's possible with all the pressure to say the case was officially closed, neither Tommy nor I ever followed up."

"Why would you have?" Drew asked, understanding what his boss was thinking. "If Chief Stanley told you the case was over, the case was over. From what you've told me about the guy, it was his way or the highway."

"But do you know what this means? If Joseph Miles was killed—presumably by the same person who killed Beverly Baker, Linda Carlson, and Penny Moss—that means the real murder got away. And Tommy and I let him."

"I don't suppose it would help if I said you were young and just doing what you were told?"

Ben was silent. He was playing through everything in his head. How could he have let this happen? The realization that because of his inattention, a killer had been on the loose for almost forty years made him sick to his stomach. The odds were pretty good that Tommy had also been murdered by the same person all these years later.

Drew could tell that his boss, his mentor, was tearing himself up inside. What had happened was in the past. And at the time, there could have been a hundred different reasons why they never got to see the photos.

"Sir…"

"I know, Drew. You're going to tell me this wasn't my fault." Ben sighed. "Everything was wrapped up in such a neat package for us. There would have been no reason to think twice about a murderer and sexual predator taking his own life if he thought we were about to figure out he was behind all the killings. We were all distracted. Exactly what the real killer wanted."

"I might not have said it all in those words, but that's pretty close. But doesn't all this mean we might have a better chance of figuring out who killed…um, who…"

"It's okay, Drew, I can handle it. Yes, this might help us figure out who killed Tommy. Except for the fact we're not the ones investigating his murder."

"We have to let the Sheriff's Department know what we found."

"True," Ben said with what Drew thought could be a slight twinkle in his eye. "But since there's no statute of limitation on murder…"

"And since all the original murders happened in Parker City…" Drew said, pretty sure he knew where his boss was going with this.

"We *can* investigate those. And if we figure out who the real killer was…"

"We figure out who killed Sheriff Mason."

The last fifteen minutes had been an emotional rollercoaster for Ben. Thinking he'd allowed the killer to get away only to come back and murder his best friend all these years later was almost more than he could bear. But quickly switching gears and looking at the situation in a different way, it provided the opening he needed to join the investigation into Tommy's death. Even if that wasn't the official case on which he was working. For the first time in the last few days, Ben felt hope.

He could already see the wheels turning in Drew's head as well, and just as he was about to give his assistant some directions, his cell phone began chirping. Looking at the caller ID, he saw that it was his deputy chief, Commander Channing.

"Morning, Paul," Ben said, answering the phone. "If you're looking for me, I'm already in the office."

Drew could only hear the chief's side of the conversation, but he could tell something was wrong by the expression on Ben's face.

Chapter Fifty-Nine

Then...

No more than an hour after the rain subsided, the dark clouds covering Parker City had completely vanished, revealing one of the brightest bluest skies Ben could remember ever seeing. It was a stark contrast to the scene upstairs in Joseph Miles's apartment.

He'd needed some fresh air, so had ducked out for a few minutes. Sitting on the stoop in front of Miles's building, he was trying to make sense of everything that had happened over the last few days. He was already mentally writing the report he was going to have to file. This was certainly not how he ever imagined his first big case turning out. Not that he'd thought his first "big case" was going to be a triple murder investigation either.

Discovering Miles hanging in his apartment had surprised both he and Tommy. Ben hadn't expected him to simply confess and go quietly, but suicide just didn't seem to fit his personality. In their first meeting at the high school, he could tell the teacher was too smug for his own good. He was young, cocky, and thought he could talk his way out of anything. Ben would have bet money on the fact the teacher would try and convince them it was all a misunderstanding. Or simply resist arrest. He and Tommy had been prepared for that.

It just went to show there was no way to actually predict a person's behavior when push came to shove. It wasn't uncommon for a cornered suspect to take their own life. But how did Joseph Miles know they would be coming for him? Why hadn't he just run?

There were still too many unanswered questions.

After discovering Miles's body, he and Tommy had quickly regrouped. They'd swept the apartment one more time to make sure no one else was there and, from what they could tell, determined that all of the doors and windows were locked. It appeared to be a pretty straightforward case of suicide. Almost textbook.

Tommy radioed it in to the station and requested assistance, while Ben started going through Miles's rooms looking for evidence to tie him to the murders. With the majority of the department's resources still dealing with the flash flooding from that morning, the response to their call was not as quick as Ben would have liked. But it did give them time to find some disturbing material.

In Miles's nightstand, Ben found a stack of Polaroid photos. There were over two dozen pictures of naked young women. Linda Carlson and Penny Moss were in the collection, along with a couple of others who they'd have to identify but were clearly around the same age. Murderer or not, the man had been a sexual predator preying on his students. The thought of him having a relationship with not one, but four girls turned Ben's stomach.

Taking the photos from his partner, Tommy said, "Well, this definitely connects him to Linda and Penny." Looking around, he held a couple of the pictures up to show they'd been taken there in Miles's bedroom.

"None of Beverly Baker, though," Ben pointed out.

"You didn't think it was going to be that easy, did you? I'm sure we'll find something to link the cases. We just need to keep looking."

It shouldn't have surprised either of them that Captain Brent was the first to arrive. He'd still been at the Moss crime scene wrapping up the investigation there, so was only a few blocks away. When he entered the apartment, he looked tired but was still very alert. Tucking his sunglasses into his pocket, his eyes scanned the room. Ben wondered what he was thinking; the man had one of the best poker faces.

Taking the captain into the bedroom so he could see Miles for himself,

Brent listened as Ben and Tommy began filling him in on what had happened since they left the Moss crime scene. As Ben was handing over the Polaroids, there was a commotion in the hallway that attracted all of their attentions. It was the medical examiner who, just like Brent, had come straight from the previous scene.

"You boys out here in Parker are keeping us pretty busy. We might have to open an office out here if this keeps up," the disheveled medical assistant said as he huffed into the apartment carrying his heavy kit. "At least it would keep me from having to drive back and forth from Baltimore every day."

They all ignored the comments.

Ben was thankful that they'd be able to take Miles's body down as soon as the M.E. finished his examination. It had been rather awkward searching the room with him hanging there, but they weren't going to touch the body. Apparent suicide or not, the state's medical examiner needed to make the final call.

Using the distraction, Ben excused himself so that he could step outside and clear his head. He was beginning to feel slightly claustrophobic in the apartment. Tommy could answer any more of Brent's questions.

Letting the sun warm his face, a few deep breaths began to relieve some of the growing tension in his chest. Ben stood and stretched his legs. The smell of the wet grass on a spring day—even if it was slightly cooler than normal—carried with it a sense of calm.

By the time he'd made it back upstairs, Miles's body had been taken down and the M.E. was conducting his initial examination.

Captain Brent handed Ben a folded piece of paper. "This was in his pocket. Suicide note. He confesses to all three of the murders."

In his last act before taking his own life, Joseph Miles scribbled out a full confession. He admitted to being the Spring Strangler. The handwriting was barely legible, but there it was in black and white.

Chapter Sixty

As word began to spread throughout the PCPD that Joseph Miles, the lead suspect in the Spring Strangler case, had committed suicide, any officer who was available made his way to the Chestnut Hill Manor apartment complex. Some had been assigned to help go through the apartment and collect evidence. Other just wanted to see firsthand what a serial killer's lair looked like. At least that's what Ben thought he'd overheard Buck LuCoco say to a couple other patrolmen lingering in the corridor outside Miles's apartment. Instead of saying anything, Ben just let it go. He didn't have the time or energy.

Ben was already frustrated with the fact the medical examiner had been in and out so quickly. No sooner had he taken Miles's body down and done a brief examination, he had it loaded in the van, along with Penny Moss, and was on his way back to Baltimore. The M.E. said it looked like suicide to him, but there would be an autopsy to confirm that one way or the other. Of course, that had been said just as Chief Stanley arrived.

"He knew he was going to get caught and didn't want to go to jail," the chief barked, chomping on his cigar. "Of course he offed himself. Makes perfect sense to me."

It was clear to everyone that Stanley was thrilled with the outcome. So much so, he actually told Ben and Tommy they'd done a "decent" job on the case.

"High praise," Tommy said with a heavy dose of sarcasm in his voice when the two were out of earshot of anyone else.

"The mayor's going to hold a press conference later today. Brent thinks we should be there," Ben said.

"You know Stanley'll be the one doing all the talking."

"I'm alright with that," Ben said, looking around the now empty bedroom. "I'm still not satisfied."

"The missing Beverly Baker connection? Yeah. I'm with you. But Stanley isn't going to let us keep investigating. All anyone cares about is that he confessed."

Ben looked up at the beam from which Miles had hung himself and asked, "The rope he used, the M.E.'s going to compare that to the marks on the girls' throats?"

"He said they'd compare the pattern, but it looked pretty close to me. It was a pretty common piece of rope. He could have picked it up at Hechingers."

Ben rubbed his face. Was he overthinking this? Should he be looking a gift horse in the mouth? Miles closed the case for them. And by him committing suicide, there'd be no trial in which some lawyer might be able to find a legal loophole to get him off on some technicality. He just hoped the nagging feeling that they were overlooking something would go away.

Chapter Sixty-One

Now...

Chief Ben Winters found himself once again on his way to a crime scene. He'd seen them all and worked on almost every type of case in his career. At this point, very little surprised him. But even after more than forty years on the job, he still had the same feeling. Adrenaline, anxiety, curiosity, frustration, and, God help him, excitement. They all combined to sharpen his senses and prepare him for whatever he was about to walk in to.

It didn't matter what the crime, there were still routines and procedures to be followed. Ben liked that. Ben liked order. Crime, in the abstract sense, was disorder and uncontrollable. But solving crimes was done by putting things in order.

Ben realized he was just trying to distract himself as his Interceptor, driven by Corporal Collins, sped through the streets of Parker City on its way to the former mayor's residence on Grandview Avenue. His was the first in a phalanx of three cruisers on their way to the scene.

Rush hour, both in the morning and evening, was becoming more and more congested. As the city grew, so did the workforce. As the workforce increased, so did the number of cars on the street. Ben remembered a time when you could drive from one end of Parker to the other in about fifteen minutes. Now, if you wanted to be on time, it was good to give yourself at least a half an hour.

The trio of police vehicles was having no difficulty maneuvering through the steady stream of cars, though. The screaming sirens helped to cut through the early morning traffic. It was still taking too long, Ben thought as he fidgeted in the passenger seat.

As was protocol, Commander Channing had been alerted to the call that came from the Olands' house that morning. He was always notified first when something potentially "big" happened. It was then up to him as to whether or not to involve the chief. Nine times out of ten, it was something that rose to the level of having to bring the city's top cop in right away. Even though Paul Channing knew that Ben would want to be brought in on every call—no matter how big or small—he was the chief of a top-rated police force made up of people who could handle anything thrown at them. However, while driving to work, when he received the call that Charlie Oland had been found bludgeoned to death in his study, Channing couldn't call Ben fast enough.

Drew deftly weaved his way through the morning traffic, guiding the squad cars behind him on a path that took them from the bustling downtown of Parker City to one of its most historic and sought-after residential neighborhoods.

A pair of PCPD cruisers and two unmarked sedans were already parked in front of the Olands' Victorian mansion. Thankfully, it didn't appear that any of the neighbors had noticed the unusual police presence yet, so the street was free of the usual crowd of onlookers that needed to be contained. Knowing that was bound to change, two uniformed officers were stationed on the front lawn, one of whom signaled for Drew to park in the driveway.

Ben was out of the car and heading for the house before Drew could even shut off the engine. The younger officer had to double-time it to catch up. Reaching the front door, Ben stopped and turned to his assistant.

"I need you to…" he started to say, then stopped. He never finished what he was saying, just turned and opened the door.

Drew closed the door behind the chief as he disappeared into the house. He knew what Ben wanted him to do. First, he made a phone call to Lieutenant Katharine Rogers, supervisor of the PCPD's Detective Unit.

Then he called her commander, Dwayne Lewis, captain of the department's Criminal Investigation Division. When the victim was someone as high profile as the city's extremely popular former mayor, the top brass was called in immediately.

With Rogers and Lewis on their way, Drew turned his attention to the uniformed officers stationed on the front lawn and the additional patrolmen who'd followed him and the chief from the station. He knew Patrol would send a supervisory officer to take command. Drew figured no less than the captain of the division would arrive soon. Until then, technically a senior patrol officer in the department, he was the highest ranking uniformed officer, so would coordinate securing the outside of the crime scene. Drew had been trained by the best and had no intension of letting his mentor down.

As he handed out assignments to the assembled patrolmen, he couldn't help but think about the situation. Why would someone kill the former mayor? Sure, he was still something of a figure around town, but nothing like he was in the past. Charlie Oland held no real power any longer. Could someone have been sending a message to his son, the current mayor and a candidate for congress? Or, Drew shuddered to think, did this have something to do with Sheriff Mason's murder and the Spring Strangler case?

Chapter Sixty-Two

Walking into the foyer of the Oland family manse triggered a flashback for Ben to the very first time he'd stepped foot in the home decades earlier. It was still one of the most stately homes he'd ever seen, even though it looked nothing like it did all those years ago. Ben remembered that Charlie Oland told him how his wife was always redecorating. It was still a grand entrance, definitely meant for show.

Then he saw the one piece he still remembered, the suit of armor standing guard outside Charlie Oland's study. Not that it had done its job last night, he thought, stepping into the room. Books and papers were tossed all around the room. Lamps lay on the floor with their cords pulled out of the electric sockets. It looked like someone had been looking for something. That's the initial impression Ben got. But looks could be deceiving, he reminded himself.

Charlie Oland's body lay on the floor next to his desk. Crouched next to it was a man Ben had come to respect very much over the last several years. He was on the younger side, but they'd all been there once. Detective Sergeant Gabe Wilson, head of the Robbery-Homicide Squad. Ben was glad to see he was already on the scene.

Detective Wilson stood when he saw Ben. "Morning, sir."

"Detective. How bad is it?"

"You can see for yourself. He took a beating."

Ben slowly stepped toward the body, careful not to touch or disturb anything. Charlie Oland was lying on his stomach, sprawled out on the study's hardwood floor with a pool of blood spreading out from under his head. His wounds were impossible to miss. What was left of the once thick mane of hair was completely covered with blood. It was a grisly sight from the back, so Ben was afraid of what the former mayor's face might look like when they were finally able to roll him over.

"I know it looks like the place was tossed, like someone was looking for something. Possibly a burglary gone wrong," Wilson said, "but this looks very personal to me."

Much like Drew, Gabe Wilson was someone on whom Ben had had his eye for a while. He was smart and intuitive. Two qualities a good detective must possess. And he was right about what they were looking at.

Such a brutal attack wasn't usually something that just happened on the spur of the moment. Criminal Psychology 101 would say something this violent meant the killer had an intense reason to do this to the victim. Or he/she was completely crazy. But for now, Ben was going to play the odds.

"What happened?" Ben asked, looking around the room for the murder weapon.

"Commander Channing and Detective Moser are taking the statements now, but earlier this morning when the Olands' housekeeper—one Mia Phillips—arrived, she noticed that the light was on here in the study. She assumed the former mayor had gotten up early and was in here reading the paper like he did some days. Apparently, he still read the actual paper," Wilson threw in. "Ms. Phillips came in to say hello and ask if the mayor wanted some coffee. When she came in, this is what she found.

"She started screaming, which woke up Mrs. Oland, who had gone to bed early last night because she wasn't feeling well. Mrs. Oland called 9-1-1 and there was a patrol car on the other side of the park." The detective motioned out the front window toward Jefferson Park across the street. There was a reason the street was named Grand*view* Avenue. All of the houses lucky enough to bear an address on this street had stunning park scenes right outside their windows.

"Officer Fischer got here in a matter of minutes," Wilson continued. "Realizing whose house this was and who the victim appeared to be, he called in the cavalry."

"That's when Commander Channing was notified," Ben said, "and you were called in."

"I was on my way to the station," the detective said. "Not really the best way to start the day."

"Did you find the murder weapon?"

"Yes. This award," he said, pointing at a bloody geometric crystal statue lying on the floor behind Charlie Oland's desk. "I'm hoping CSU will be able to get a print off it."

Ben knelt down so he could get a closer look. The trophy was from the Parker County Chamber of Commerce thanking Oland for all the work he had done throughout his career for the businesses in and around the city. The deep red smears of blood stood out sharply on the bluish crystal. He saw lots of streaks and smudges, but nothing that looked like a fingerprint to the naked eye.

He hadn't wanted to think that this could be somehow related to Tommy's murder, but how could that thought not have crossed his mind? If Oland was killed by the same person, they hadn't found any prints on the knife used to attack Tommy, so he wasn't going to hold his breath that they'd find any on the award.

Chapter Sixty-Three

As an octogenarian, Mary Ann Oland was still a stunning woman. Her bright red hair, a feature for which she had always been known, was as vibrant as ever. Whether it was natural or the product of hours in a salon chair, only she knew. Always a strong woman—the power behind the throne, many said—the city's former first lady was in tears as Ben found her and Commander Paul Channing in the sitting room down the hall.

It was the same sitting room in which he'd first met the woman and her twins. Instead of the flowery and pastel décor, the room, like all the rest in the house, had been redecorated several times. The walls were now covered with a sage color and paintings of country scenes. The furniture, cream colored and overstuffed, was plush and comfortable. It was all soft and elegant. Ben always had the feeling this was the room in which Mary Ann Oland must have spent most of her time.

When she saw Ben standing in the doorway, Mary Ann used the hand stitched embroidered handkerchief to wipe her eyes. Her face was a mixture of unbearable anguish and disbelief. Without saying a single word, she asked Ben, "How could this have happened?"

For the last several days, Ben had been living with the pain of losing his oldest and closest friend. It was, without question, one of the worst feelings he'd ever experienced. But the thought of losing Natalie was unthinkable. He couldn't even begin to imagine what Mary Ann was feeling, having been married to Charlie for sixty years. Just thinking about the possibility of Nat not being there made his chest tighten to a point where he couldn't breathe.

Shaking off the horrifying specter of losing the love of his life, Ben nodded to his deputy and took a seat next to Mary Ann Oland. The two had become acquaintances over the years, as much as he and the former mayor had. They'd see each other at functions around town, attend some of the same parties, so were friendly but far from friends. Which is why Mary Ann reaching over and taking Ben's hand in hers was surprising.

The deputy chief decided to give the two a few minutes alone, so ducked out to find Detective Moser and see if he'd learned anything from the housekeeper.

As the latch on the door clicked shut, Ben started to say how sorry he was for her loss but couldn't get the words outs before Mary Ann threw herself into his arms, sobbing.

Sometimes, the job of a cop was to be tough. Other times, they literally needed to provide a shoulder to cry on. It was clear Ben wasn't going to be able to get any information out of her at the moment, so thought it better to offer her some comfort. After several more minutes of tears, Mary Ann began to calm down. Ben could feel the tension in her body start to easy slightly. He was sure there'd be another wave of crying to come, so decided to see if he could get one or two questions answered.

Ben didn't want to push too hard, he just wanted to know what had happened the night before. According to her, it was a normal evening. Except for the fact she wasn't feeling well, so had taken some medicine and gone to bed shortly after dinner. Even if she hadn't gone to bed early, she said it wasn't uncommon for her husband to stay up late watching television or reading. There were times he'd fall asleep on the sofa in his study and never make it to bed. When she woke up at three in the morning and he wasn't in bed, she never thought anything of it. She just rolled over and went back to sleep. The medicine had knocked her out, so she never heard anything after going to bed.

"Had Charlie said anything to you in the last few days about anything being out of the ordinary? Anything happening that he was concerned about?" Ben asked.

"Nothing that he told me about," she offered, trying to think of something that could help. "There was the business with the sheriff's death. He was upset about that."

"That shook us all up," Ben said.

"Of course it did. I'm sorry," Mary Ann said, clearly realizing with whom she was speaking.

Ben gave her a gentle smile to let her know it was all right.

Squeezing her hand, Ben said, "I'm going to have someone come in to sit with you. I'm just going to step out to speak with my detectives and see if they've found anything. Can I have someone get you anything?"

She shook her head and turned to look out into the garden. Spring was in full bloom just outside. Flowers of every color in the rainbow looked back at them through the window.

"I've always thought you had a beautiful garden," Ben said. "Ever since the very first time I saw it."

"Is that what this is about?"

Ben had turned to leave but was stopped in his tracks by her question. He looked back at her. Her gaze still focused out the window.

"I'm sorry?" Ben wasn't sure he'd heard her correctly.

Slowly turning, she looked directly into his eyes. Gone was the sadness, replaced by a steely determination. She'd had her moment to grieve. It was time for her to regain her composure.

"Is that what this is about?" she asked again. "The first time you saw my garden was when you came here to question Gregory about that girl's murder. I may be old, but I haven't forgotten. The Spring Strangler...does my husband's murder have something to do with that? First the sheriff, your former partner, now Charlie? You may think I was just a politician's wife, but it isn't hard to connect the dots and put the pieces together. Two very public men have now been killed and the only thing they had in common was that damn case. Don't tell me you haven't already made the same connection, Ben."

He wasn't sure what to say. His gut was telling him that everything that had happened in the last few days must be related to the '81 case. But there was no proof to back that up. And at that moment, he had no idea why anyone involved in the Strangler case would have any reason to kill the former mayor. Unless he'd been involved somehow, but he'd never been a suspect. Things weren't making any sense. Maybe he was wrong and Charlie Oland's murder had nothing to do with Tommy's? Tommy had been strangled. Oland was bludgeoned.

Ben's head was starting to spin.

"I have no idea if the two murders are connected to each other or the case from 1981," Ben finally answered. "I just don't know."

Chapter Sixty-Four

en found Detective Wilson briefing Captain Lewis and Lieutenant Rogers in the hallway. Lewis, a bulldog looking man, was gesturing excitedly as Wilson simply nodded his head. Rogers, a much less excitable figure than her captain, raised an eyebrow at whatever he'd just said. Ben wanted to speak with Detective Wilson again, but first, he needed to find Commander Channing.

The deputy chief was in the study overseeing the work of the Crime Scene Unit. They'd arrived in full force with all of their equipment and personnel and, as instructed, immediately began processing the scene. Several additional uniformed offers had arrived and were assisting the CSU techs.

Even though there was a flurry of activity happening in the grand old manor, it was completely organized. Everyone had their job, and each job had a purpose. Every inch of the former mayor's study was being photographed and dusted for prints. The papers strewn all over the floor were being collected and bagged to take back to the station, as was the award which had been used to kill Charlie Oland.

The medical examiner, who Ben hadn't realized was already there working, was performing her initial examination of the body. She'd be able to give them an idea of when Oland had been killed so they could start building a timeline. Having an idea of when the murder was committed was always an important starting point. When Mary Ann Oland had gone to bed between seven and seven-thirty, her husband was still alive. About twelve hours later, when Mia Phillips arrived for work, he was dead.

Hopefully they could narrow that window.

What would help was if the uniformed officers canvassing the neighborhood could turn something up. Going from door-to-door, up and down the street, they were looking for someone who had seen anything out of place the previous evening. Ideally, one of the neighbors had seen someone coming or going from the Olands' house.

Ben watched from the doorway as the CSU team worked its way around the study. Next to him on the wall were framed newspaper articles about the family from over the years. One of which was the feature from the *Herald-Dispatch*'s Home and Garden section about the major renovation the house underwent in the early '80s.

Something in the photo caught Ben's attention. It was a picture of Charlie, Mary Ann, and the twins standing together in the parlor across the hall. Mary Ann, with a bright smile, was holding a stack of fabric swatches, the mayor, a roll of wallpaper. It was obviously a posed picture. Neither Greg nor Gary, standing behind their parents, looked too excited. There was something about the photo nagging at the back of Ben's mind. It wasn't like he hadn't seen it before. There was a copy of it in Tommy's file. And he remembered when they'd come to interview Greg about Linda Carlson's death, how the house was in the process of being renovated. So why was this photo bothering him now?

Asking one of the CSU techs for a pair of latex gloves so he wouldn't contaminate anything with his own fingerprints, he was about to take the framed article off the wall to get a closer look when Commander Channing cleared his throat. Ben had been so engrossed in the photo he hadn't noticed the deputy chief walk over to him with a piece of paper in a plastic evidence page.

"Ben, I think you should see this," Channing said. "They found this in the fireplace. It didn't burn all the way. And I don't think anyone here is old enough to understand what this means."

Puzzled, Ben took the bag. The paper was old to start with, but after someone had tried to burn it, it was now charred as well. The edges had all been burned away, but there was still more than enough left to see that it was a rather explicit love letter. A love letter to "Charlie"…from "Beverly."

It felt like his heart stopped mid-beat. Yet his mind was racing. Puzzle pieces that had been floating around in his subconscious for almost four decades were beginning to fall into place. Just as Ben was about to instruct his deputy chief to personally take the piece of evidence back to the station and make sure it was safely locked away, the unmistakable voice of Greg Oland could be heard outside cutting through all the commotion. Ben had been dreading this moment.

Chapter Sixty-Five

Then...

The massive headline on the front page of the *Herald-Dispatch* read "Strangler Commits Suicide!" The paper, through the article's author—Roger Benedict—was declaring an end to the terror of the last several days. At the same time, the article made certain to point out that even though the police had determined the identity of the Spring Strangler, it was the killer himself who took his own life, thus ending his killing spree.

Ben folded the paper and tossed it on his desk. If he'd been able to light a fire in the trash can, he would have burned the damn thing. But with his luck, the entire building would have caught on fire and burned to the ground. With as many people who smoked in the building, he was amazed there hadn't been a fire already.

He knew he should have been feeling better about the fact the case was over. But three women were dead and the killer, while being stopped, hadn't really been brought to justice. At least in his mind. Though there were many others in the city who disagreed.

The press conference the day before, which had been attended by press from all over the region, including the *Washington Post*, had been a hugely successful for the mayor and police chief. Yes, Ben and Tommy's efforts were mentioned, but in the way Stanley framed it, one would think he'd been out on the streets personally going door-to-door hunting down the killer.

After filing his reports yesterday, Ben had gone home early. Not that he'd really been given a choice. Captain Brent told him in no uncertain terms he should go home and get some sleep. Unfortunately, getting sleep and recharging his batteries was the last thing he'd been able to accomplish. All he did was lie in bed and rerun every minute of the last few days in his head.

Tommy, for his part, hadn't really said much after the two finally left Joseph Miles's apartment, except to offer to write up the reports. Something he never did. He'd spend most of the afternoon up until the press conference quietly organizing the case file for when it was ready to be sent off to Room B-114, the Records and Archives Room in the bowels of the building.

How he spent his evening, Tommy wouldn't tell Ben, but his partner expected it was in the company of Shirley from Dispatch or some other lucky lady he'd crossed paths with at some point. But when Ben got to the office that morning, Tommy was already at his desk typing away on the computer that he hated so much.

Even though the case was now officially closed, as per Chief Stanley's decree, Ben was still waiting to see the autopsy reports on both Penny Moss and Joseph Miles. However, since the case wasn't a top priority any longer, he wasn't expecting them in for a few days. Ben just wanted to make sure they hadn't missed anything. He wanted to cross all his T's and dot all his I's before *he* put the case to rest.

There were several telephone messages waiting for him on his desk. All were from reporters looking to speak with him and Tommy about the case. One was from the *San Francisco Chronicle*. Ben was surprised anyone on the west coast was interested in what had happened in Parker City. But then again, San Francisco had been faced with its own series of horrifying murders not too long ago. It could have created an unhealthy fascination with the macabre, Ben thought. He tore all of the messages up and threw them away.

"Is this how it feels after closing a big case?" Tommy asked, throwing a crumbled up paper ball into the trashcan like he was shooting hoops. "Shouldn't we be feeling more excited?"

Ben knew exactly what he meant. If nothing else, there should have been a feeling of relief knowing there would be no more murders. But Ben just felt empty. Joseph Miles hanging himself wasn't the closure he'd wanted.

"Some of the guys are getting together for drinks across the street after shift. They asked if we wanted to go."

Ben slowly turned, raised his eyebrow at his partner, and said, "They asked if *we* wanted to go."

Tommy just shrugged.

Before Ben had a chance to say anything else, his phone rang. It was Lieutenant Dennis.

"Winters, two guys just robbed the Fifth Street branch of South Mountain B&T. Brent wants you and Mason to get over there. Don't fuck this up."

Chapter Sixty-Six

Now...

Ben finally made it back to his office after first, an hour of talking to Greg Oland and filling him in on what little information they'd been able to collect in such a short amount of time, and then doing the same with Gary Oland. The difference in the two encounters was that the mayor listened to what his police chief had to say and seemed genuinely stunned and upset by his father's murder. His brother, on the other hand, was a pompous ass. Gary shouted at Ben, threatened to have Commander Channing fired, and berated Captain Lewis, Lieutenant Rogers, and Detective Wilson straight down the line.

It wasn't until his brother finally had enough and, uncharacteristically, stood up to his twin and told him in no uncertain terms he needed to shut his mouth or he'd have him removed from the scene, that Gary relented and ended his tirade. Ben still couldn't get over the difference in the two Oland boys, how they could be twins and look exactly alike yet have such completely different personalities.

Greg, whether it was sincere or not, always seemed caring and compassionate. Sometimes to a fault. Sure, he was a politician and could give a barn burning speech, but for the most part, he was reserved and reflective. Gary was the pit bull who attacked first and never asked any questions later. His natural instinct was to go on the offensive. It was easy to see why Greg Oland had become the public face of the family, and Gary worked behind the scenes.

Talking with the brothers, Ben could only give them what information he had at the time, which wasn't that much since the scene was still being processed. What he hadn't told them about was the love letter that had been found burned in the fireplace. He'd also instructed the deputy chief not to discuss the piece of evidence either. It would be in the report, but he didn't want anyone knowing about it yet.

In the last few hours, two huge pieces of information had been revealed. First, Joseph Miles hadn't killed himself. In all likelihood, that meant he was not the Spring Strangler. Second, Charlie Oland and Beverly Baker had had an affair. With the date of the letter burned off, for all Ben knew, they could have been having the affair up until the day she'd been killed.

If they'd had that information back in 1981, how would that have changed the way he and Tommy were looking at the case?

That certainly connected Charlie Oland to Beverly Baker. If she was threatening to go public with the affair, he would want to keep her quiet. But what would his reason for killing Linda Carlson and Penny Moss have been?

Ben sat tapping his fingers on the desk as he let the wheels turn in his head.

There was one person throughout the entire case that always seemed to know more than anyone else. It pained Ben to admit, but he needed to talk with Roger Benedict and have a real conversation, not a head-butting, sparring match. Thinking back, he remembered the reporter saying he'd recently spoken with Tommy? Could Benedict be the "someone" Tommy spoke to about the case?

Ben picked up his phone and hit the button for Drew's extension.

"Yes, sir?"

"Didn't you say that Roger Benedict called and wanted to set up an appointment?"

Ben could hear his assistant typing something on his keyboard. "Yes. He called last Tuesday evening." Then cautiously asked, "Why?"

Knowing the history between the two men, he was surprised that his boss wanted to speak to him.

"I need to meet with him. I have a feeling he's the person Tommy spoke to that got him thinking about the case. Can I get that number?"

"Do you want me to call him and set up a meeting?" Drew asked.

Ben sighed. "No. I need to do this one myself."

Chapter Sixty-Seven

Before meeting with Roger Benedict that evening, Ben changed out of his uniform into a spare button-down shirt and slacks he kept in the office. The chief's uniform tended to attract too much attention. So with his Ravens cap and windbreaker on, he hoped to blend into the crowd as much as possible when he met with the editor. Neither man wanted to meet at the others' office, so they agreed on the Java Bean—a coffee shop literally halfway between the Parker City Police Department and the *Herald-Dispatch* offices.

Usually an extremely busy spot during the workday, at dinner time the crowd thinned out considerably. There were only a couple other patrons in the shop when Ben arrived. One was clearly a frazzled college student working on a paper. She'd practically built a fort out of books around her table, making it clear she did not want to be disturbed. The other was a woman in a sharp business suit sipping a latte and scrolling through screens on her tablet. She didn't need the physical barrier telling people to leave her alone. The message was clear from her demeanor.

At a table in the back corner of the shop, almost completely out of view, Ben saw Benedict sitting behind a copy of that day's *Herald-Dispatch*. Ben had to seriously think about the last time he'd seen a physical copy of the paper. He'd joined all the rest who liked getting their news online. Plus, after his dealings with the *Herald-Dispatch* over the years, he preferred not to give them any of his money through a subscription. His distaste for the paper was mostly because of the man he was about to sit down with.

The irony of the situation was not lost on Ben. During the murders back in '81, it infuriated Ben that the reporter seemed to have more information than he and Tommy. Now he needed that information and was glad someone might have the missing piece of the puzzle he needed. Even if it was Benedict.

Before sitting down, Ben ordered a black coffee from the barista behind the counter. At first, she seemed slightly confused when he didn't ask for some half-caf, no-foam, extra espresso shot type of drink. She wasn't used to pouring a simple cup of black coffee.

As Ben slid into the seat opposite the former reporter, Benedict folded the paper he'd been reading and laid it on the table between them. Ben smiled when he saw the fancy looking beverage in front of Benedict. It figured.

"So, you wanted to talk?" Roger Benedict started. "It's probably been a hell of a day for you, Chief. Do you have any leads on who killed Oland?"

There was just something in his eyes that made Ben want to punch him in the face. He was goading him. It was the same tone he always used when he appeared at one of the crime scenes, like he knew something no one else did.

"First of all, thank you for agreeing to talk to me," Ben began, thinking a diplomatic, friendly approach may be the best way to get the information he needed. The less adversarial this conversation was, the better. "But this is all off the record. I'm not here for an interview. I'm here because I need to ask *you* a question."

Benedict's eyes narrowed as he leaned back in his seat.

"That's a twist. I'm a little surprised you didn't have any of your boys in blue and gray drag me down to the station. I seem to remember that happening once before."

"Look, there isn't time for this, Roger. You and I are too old and have seen and been through too much to keep playing these games."

Ben saw the expression on the other man's face completely change. The jackass smirk disappeared and was replaced with something Ben hadn't seen before. Could it be a look of understanding, perhaps? Obviously, Ben's tone and body language explained how serious the situation was.

"Ask away," Benedict said.

"Why did you originally leave Parker?"

That clearly wasn't the question the newspaper man was expecting. "After the articles I wrote about the Strangler case, I got a great offer from another paper. I didn't want to stick around Parker all my life. What were the odds something that big would ever happen around here again?"

It was always about the next big story with this guy, Ben thought. "Now you're back. I guess you've changed your mind about Parker."

"Well, Chief. You know as well as anyone how wrong I was about the kind of stories I could have kept writing if I stayed in town. I just didn't know that at the time. I would never have guessed what kind of dark secrets Parker City had buried."

Ben didn't want to get off topic. So he quickly asked, "Did you talk to Tommy recently?"

Benedict bit his lower lip before answering. "Yeah. The beginning of last week."

"Who called who?"

"What difference does that make?"

"A big difference. Did you call him or did he call you?"

"He called me. Like you, he said he had to ask me some questions."

Ben took a moment to think before he asked his next question.

"What did you ask you about?"

"Come on, Chief." Benedict's eyes narrowed. "You're supposed to be this great investigator. You can do better than that."

Niceties and trying to be diplomatic be damned. "Did he ask you if you were the Spring Strangler?"

Benedict laughed. "Tom Mason could be a pretty in-your-face guy, but no, he didn't ask me if I was the Strangler. Is that why you're here?"

"No. But if Tommy called you, then I know you *aren't* the Strangler. But you *were* at the top of our list of suspects at the time."

Benedict's brow wrinkled as he let that sink in. "You found the killer thirty years ago. And Joseph Miles killed himself. Why would the sheriff have asked me if I was the killer when I talked to him *last* week?"

The two men's eyes locked. Ben decided he needed to lay all his cards on the table.

"Tommy and I weren't one hundred percent satisfied with the way the case ended. We didn't think there was enough evidence to tie Miles to all three murders."

"Even though he left a suicide note?"

Nodding, Ben said, "Just recently, some information has come up. It calls into question whether he killed himself or whether someone murdered him and made it look like suicide." He could see that he finally had information the former reporter didn't. The tables had turned. So Ben pressed on. "What else did Tommy ask you?"

Benedict bit his lower lip again, stalling for time so he could think about what he'd just been told. After finishing what was left of his caramel macchiato, he said, "The sheriff asked if there was any information I had about anyone involved in the Strangler case that was never published. I thought it was kind of an odd question."

"Was there ever any information you had that you didn't publish?"

"Yes and no."

The frustration in Ben's voice was clear. "What's that supposed to mean?"

"Like I told the sheriff...I didn't know it at the time the murders were happening, but shortly *after* Miles hung himself, I was working on another... project and started hearing rumors that Beverly Baker had been having an affair with someone who couldn't afford the scandal if it ever came out. Boy, things were different back then. Nowadays, no one would care about an affair like that. Hell, most people just expect it."

"Who was she having the affair with?"

"Charlie Oland."

Hearing that, it all made sense. For whatever reason, it was the trigger Ben needed. The puzzle pieces were finally all fitting together. Charlie and Beverly...what had caught his eye in the photo at the Oland house...how Joseph Miles could have been killed and framed to look like the Strangler... the connection between the three victims! It all made sense to him now. It all *finally* made sense.

Chapter Sixty-Eight

The flood of emotions that continued to wash over Ben as he raced back to the station would have been impossible for him to put into words. In the last twelve hours, he'd discovered the crucial pieces of information that allowed him to solve a case almost forty years old—a case that had also cost the lives of his best friend and, in all probability, the city's popular former mayor.

After meeting with Benedict, he would have liked nothing more than to have left the coffee shop, called in his S.W.A.T. team, and raided the home of the real Spring Strangler. Unfortunately, he knew to be able to make an arrest, he was going to need the evidence to back it up. Which is why he needed to go through Tommy's case file one more time. After he did, he was certain he'd have everything he needed to bring down the man who killed Beverly Baker, Linda Carlson, Penny Moss, Joseph Miles, Charlie Oland… and Tommy.

The bright red-and-blue flashers on the dashboard gave the signal for all other cars on the road to let Ben pass. For the second time that day, Ben found himself weaving through Parker City's downtown traffic. Luckily, at dinnertime, it was much thinner than during morning rush hour. Ben still needed to be mindful of the pedestrians, however. At this hour, the sidewalks were filled with restaurant-goers coming to and from all of the fine eateries downtown. Anyone of who could decide not to cross the street at the corner and dart out between two parked cars in the middle of a block.

Easing past the Harlequin Performing Arts Center, Ben hit the button on the digital dash screen to call home. All he told Natalie was that he didn't know when he'd be home and not to wait up. She'd understand everything in the morning.

Once at the station, Ben took the stairs two at a time to get to his office. As he'd hoped, Drew was at his desk working. For once, Ben didn't say anything about him working through dinner. He was going to need his help.

In a rapid fire manner, Ben brought his assistant up to speed on what he'd learned.

Listening intently, hanging on the chief's every word, the corporal's eyes widened as Ben laid everything out for him. Thinking about it, it all made perfect sense now.

"What do you need me to do?" Drew asked.

Ben rattled off a list of items he needed—specific documents from Tommy's case file, the medical examiner's report Drew had obtained from the Sheriff's Department on Tommy's murder, and the remains of the love letter between Charlie Oland and Beverly Baker he'd sent back with Commander Channing.

Once Drew was off pulling together everything on his list, Ben scrolled through the contacts on his cell phone until he came to one of the many private numbers he'd acquired over all his years in law enforcement. He needed to call in a big favor from an old friend.

Chapter Sixty-Nine

One last time, Ben Winters reexamined the Spring Strangler case. This time, he had the information he didn't have in 1981, as well as nearly forty more years of experience. Had he and Tommy not been so young and inexperienced, had Chief Stanley and Mayor Oland not put the pressure on them to close the case, had one of them seen Joseph Miles's autopsy photos, maybe things would have turned out differently. But as they say, hindsight is always twenty-twenty.

There was no question in Ben's mind what he needed to do. Even though he was well aware of the firestorm, he would be bringing down on himself and the department. But since he was so close to retirement anyway, he thought he might as well go out with a bang.

As he gave Drew his final instructions, Ben buckled the shoulder holster he wore when he wasn't in his uniform, then pulled his windbreaker over it. Hopefully, there would be no need to flash the gun around. But just in case, he didn't want to be without it.

Once he left his office, everything seemed to happen in slow motion—leaving the building, getting into the car, turning into the evening flow of vehicles heading across the city.

No lights or sirens cleared the way this time. He didn't want to alert the killer and let him know he was coming. He'd gotten away with what he'd done for decades. The silent approach would allow him to keep thinking that. For once, Ben had the element of surprise on his side.

Pulling up in front of the house, Ben took a deep breath. He'd done this hundreds of times. There was no reason for this time to be any different.

Even though he was well aware that it was. Gritting his teeth, Ben pushed the door open, allowing the crisp spring night air to fill the car.

Ben walked along the cobblestone path leading from the sidewalk up to the house's front door. It was another of the city's stately homes that had been built just prior to the turn of the previous century. The property, surrounded by an intricately molded wrought-iron fence, consisted of the main house and a four car detached garage, separated by a brick courtyard. The mansion, renovated and rebuilt several times over its one hundred plus years, was a three-story life-sized brick dollhouse.

Ben noticed the lilacs blooming in the carved stone flower boxes on either side of the front door, which in itself was a work of art. He'd heard the story about it a few times. Hand carved by a craftsman in New England, the inset stained glass came from a church that had been sacked during the Revolutionary War.

Ringing the bell, Ben turned and looked down East Branch Avenue toward his own home several blocks away. The street lamps illuminated the historic homes, giving each its own magnificent glow as if it were the central feature in a Thomas Kinkade painting.

Hearing the door open behind him, Ben turned and came face to face with the man responsible for the death of his best friend. He had to resist the urge to pull his gun and deliver a criminal sentence right there on the front porch. Resist he did.

Instead, he said, "Greg, we need to talk," and walked past the mayor into the house.

Chapter Seventy

"Not that I mind you calling me 'Greg,'" he said, "but you've never done it before."

The mayor appeared far from his normal polished self. Ben hardly recognized the man standing before him. He looked older, the creases on his brow deeper with dark circles under his eyes. His powder blue dress shirt unbuttoned, its tails hanging freely over his belt revealing a white undershirt. No, this was not the Mayor Gregory Oland he was used to seeing.

His appearance would easily have been explained away by the horrific murder of one of his parents earlier today, except for his role in the killing.

"Do you have news about my father's…" He couldn't bring himself to finish the question.

Ignoring this, Ben asked one of his own. "Is Theresa home?"

"No. She's with my mother. I just came home to change. Why? Ben, what's wrong? Is this about my father?"

"In a manner of speaking," Ben answered, laying the folder he was carrying on the table in the center of the foyer.

"Chief, I don't know what that means, and it's getting late. Do you have a suspect or not? I'm really in no mood to play games."

"We do have a suspect. Yes," Ben answered coolly.

Ben never took his eyes off Oland. With a single finger, Ben flipped open the folder on the table.

After an uncomfortable moment of silence, Greg Oland finally asked, "Well? Who is it?"

"The same person who killed Tommy."

The blood drained from the mayor's face. "What?"

"The same person who killed Beverly Baker. And Linda Carlson. And Penny Moss. And the same person who killed Joseph Miles. Remember them?"

"I don't understand? Ben, if this is some sort of joke…"

"It's far from a joke. But you know that. Don't you, Greg?"

"I don't know what you're playing at, Chief Winters. But I have had a very long day, so I suggest you leave now."

Ben didn't move a single muscle. He wasn't going anywhere. Picking up the top sheet of paper in the folder, he asked, "Where were you last Thursday evening? After the reception for Tommy's retirement?"

"I was here. I decided to have an early night and came home after the event."

"I called you from Tasker Valley Memorial to tell you about the incident there. You didn't answer your cell phone."

"I might have had the ringer turned off or was in the bathroom. I don't know. So what?"

"Your voicemail picked up. I left you a message. Remember?" Ben didn't let him answer. "The point is the call connected, leaving an electronic marker of your location out there in the universe for anyone who could find it. And I don't mean the kind of general cell tower triangulation we use at the department. Tommy and I have an old friend that once hinted to us about a highly classified, and very controversial program that could actually locate the *exact* location of a cell phone. Well, within a couple of feet, at least.

"Lucky for me, I know someone who has that sort of ability. Well, *he* doesn't, but he has people that work for him that can do it in a snap. You remember I introduced you to Alan at Tommy's retirement party? The Director of the FBI? It's amazing the kind of capabilities the Bureau has that they don't want people to know about."

Greg Oland's eye narrowed. The chief allowed the revelation of this high-tech surveillance program to hang in the air. Then he tightened the noose.

"Alan and his tech boys were able to locate your cell phone."

Ben noticed a slight tremor in the mayor's hands.

"Using your phone's electronic data footprint—their words, not mine—they were able to pinpoint where you were when I called you from the hospital. If people only knew about the true abilities of the Bureau, they would be amazed…and terrified. But it comes in handy when tracking down terrorists…and murdering pieces of shit."

Ben laid the sheet of paper on the table and slid it across the polished surface to the mayor.

Pointing at the sheet baring the official seal of the Federal Bureau of Investigation, Ben said, "That's where your cell phone was. But you already know where you were. You were at Tommy's house. In fact, you were in his back yard to be more precise. I told you, this program is scary. The minute the call I made connected with your voicemail, they were able to nail you. Can you believe that?

"Before you ask, being that you are the county's former state's attorney, we went about tracking your phone completely legally. The warrant was all signed, sealed, and delivered in a timely fashion. Again, it helps that it was the director himself asking for the paperwork to be expedited."

He paused to take another piece of paper from the file. It was Tommy's autopsy report. "According to the FBI, you were at Tommy's house around the time the medical examiner says he was killed. Not here at home like you said."

The color was returning to Greg Oland's face. The blood was clearly pumping through his veins now as a line of perspiration began forming on his forehead. And under his blue dress shirt, a spot of dark crimson appeared, standing out against the white of his undershirt.

A third piece of paper sailed across the walnut inlaid table.

"There were two types of blood on the knife used to stab Tommy. His and the killers. But you know that too. You know Tommy didn't go down without a fight. He used the same knife you stuck in his stomach to cut you."

Ben walked around the table and grabbed the mayor's side. "My guess is that he got you right here where it looks like you have a pretty serious injury."

Greg Oland jerked backward, slamming into the door behind him.

"What are you doing, you sonofabitch?" Oland barked.

"You killed Tommy because he figured out you were the Spring Strangler."

From behind him, Ben heard the hammer of a gun click into place and a familiar voice say, "You're only half right about that, Chief."

Ben turned to see Gary Oland standing in the hallway aiming a .9mm square at his chest.

Chapter Seventy-One

"Do you honestly think my brother could have killed all those people by himself?" Gary Oland asked in a stone-cold tone. "Greg has always needed someone behind him urging him along. Whispering in his ear, telling him what he needs to do. That's how he's gotten where he is today."

There was something about the look on the mayor's face that told Ben while he had been involved in the murders all the way, his brother might really be the one calling the shots. Ben couldn't tell if it was relief that the secret had finally come out or fear that they'd been caught. What he knew for certain was that Greg was definitely the weaker of the two Oland twins.

Turning to the mayor, he asked, "So why'd you do it? Why'd you kill all of them? I mean, Miles had to go so that it looked like his guilt got the better of him. But what started all of this?"

The muscles around Greg's eyes were trembling as Ben stared him down. Slowly his jaw began to twitch as he was getting ready to break. But before he could finally bring himself to say anything, to explain what caused the horrific actions decades earlier, his brother broke the tense silence.

"The women were all whores and needed to be put in their place. That bitch Beverly almost destroyed our parents' marriage and those sluts from school…" Gary's voice trailed off. His reaction had been so visceral, so vile—just the mention of the three women that had been killed made him seethe. "They deserved what happened to them. So did Miles. Sleeping with his students? He set himself up as far as I'm concerned."

There it was—the break between the two. Up until that moment, Gary had been speaking for both he and his brother. But he just said, "as far as *I'm* concerned." Joseph Miles might have been the fall guy, but Greg Oland was the real patsy, being controlled like a puppet by his twin brother.

"And Tommy?" Ben asked. "Did he figure all of this out? That's why you two killed him?"

"Oh, no. Greg took care of the sheriff all by himself. He overheard you two talking at the reception. About how he figured something out. So, my dear, inept brother…for the first time in his life…decided to handle something on his own. And he *fucked it up!*"

For a split second, it looked as though Greg might defend himself. His jaw set, his chest raised, but the moment came and went without him saying a word. Gary steamrolled on, remaining firmly in control.

"He got himself stabbed. And if that wasn't bad enough, he left the knife behind! It was only going to be a matter of time before someone put it all together. Which is what happened."

"Which is why Greg had to kill your father." Ben didn't ask. It made sense. He must have always had his suspicions. Even during the murders, there must have been something in the back of his mind telling him that one or both of his boys were involved. That would be another reason he was so quick to close the case when everyone thought Miles hung himself.

To Ben's surprise, Greg Oland finally spoke. "I didn't kill my father. I have no idea who did. I could never hurt him. He didn't know anything about this."

"Yes, he did, you idiot," Gary shouted. "He figured it out. He called me yesterday and said he needed to talk. When I got to the house, he said he knew one of us was involved. He had those damn letters from Beverly all over his desk."

The realization struck the mayor like a lightning bolt. For the second time that evening, all the color drained from his face. Taking a very unsteady step toward his brother, almost inaudibly, he said, "You killed him. You killed Dad? What would have happened if Mother walked in?"

His brother shrugged. There was no register of emotion on his face.

"How could you? How could you kill him?"

"I did what needed to be done. Then I threw those fucking letters in the fire. But I'm curious, Chief. How did *you* figure it out?"

Ben pointed back to the file folder on the table. There was one last piece of paper he hadn't shown them yet, the copy of the *Herald-Dispatch* Home and Garden Section article.

"Tommy had a copy of that article in his case file. I didn't think much of it. We were even at your house while that renovation was going on. But it's when I saw the article again in your father's study that something in the photo kept nagging at me. The curtains behind the four of you. More specifically, the thick corded tiebacks with the big tassels on them. Hell, I have them in my house. But out of context, they didn't mean anything. It might not have been those exact ones, maybe one of the old ones your mother was getting rid of, but that's what you used to strangle Linda and Penny."

A wicked grin spread across Gary Oland's lips. Was he impressed, Ben wondered.

"So, with that and the fragment of one of those letters we found in the fire—oh, I didn't tell you that we found that," Ben answered with his own smirk, "all the pieces fell into place."

"Bravo, Chief Winters. I'd say I was impressed, but it did take you almost forty years to figure it out. So, how impressed should I really be if you think about it?"

"Gary Oland, Greg Oland," Ben began, "you are under arrest for the murders of Beverly Baker, Linda..."

"Excuse me, Chief," Gary interrupted with a chuckle. "I'm the one standing here with a gun. How exactly do you think you're going to arrest us? I mean, we pretty much answered your questions and you've answered ours. So it's time for me to put a bullet in your head."

For the first time that night, Ben smiled. It might have taken forty years, but he'd solved the case that had haunted him and his partner their entire careers and even cost one of them his life. In one of his darkest moments after Tommy's death, he'd promised to find whoever killed him. He was true to his word.

"The one thing you're forgetting," Ben said, "is that this isn't a movie." He gestured around the foyer. "I'm not some hotheaded detective who doesn't follow procedure and charges in after the killer without backup. I'm the chief of a very, *very* good police force. I have the entire house surrounded and they've been listening to every word that's been said in here tonight."

Ben casually opened his windbreaker to reveal the radio he'd concealed. "I really didn't think it was going to be this easy to get you to confess. I guess I owe you a dollar, Drew," he said into the receiver.

With that, blinding beams of light surged through every window in the house as the PCPD S.W.A.T. team lit up the Victorian mansion with tactical floodlights. So bright and intense, all color washed away, leaving in its place a stark white glow.

Greg Oland covered his eyes and began to stumble down the hallway.

His brother had a completely different reaction. Fire erupted in Gary Oland's eyes. Ben couldn't imagine how the man thought he would get away with killing the police chief, but that seemed to be his end game.

It took Gary only a second to raise his gun from aiming at Ben's chest to his head. It took Ben a few seconds more to reach for the gun under his windbreaker. Seconds that cost because as he reached for his weapon, he heard the unmistakable crack of a gunshot. Bracing himself for the expected blow from the searing lead flying through the air, he watched instead as a hole exploded in Gary Oland's shoulder, sending the .9mm crashing to the floor.

At that moment, all hell broke loose. The front door burst open nearly flying off its hinges, windows could be heard shattering in other rooms, all as a swarm of heavily armed officers clad in black tactical gear stormed the house.

Gary Oland collapsed to his knees, clutching his shoulder as blood spilled down his side. Behind him, gun drawn and still trained on his target, was Corporal Drew Collins, who had snuck into the house from the rear while the chief went in through the front. If there was anyone Ben was going to trust to have his back when he went into the house to confront Oland, it was Drew. Which is why Ben knew he was never in any real danger.

As a pair of S.W.A.T. officers yanked Gary Oland to his feet, not caring about the pain shooting through his body by the jerking of his arm, Ben stepped up to him and whispered in his ear, "Never pick a fight with someone who can answer the question 'you and what army'?"

Chapter Seventy-Two

News of the mayor's arrest sent shock waves through Parker City. As the details surrounding the event slowly began trickling out, shock was replaced by horror as residents learned about the mayor and his brother's actions when they were teenagers. Then to find out one twin killed the sheriff and the other his own father to cover up the decades old murders, it was like something out of a movie. Almost unbelievable.

Those were Drew Collins's exact words as he reread the article on his tablet while sitting in the chief's office the afternoon after the arrests. He and the chief had been up all night dealing with the immediate fallout. This was the first chance they'd had to sit down. Now, with very strong cups of coffee in front of them, Drew was updating Ben on the media reaction.

Once again, Ben Winters found himself right where he didn't want to be. On the front page of the papers. Or, at least, their home pages. From the *Herald-Dispatch*, to the *Washington Post*, to the *New York Times*, across the pond to the *London Daily Mail*, the story was a sensation. Even the national news channels were running pieces on Parker City's dark secret and the police chief who finally brought a killer to justice.

"They really are taking a lot of liberties, aren't they?" Drew said, reading one of the headlines. "Maybe you should talk to one of them and set things straight."

Ben shook his head.

"I don't want this story to be about me. We're going to be releasing an official statement from the department tonight. It will have all the facts we can share at this point and hopefully clear up some of *these* dramatic details."

"Okay, but you can answer a few questions for me, though?" Drew turned off his tablet. "What started all of this?"

"It was Gary. He found out that his father and Beverly Baker were having an affair. He convinced his brother they needed to do something about it. And then he decided every woman he thought wronged them needed to be punished. The mayor started singing like a canary the minute they got him into an interrogation room. By the way, his campaign for congress is over."

"You think?" asked Drew with a wry smile.

"For the most part, it was Greg who actually strangled all the women, but Gary was right there beside him, urging him on. The two have always been inseparable. Greg's been the friendly, outgoing one but Gary was always the one calling the shots from the shadows."

"Okay, so I guess I get it. Teenage hormones, a psychotic tendency, they start killing. Why'd they kill Joseph Miles?"

"He was the perfect scapegoat. Even then, these boys were politically astute. If you don't want to get caught, you need someone else to blame. In this case, it turns out they had the perfect candidate. Who better to pin all the murders on than a teacher sleeping with his students? Linda Carlson broke up with Greg *because* she was seduced by Miles. Gary didn't have a hard time convincing his brother Miles needed to be punished too."

Drew was absorbing all of this. One thought after another kept coming to him.

"How did they know about Miles and his affairs with the girls?"

"Come on, Drew," Ben said. "Think about when you were in school. All the gossip? The kids knew everything. If he'd been sleeping with just *one* of his students, maybe, just *maybe* it could have been kept secret. But more than one, it was only a matter of time before everyone found out.

"When we found Miles hanging in his apartment, we just assumed—and were encouraged—to believe Miles figured it was only a matter of time before he was caught, so he hung himself. It wasn't an unreasonable idea.

"Not to mention, how would someone have killed him? Miles was a young, athletic guy. He would have put up a fight. Unless there were *two* younger, and more athletic guys who were able to overpower him. They strangled him, then strung him up so it looked like a suicide. After seeing the autopsy photos, the two sets of bruising, it makes perfect sense looking back at it."

"It's just unbelievable," Drew murmured.

Before Drew could ask another question, Ben took his opportunity to say, "I think it's time we both head home and get some sleep. We'll have plenty of time to talk about all of this."

As Ben began collecting his things, Drew picked up the empty coffee mugs and his tablet and started for the door. Then he stopped.

"Chief, the FBI program that can pinpoint the exact location of a cell phone? Is that real or were you just bluffing?"

Ben looked at his young assistant and smiled.

"I couldn't possibly confirm nor deny the existence of such a resource."

Chapter Seventy-Three

The funeral for Sheriff Tom Mason was held at St. Joseph's Episcopal Church across from Jefferson Park. In addition to the part it had played in the case back in '81, it was also the location of Tommy's third wedding. Interestingly, it was his only church wedding as the first two Mrs. Masons had tied the knot with him at the Parker County Courthouse. All three times, Ben had been there at his side. And that's exactly where he was now as the coffin was being carried out to the hearse. Tommy's final journey would take him on a path from St. Joe's across town past the old Parker City Police headquarters on to the Sheriff's Department and finally to Rosehill Gardens where he would be laid to rest.

The somber event drew hundreds of people wishing to pay their respects to one of the county's most respected figures. From the Governor of Maryland to the Director of the Federal Bureau of Investigation to all three former Mrs. Masons, it was a who's who of Tommy's life and career. Even Andrew and Emma, Ben's children, came home for the service.

Once again, for the second time in a week, Ben found himself standing in front of a large crowd praising his friend. Though he was not a particularly religious man, Ben knew that Tommy was watching over the whole affair shaking his head with that smartass grin of his on his face.

As the sun was just beginning to set over the mountains, Natalie let go of Ben's hand and started back to the car so he could have a final moment alone with Tommy at the gravesite. For the last week, she'd seen him try to push himself and work through the pain and grief she knew he was feeling. She just wanted him to be able to have some closure.

Alone at the grave, for the first time all week, Ben felt his eyes begin to swell with tears. Instead of fighting the emotions, he finally allowed himself to accept what had happened. Events had occurred so long ago that brought them to this very moment. Had things been done differently, Ben began to think, then stopped himself. Second guessing wasn't in his nature, and it certainly would have pissed Tommy off.

There was no way he would ever forget everything they'd been through—the good, the bad, and the ugly. It had been a wild ride.

Wiping a tear from his cheek, Ben laid his hand on the top of Tommy's simple tombstone and said a silent prayer for his best friend. In that moment, he felt the grief disappear, replaced by a sense of calm and, dare he say, peace.

As if almost on cue, the cell phone in his pocket began to vibrate. Not his personal cell, his official PCPD phone. The one that would only be ringing right now if there was an emergency that demanded the attention of the chief of police.

With one last look at the tombstone, Ben smiled, turned, and answered the phone. "Chief Winters."

A Note from the Author

When I sat down and began writing *Now & Then*, I knew Parker City was going to be as much of a character in the story as Ben and Tommy. To make the setting as real as possible, like many writers, I looked around for inspiration. Well, I didn't have to look very far. For anyone who lives in or around Frederick, Maryland (or Frederick County), you should be able to see a good number of familiar locations in this book (not to mention in the coming stories). They may not have the same name or be in the exact same location as they are in real life, but I can't deny that Parker City is a highly fictionalized version of the City of Frederick. Why did I do this? Because Frederick has such a rich history from which to draw. From its buildings to its residents, Frederick is not only an incredible place to live and work, it has everything a mystery writer could dream of for inspiration.

About the Author

When not sitting in his library devising new and clever ways to kill people (*for his mysteries*), Justin can usually be found at The Way Off Broadway Dinner Theatre, outside of Washington, DC, where he is one of the owners and producers. In addition to writing the Parker City Mysteries Series, he is also the mastermind behind Marquee Mysteries, a series of interactive mystery events he has been writing and producing for over fifteen years. Justin and his wife, Jessica, live along Lake Linganore outside of Frederick, Maryland.